I0599405

Uriah Smith

The Marvel of Nations

our country, its past, present, and future, and what the scriptures say of it

Uriah Smith

The Marvel of Nations
our country, its past, present, and future, and what the scriptures say of it

ISBN/EAN: 9783337227005

Printed in Europe, USA, Canada, Australia, Japan

Cover: Foto ©Andreas Hilbeck / pixelio.de

More available books at **www.hansebooks.com**

Yours very truly,
Uriah Smith.

THE MARVEL OF NATIONS.

OUR COUNTRY.

ITS PAST, PRESENT, AND FUTURE.

OUR NATIONAL EMBLEM.

THE MARVEL OF NATIONS.

OUR COUNTRY:

ITS PAST, PRESENT, AND FUTURE,

AND

WHAT THE SCRIPTURES SAY OF IT.

By URIAH SMITH,

Professor of Biblical Exegesis in Battle Creek College, Thirty Years Editor "Review and Herald," Author of "Thoughts on Daniel and the Revelation," "Man's Nature and Destiny," "Parliamentary Rules," etc.

Fiftieth Thousand.

REVIEW & HERALD, PUBLISHERS,
BATTLE CREEK, MICH.;
PACIFIC PRESS, OAKLAND, CAL.;
PRESENT TRUTH, GREAT GRIMSBY,
ENGLAND.

1886.

" Westward the Course of Empire takes its way,
  The first four Acts already past,
A fifth shall close the drama with the day,---
  Time's noblest offspring is the Last."

—BISHOP GEORGE BERKELEY.
WRITTEN ABOUT 1726.

PREFACE

E have a right to presume that every intelligent and patriotic citizen of the Great American Republic, feels an interest in all that pertains to his country—in what it has been, is, and is to be. While he looks with just pride on its past unparalleled progress and noble achievements, and surveys with satisfaction its present position of national exaltation and influence, with its free government, immense wealth, and exhaustless resources, he cannot be indifferent to probabilities affecting its future, so far as they may be legitimately calculated from lessons of history, from principles established in our own Constitution, and from the tendency of influences already actively and widely at work in different parts of our land.

In this direction, the mind of every one must turn with peculiar interest; and while many unquestionable conclusions relative to our future may be established on the grounds already referred to, we believe there is another source of instruction, almost wholly overlooked or ignored, which sets forth more explicitly and more fully startling developments which days not far to come have in store for us. It is designed in this work to call particular attention to these matters.

We do not purpose here to enter largely into the history of this government. There are works already published which leave nothing to be desired in this direction. Neither is it our object to make in these pages either political economy, arithmetic, or geography, a specialty, though something will be referred to under each head. The leading title of the book is given as "The Marvel of Nations;" and we propose to inquire somewhat into the significance of this "marvel." If we believe that there is a God who rules in the kingdoms of men (Dan. 5 : 21), we must look for his providential hand in human history, in the rise, career, and fall of the nations and peoples of the world. But as a prominent and inevitable object in this line of thought lies the inquiry, what providential design we are to look for in a nation which has been so suddenly and rapidly developed as this has been, and what grand purpose God has to work out through this goodly heritage of ours. This inquiry will not be pressed even to the verge of fancy or speculation; for, if we mistake not, enough will be found to instruct us, perhaps surprise us, on these points, in the solid and sober realm of fact.

Many of the most studious, careful, and critical minds of the present generation, have been led to the conclusion that numerous lines of prophecy, spanning many ages and embracing many lands, find their focal point in our own times; may we not add, also, in our own country? Certainly, the present age seems to be illuminated by the light of current prophetic fulfillments above all others. Here we find the most emphatic touches of the inspired pencil; and the events to transpire and the agents therein concerned are brought out in a most vivid and startling light. Has the United States any part to act in these scenes? What do the Scriptures say on this question? None but those who do not believe that God ever foretells the history of nations, or that his providence ever works in their development and decline, can fail to be interested in a consideration of these topics.

That this little treatise is exhaustive of the subject which it es says to bring briefly before the reader, is not claimed; but many facts are presented which are thought to be worthy of serious consideration, and enough evidence, it is confidently hoped, is produced in favor of the positions taken to show the reader that the subject is not one of mere theory, but one of the highest practical importance, and so enough to stimulate thought, and lead to further inquiry.

If the views presented in the following pages are correct, the subject is destined soon to become one of absorbing interest; and information respecting it is necessary to an understanding of our duties and responsibilities in the solemn and important times that are upon us. In this light we commend it to the candid and serious attention of the reader.

U. S.

Battle Creek, Mich.,
August, **1885.**

CONTENTS.

CHAPTER I.

EXPECTATIONS AND PREDICTIONS OF EMINENT MEN.

CHAPTER II.

A CENTURY'S PROGRESS.

CHAPTER III.

POLITICAL AND RELIGIOUS INFLUENCE OF THE NATION.

[vii]

CHAPTER VII.

WHEN MUST THE GOVERNMENT INDICATED BY THIS SYMBOL ARISE?

CHAPTER VIII.

THE UNITED STATES HAS ARISEN IN THE EXACT MANNER INDICATED BY THE SYMBOL.

CHAPTER IX.

THE TWO GREAT PRINCIPLES OF THE GOVERNMENT.

CHAPTER X.

INCONSISTENT UTTERANCES.

—◦—

CHAPTER XI.

HE DOETH GREAT WONDERS.

—◦—

CHAPTER XII.

CHURCH AND STATE.

—◦—

CHAPTER XIII.

THE SUNDAY QUESTION.

CHAPTER XIV.

INDICATIONS OF COMING CHANGES.

LIST OF ILLUSTRATIONS.

——◄►——

[xii]

OUR COUNTRY:

ITS PAST, PRESENT, AND FUTURE.

CHAPTER I.

EXPECTATIONS AND PREDICTIONS OF EMINENT MEN.

IT is but a little more than one hundred years since the nation known as "THE UNITED STATES OF AMERICA" began to exist. A hundred years is not a long period in the history of nations. Let the eye run back upon the path of history, and mark the condition of nations when only a hundred years of age. Ancient Rome, the most notable of them all, when it had attained the age of a hundred years, was scarcely known outside the few provinces of Italy which composed its territory. Not so with this new empire of the West. Ere a hundred years had elapsed, its fame had encircled the earth, exciting the wonder and envy of the aged and stagnant kingdoms of other lands. It began with a few small settlements of earnest men, who, fleeing from the religious intolerance of the Old World, occupied a narrow area along our Atlantic coast. Now, a mighty nation, with a vast expanse of territory stretching from ocean to ocean, and from regions almost arctic on the north to regions as nearly torrid on the south, embracing more square leagues of habitable land than

[13]

Rome ruled over in its palmiest days, after more than seven centuries of growth, here holds a position of independence and glory among the nations of the earth.*

And the sound of this new nation has gone into all the world. It has reached the toiling millions of Europe; and they are swarming to our shores to share its blessings. It has gone to the islands of the sea; and they have sent their living contributions to swell its busy population. It has reached the Orient, and opened, as with a pass-word, the gates of nations long barred against intercourse with other powers; and China and Japan, turning from their beaten track of forty centuries, are looking with wonder at the prodigy arising across the Pacific to the east of them, and catching some of the impulse which this growing power is imparting to the nations of the earth.

Precisely one hundred and nine years ago, with about three millions of people, the United States became an independent government. It has now a population of over fifty-five millions of people, and a territory of more than three and a half millions of square miles. Russia alone exceeds this nation in these particulars, having thirty millions more of people, and, including the vast and dreary regions of Siberia, nearly five millions more square miles of territory.†

---

* In a speech at the "Centennial Dinner" at the Westminster Palace Hotel, London, July 4, 1876, J. P. Thompson, LL. D., speaking of the United States, said: "They have proved the possibility of free, popular government upon a scale to which the Roman Republic of five hundred years was but a province."—*The United States as a Nation*, p. xvii.

† The area of the two countries is given in "Lippincott's Gazetteer of the World," as follows:—

United States, ... 3,580,242 square miles.
Russia, ... 8,352,940 square miles.

Of all other nations on the globe whose laws are framed by legislative bodies elected by the people, Brazil, which has the largest territory, has but little more than three millions of square miles ; and France, the most populous, has not by many millions so great a number of inhabitants as our country. So that in point of territory and population combined, it will be seen that the United States now stands at the head of the self-governing powers of the earth.

Occupying a position altogether unique, this government excites equally the astonishment and the admiration of all beholders. The main features of its history are such as have had no parallel since the distinction of nations existed among men.

1. No nation ever acquired so vast a territory in so quiet a manner.

2. No nation ever rose to such greatness by means so peaceable.

3. No nation ever advanced so rapidly in all that constitutes national strength and capital.

4. No nation ever rose to such a pinnacle of power in a space of time so incredibly short.

5. No nation in so limited a time has developed such unlimited resources.

6. No nation has ever existed, the foundations of whose government were laid so broad and deep in the principles of justice, righteousness, and truth.

7. No nation has ever existed in which men have been left so free to worship God according to the dictates of their own consciences.

8. In no nation and in no age of the world have the arts and sciences so flourished, so many improvements been made, and so great successes been achieved in the arts both of peace and war, as in our own country during the last fifty years.

9. In no nation and in no age has the gospel found such freedom, and the churches of Christ had such liberty to enlarge their borders and develop their strength.

10. No age of the world has seen such an immigration as that which is now pouring into our borders from all lands the millions who have long groaned under despotic governments, and who now turn to this broad territory of freedom as the avenue of hope, the Utopia of the nations.

The most discerning minds have been intuitively impressed with the idea of the future greatness and power of this government. In view of the grand results developed and developing, the discovery of America by Columbus, not four hundred years ago, is set down as "the greatest event of all secular history."

The progress of empire to this land was long ago expected.

Sir Thomas Browne, in 1682 predicted the growth of a power here which would rival the European kingdoms in strength and prowess.

In Burnaby's "Travels through the Middle Settlements of North America in 1759 and 1760," published in 1775, is expressed this sentiment :—

"An idea, strange as it is visionary, has entered into the minds of the generality of mankind, that empire is traveling westward ; and every one is looking forward with eager and impatient expectation to that destined moment when America is to give the law to the rest of the world."

John Adams, Oct. 12, 1775, wrote :—

"Soon after the Reformation, a few people came over into this New World for conscience' sake. Perhaps this apparently trivial incident may transfer the great seat of empire to America."

On the day after the signing of the Declaration of Independence, he wrote :—

"Yesterday the greatest question was decided which was ever debated in America, and a greater, perhaps, never was, nor will be, decided among men."

In 1776, Galiani, a Neapolitan, predicted the gradual decay of European institutions, to renew themselves in America. In 1778, in reference to the question as to which was to be the ruling power in the world, Europe or America, he said,—

"I will wager in favor of America."

Adam Smith, of Scotland, in 1776 predicted the transfer of empire to America.

Governor Pownal, an English statesman, in 1780, while our Revolution was in progress, predicted that this country would become independent, and that a civilizing activity, beyond what Europe could ever know, would animate it ; and that its commercial and naval power would be found in every quarter of the globe. Again he said :—

"North America has advanced, and is every day advancing, to growth of state, with a steady and continually accelerating motion, of which there has never yet been any example in Europe."

David Hartley wrote from England in 1777 :—

"At sea, which has hitherto been our prerogative element, they [the United States] rise against us at a stupendous rate ; and if we cannot return to our old mutual hospitalities toward each other, a very few years will show us a most formidable hostile marine, ready to join hands with any of our enemies."

Count d'Aranda, one of the first of Spanish statesmen, in 1783 thus wrote of this Republic :—

"This Federal Republic was born a pygmy, so to speak. It required the support and forces of two powers as great as Spain and

France in order to attain independence. A day will come when it will be a giant, even a colossus, formidable in these countries."*

Sir Thomas Browne, referred to above, in 1684 published certain "Miscellany Tracts," one of which, entitled "The Prophecy," is the one which contains his reflections on the rise and progress of America. Dr. Johnson says of it: "Browne plainly discovers his expectation to be the same with that entertained lately with more confidence by Dr. Berkeley that 'America will be the seat of the fifth empire.'" It is in verse, and the lines relating to America are :—

"When New England shall trouble New Spain,
When America shall cease to send out its treasure,
But employ it at home in American pleasure;
When the new world shall the old invade,
Nor count them their lords, but their fellows in trade."
        —*Duyckinck's American Literature,* vol. i., p. 179.

In 1773 the Bishop of St. Asaph (Wales) before the Society for the Propagation of the Gospel in Foreign Parts, said :—

"The colonies of North America have not only taken root and acquired strength, but seem hastening, with an accelerated progress, to such a powerful state as may introduce a new and important change in human affairs."—*Id.*

The transfer of religion to this land, and its revival here, was also expected. George Herbert in a poem entitled "The Church Militant," published in 1633, said :—

"Religion stands on tiptoe in our land,
Ready to pass to the American strand."—*Id.*

Of these prophecies, some are now wholly fulfilled,

---

* These quotations are from an article by Hon. Charles Sumner, entitled "Prophetic Voices about America," published in the *Atlantic Monthly* of September, 1867.

and the remainder far on the road to fulfillment. This infant of yesterday stands forth to-day a giant, vigorous, active, and courageous, and accepts with dignity its manifest destiny at the head of powers and civilizations.

A question of thrilling interest now arises. This government has received recognition at the hands of men sufficient to satisfy any ambition. Does the God of heaven also recognize it, and has he spoken concerning it? In other words, does the prophetic pen, which has so fully delineated the rise and progress of all the other great nations of the earth, pass this one by unnoticed? What are the probabilities in this matter? As the student of prophecy, in common with all mankind, looks with wonder upon the unparalleled rise and progress of this nation, he cannot repress the conviction that the hand of Providence has been at work in this quiet but mighty revolution. And this conviction he shares in common with others.

Governor Pownal, from whom a quotation has already been presented, speaking of the establishment of this country as a free and sovereign power, calls it—

"A revolution that has stranger marks of *divine interposition*, superseding the ordinary course of human affairs, than any other event which this world has experienced."

De Tocqueville, a French writer, speaking of our separation from England, says :—

"It might seem their folly, but was really their fate ; or, rather, the providence of God, who has doubtless a work for them to do in which the massive materiality of the English character would have been too ponderous a dead weight upon their progress."

Geo. Alfred Townsend, speaking of the misfortunes

that have attended the other governments on this continent (New World and Old, p. 635), says :—

"The history of the United States was separated by a beneficent Providence far from the wild and cruel history of the rest of the continent."

Again he says :—

"This hemisphere was laid away for no one race."

Mr. J. M. Foster, in a Sermon before the Reformed Presbyterian Church in Cincinnati, O., Nov. 30, 1882, bore the following explicit testimony to the fact that the hand of Providence has been remarkably displayed in the establishment of this government :—

"Let us look at the history of our own nation. The Mediator long ages ago prepared this land as the home of civil and religious liberty. He made it a land flowing with milk and honey. He stored our mountains with coal, and iron, and copper, and silver, and gold. He prepared our fountains of oil, planted our forests, leveled our plains, enriched our valleys, and beautified them with lakes and rivers. He guided the Mayflower over the sea, so that the Pilgrim Fathers landed safely on Plymouth Rock. He directed the course of our civilization, so that we have become a great nation."

Plymouth Rock.

The spot where the PILGRIM FATHERS landed from the "Mayflower," Dec. 21, 1620. A portion of this granite rock has been removed from the water-side, and located in front of Pilgrim Hall, protected by an iron fence. The original portion on Water Street, is covered by a suitable canopy, in the top of which are the bones of the original settlers. Plymouth is 37 miles southeast from Boston, Mass.

CHAPTER II.

A CENTURY'S PROGRESS.

HAVE the foregoing predictions been justified, and the expectations of these great men been fulfilled? Every person whose reading is ordinarily extensive has something of an idea of what the United States is to-day; he likewise has an idea, so far as words can convey it to his mind, of what this country was at the commencement of its history. The only object, then, in presenting statistics and testimony on this point, is to show that our rapid growth has struck mankind with the wonder of a constant miracle.

Said Emile de Girardin in *La Liberte* (1868) :—

"The population of America, not thinned by any conscription, multiplies with prodigious rapidity, and the day may before [long be] seen, when they will number sixty or eighty millions of souls. This *parvenu* [one recently risen to notice] is aware of his importance and destiny. Hear him proudly exclaim, 'America for Americans!' See him promising his alliance to Russia; and we see that power, which well knows what force is, grasp the hand of this giant of yesterday.

"In view of his *unparalleled progress and combination*, what are the little toys with which we vex ourselves in Europe? What is this needle gun we are anxious to get from Prussia, that we may beat her next year with it? Had we not better take from America the principle of liberty she embodies, out of which have come her citizen pride, her gigantic industry, and her formidable loyalty to the destinies of her republican land?"

The *Dublin* (Ireland) *Nation*, already quoted, about the year 1850 said :—

"In the East there is arising a colossal centaur called the Russian empire. With a civilized head and front, it has the sinews of a huge barbaric body. There one man's brain moves 70,000,-000. [In 1870, 87,795,987.—*Lippincott.*] There all the traditions of the people are of aggression and conquest in the West. There but two ranks are distinguishable—serfs and soldiers. There the map of the future includes Constantinople and Vienna as outposts of St. Petersburg.

"In the West, an opposing and still more wonderful American empire is emerging. We islanders have no conception of the extraordinary events which amid the silence of the earth are daily adding to the power and pride of this gigantic nation. Within three years, territories more extensive than these three kingdoms [Great Britain, Ireland, and Scotland], France, and Italy put together, have been quietly, and in almost 'matter-of-course' fashion, annexed to the Union.

"Within seventy years, seventeen new Sovereignties, the smallest of them larger than Great Britain, have peaceably united themselves to the Federation. No standing army was raised, no national debt was sunk, no great exertion was made, but there they are. And the last mail brings news of three more great States about to be joined to the thirty,—Minnesota in the northwest, Deseret in the southwest, and California on the shores of the Pacific. These three States will cover an area equal to one-half of the European continent."

Mitchell, in his "School Geography" (fourth revised edition), p. 101, speaking of the United States, says :—

"It presents the most striking instance of national growth to be found in the history of mankind."

Let us reduce these general statements to the more tangible form of facts and figures. A short time before the great Reformation in the days of Martin Luther, not four hundred years ago, this western hemisphere was discovered. The Reformation awoke the nations, that were fast fettered in the galling bonds of superstition, to the fact that it is the heaven-born right of every man to worship God according to the dictates of his own conscience. But rulers are loth to lose their power, and religious intolerance still oppressed the people. Under these circumstances, a body of religious heroes at length determined to seek in the wilds of America that measure of civil and religious freedom which they so much desired. Two hundred and sixty-five years ago, Dec. 22, 1620, the Mayflower landed one hundred of these voluntary exiles on the coast of New England. "Here," says Martyn, "New England was born," and this was "its first baby cry,—a prayer and a thanksgiving to the Lord."

Another permanent English settlement was made at Jamestown, Va., thirteen years before this, in 1607. In process of time other settlements were made and colonies organized, which were all subject to the English crown till the declaration of independence, July 4, 1776.

The population of these colonies, according to the *United States Magazine* of August, 1855, amounted in 1701, to 262,000 ; in 1749, to 1,046,000 ; in 1775, to 2,803,000. Then commenced the struggle of the American colonies against the oppression of the mother country. In 1776, they declared themselves, as in justice and right they were entitled to be, a free and independent nation. In 1777, delegates from the thirteen original States,—New Hampshire, Massachusetts, Rhode Island, Connecticut, New York, New Jersey, Pennsylvania, Delaware, Maryland, Virginia, North Carolina, South Carolina, and Georgia,— in Congress assembled, adopted Articles of Confederation. In 1783, the war of the Revolution closed with a treaty of peace with Great Britain, whereby

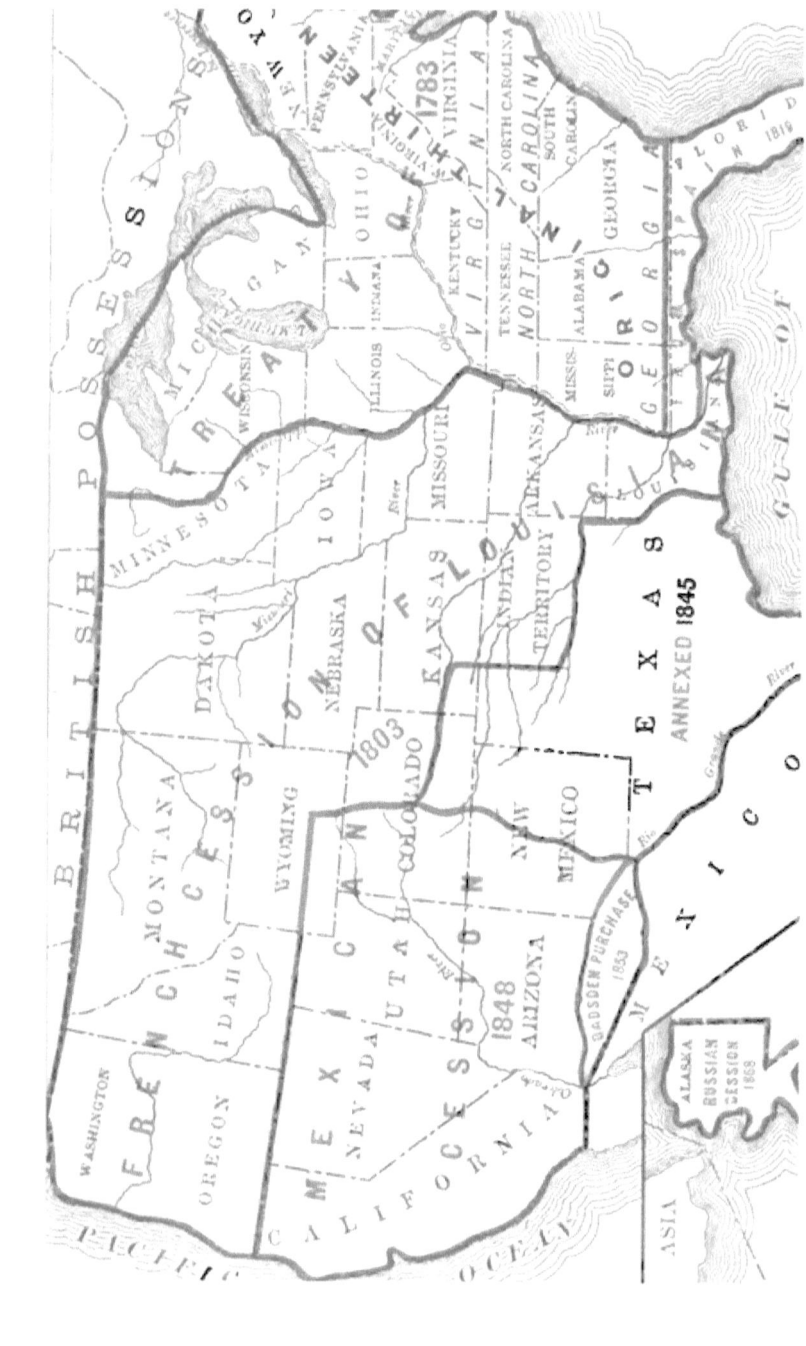

our independence was acknowledged, and territory ceded to the extent of 815,615 square miles. In 1787 the Constitution was framed, and ratified by the foregoing thirteen States ; and on the first day of March, 1789, it went into operation. Then the American ship of State was fairly launched, with less than one million square miles of territory, and about three millions of souls.

Such was the situation when our nation took its position of independence, as one of the self-governing powers of the world. Our territorial growth since that time has been as follows : Louisiana, acquired from France in 1803, comprising 930,928 square miles of territory ; Florida, from Spain in 1821, with 59,268 square miles ; Texas, admitted into the Union in 1845, with 237,504 square miles ; Oregon, as settled by treaty in 1846, with 380,425 square miles ; California, as conquered from Mexico in 1847, with 649,762 square miles ; Arizona (New Mexico), as acquired from Mexico by treaty in 1854, with 27,500 square miles ; Alaska, as acquired by purchase from Russia in 1867, with 577,390 square miles. This gives a grand total of three million, six hundred seventy-eight thousand, three hundred and ninety-two (3,678,-392) square miles of territory, which is about four-ninths of all North America, and more than one-fifteenth of the whole land surface of the globe.

And while this expansion has been thus rapidly going forward here, how has it been with the other leading nations of the globe ? Macmillan & Co., the London publishers, in announcing their "Statesman's Year Book" for 1867, make an interesting statement of the changes that took place in Europe during the half century between the years 1817 and 1867. They say :—

"The half century has extinguished **three** kingdoms, **one** grand duchy, eight duchies, four principalities, one electorate, and four **republics**. **Three** new kingdoms have arisen, and **one** kingdom has **been** transformed into an empire. There are now forty-one states in Europe against fifty-nine which **existed in 1817**. Not less remarkable **is** the territorial extension of the superior states in the world. **Russia has annexed 567,361 square miles; the United** States, 1,968,009; **France**, 4,620; **Prussia, 29,781; Sar-**dinia, expanding into Italy, has increased by **83,041;** the Indian empire **has been augmented by 431,616. The** principal states that have **lost territory are Turkey, Mexico, Austria, Denmark, and** the Netherlands."

We ask the especial attention of the reader to these particulars. During the last half century, twenty-one governments have disappeared altogether, and only three new ones have arisen. Five have lost in territory instead of gaining. Only five, besides our own, have added to their domain. And the one which has done the most in this direction has added only a little over half a million of square miles, while we have added nearly two millions. Thus the United States government has added over fourteen hundred thousand square miles of territory more than any other single nation, and over eight hundred thousand more than have been added by all the other nations of the earth put together.

In point of population, our increase since 1798, according to the census of the several decades, has been as follows: In 1800, the total number of inhabitants in the United States was 5,305,925; in 1810, 7,239,-814; in 1820, 9,638,191; in 1830, 12,866,020; in 1840, 17,069,453; in 1850, 23,191,876; in 1860, 31,445,089; in 1870, 38,555,983; in 1880, 50,000,000; and now

(1885) estimated as not less than 55,000,000. These figures are almost too large for the mind to grasp readily. Perhaps a better idea can be formed of the rapid increase of population by looking at a few representative cities. Boston, in 1792, had 18,000 inhabitants; it now has [census of 1880] 362,839; New York, in 1792, 30,000; now, 1,206,299. Chicago, about fifty years ago, was a little trading post, with a few huts; but yet it contained at the time of the great conflagration in October, 1871, nearly 350,000 souls, and now has 650,000. (See illustrations.) San Francisco, fifty years ago, was a barren waste, but contains to-day 233,956 inhabitants.

Our industrial growth has been equally remarkable. In 1792, the United States had no cotton-mills; in 1850, there were 1,074, employing 100,000 hands. Only fifty-five years ago the first section of the first railroad in this country—the Baltimore and Ohio—was opened to a distance of twenty-three miles.* We had, Jan. 1, 1883, 115,634 miles in operation, costing

---

* The first timid experiment in railroads was a tramway in Quincy, Mass., built in 1826, chiefly by Thomas H. Perkins and Gridley Bryant, of Boston. Its only purpose was for the easier conveyance—by horses—of building-stone from the granite quarries of Quincy to tide-water. It was the germ, however, of a mighty movement in this country. The first railway in America for passengers and traffic—the Baltimore and Ohio—was chartered by the Maryland Legislature in March, 1827. The capital stock at first was only half a million dollars, and a portion of it was subscribed by the State and the city of Baltimore. Horses were its motive power, even after sixty-five miles of the road were built. But in 1829 Peter Cooper, of New York, built a locomotive in Baltimore which weighed one ton, and made eighteen miles an hour on a trial trip to Ellicott's Mills. In 1830 there were twenty-three miles of railway in the United States, which were increased the next year to ninety-five, in 1835, to one thousand and ninety-eight, and in 1840, to nearly three thousand.—*Bryant's History of the United States,* vol. iv., p. 314.

Chicago as It Appeared in 1833. (See p. 27.

The Great Chicago Fire, 1871. (Loss $150,000,000. See p. 27.)

[28]

$5,750,000,000. It was only forty-five years ago that the magnetic telegraph was invented. Now the esti- mated length of telegraph wire in operation is over 250,000 miles. In 1833, the first reaper and mower was constructed, and in 1846 the first sewing-machine was completed. Think of the hundreds of thousands of both of these classes of machines now in use. And there are now more lines of telegraph and railroad projected and in process of construction than ever before, and greater facilities and larger plans for man- ufactories of all kinds than at any previous point of time. And should these industries increase in the same geometrical ratio for a few years, the figures we now chronicle would then read about as the records of a century ago now read to us.

Since the last edition of this work was issued, the electric light, the phonograph, the microphone, and the telephone have appeared in this country, and as- tonished the world with their marvelous achievements. And recently notices appeared in the papers of a new application of electricity, by which one is actually en- abled to *see* the person who is addressing him at the other end of the telephone, many miles, perhaps, away. This would seem to be reaching the last possible re- sults in the way of the annihilation of time and space in regard to both hearing and seeing.

We take the following article from "The Centen- nial History of the United States," published in 1876 at Hartford, Ct., pp. 768–779 :—

"Here, on the verge of the centennial anniversary of the birth of our Republic, let us take a brief review of the material and in- tellectual progress of our country during the first hundred years of its political independence.

"The extent of the conceded domain of the United States, in

ort nieuw Amsterdam op de Manhatans.

First Dutch Settlement of New York (New Amsterdam) 1612.
(See p. 27.)

New York in 1648. (See p. 27.)

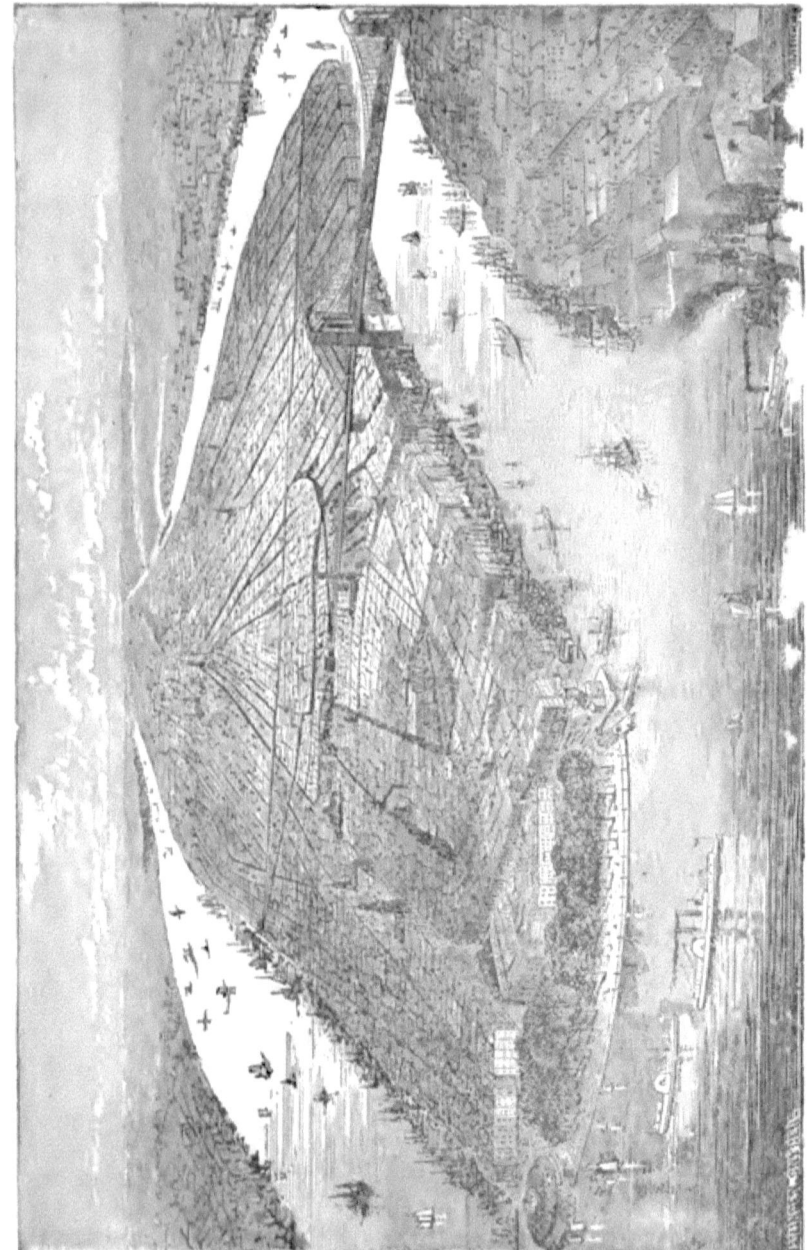

1776, was not more than *half a million* square miles ; now [when the word *now* appears in this relation it means the year 1875] it is more than *three million, three hundred thousand* square miles. Its population then was about a *million and a half ;* now it is *forty million.*

"The products of the soil are the foundations of the material wealth of a nation. It has been eminently so with us, notwithstanding the science of agriculture and the construction of good implements of labor were greatly neglected until the early part of the present century.

"A hundred years ago the agricultural interests of our country were mostly in the hands of uneducated men. Science was not applied to husbandry. · A spirit of improvement was scarcely known. The son copied the ways of his father. He worked with no other implements and pursued no other methods of cultivation ; and he who attempted a change was regarded as a visionary or an innovator. Very little associated effort for improvement in the business of farming was then seen. The first association for such a purpose was formed in the South, and was known as the 'South Carolina Agricultural Society,' organized in 1784. A similar society was formed in Pennsylvania the following year. Now there are State, county, and even town agricultural societies in almost every part of the Union.

"Agricultural implements were rude and simple. They consisted chiefly of the plow, harrow, spade, hoe, hand-rake, scythe, sickle, and wooden fork. The plow had a clumsy, wrought-iron share with wooden mold-board, which was sometimes plated with old tin or sheet-iron. The rest of the structure was equally clumsy; and the implement required in its use, twice the amount of strength of man and beast that the present plow does. Improvements in the construction of plows during the past fifty years save to the country annually, in work and teams, at least $12,000,000. The first patent for a cast-iron plow was issued in 1797. To the beginning of 1875, about four hundred patents have been granted.

"A hundred years ago the seed was sown by hand, and the entire crop was harvested by hard, manual labor. The grass was cut with a scythe, and 'cured' and gathered with a fork and hand-rake. The grain was cut with a sickle, threshed with a flail or the treading of horses, and was cleared of the chaff by a large clamshell-shaped fan of wicker-work, used in a gentle breeze. The

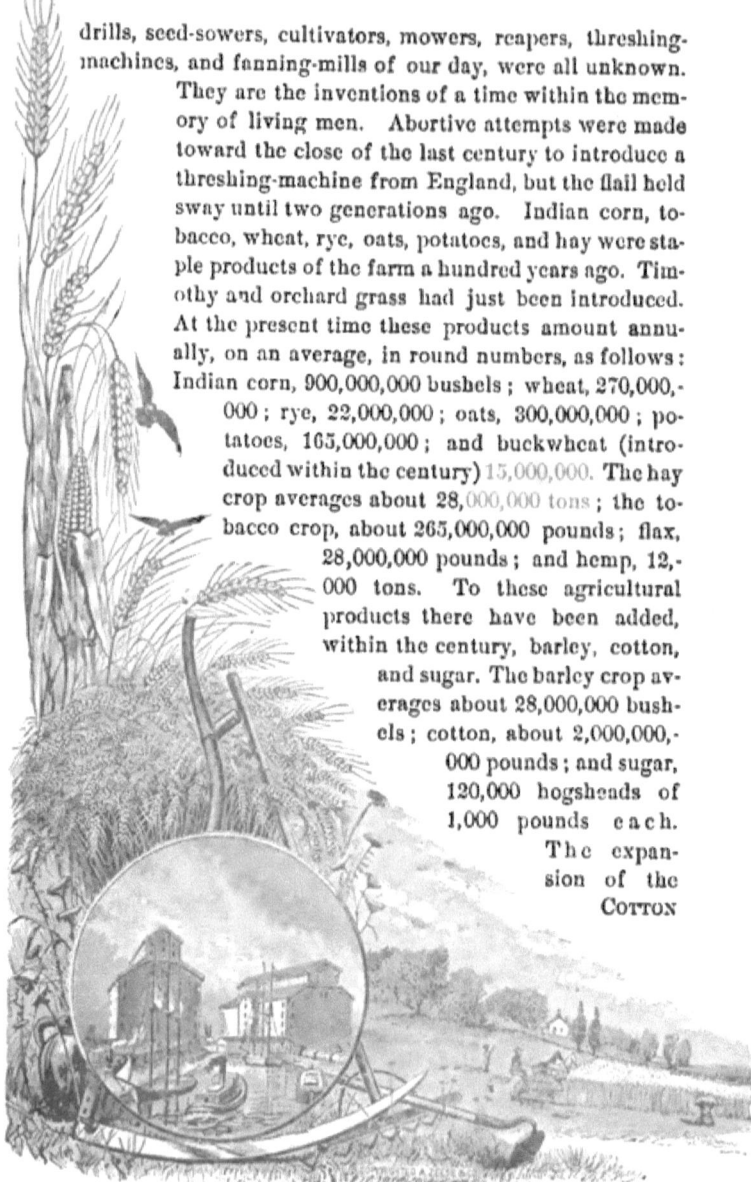

drills, seed-sowers, cultivators, mowers, reapers, threshing-machines, and fanning-mills of our day, were all unknown. They are the inventions of a time within the memory of living men. Abortive attempts were made toward the close of the last century to introduce a threshing-machine from England, but the flail held sway until two generations ago. Indian corn, tobacco, wheat, rye, oats, potatoes, and hay were staple products of the farm a hundred years ago. Timothy and orchard grass had just been introduced. At the present time these products amount annually, on an average, in round numbers, as follows: Indian corn, 900,000,000 bushels; wheat, 270,000,000; rye, 22,000,000; oats, 300,000,000; potatoes, 165,000,000; and buckwheat (introduced within the century) 15,000,000. The hay crop averages about 28,000,000 tons; the tobacco crop, about 265,000,000 pounds; flax, 28,000,000 pounds; and hemp, 12,000 tons. To these agricultural products there have been added, within the century, barley, cotton, and sugar. The barley crop averages about 28,000,000 bushels; cotton, about 2,000,000,000 pounds; and sugar, 120,000 hogsheads of 1,000 pounds each. The expansion of the COTTON culture has been marvelous. In 1784, eight bales of cotton sent to England from Charleston were seized by the custom-house authorities in Liverpool, on the ground that so large a quantity could not have come from the United States. The progress of its culture was slow until the invention of the gin, by Mr. Whitney, for clearing the seed from the fiber. It did the work of many persons. The cultivation of cotton rapidly spread. From 1792 to 1800, the amount of cotton raised had increased from 138,000 pounds to 18,000,000 pounds, all of which was wanted in England, where improved machinery was manufacturing it into cloth. The value of slave labor was increased, and a then dying institution lived in vigor until killed by the civil war. The value of the cotton crop in 1792 was $30,000 ; now its average annual value is about $180,000,000.

"Fruit culture a hundred years ago was very little thought of. Inferior varieties of apples, pears, peaches, plums, and cherries were cultivated for family use. It was not until the beginning of the present century that any large orchards were planted. The cultivation of grapes and berries was almost wholly unknown fifty years ago. The first horticultural society was formed in 1829. Before that time fruit was not an item of commercial statistics in our country. Now, the average annual value of fruit is estimated at $40,000,000. Our grape crop alone exceeds in value $10,000,000.

"Improvements in live stock have all been made within the present century. The native breeds were descended from stock sent over to the colonies, and were generally inferior. In 1772 Washington wrote in his dairy: 'With one hundred milch cows on my farm, I have to buy butter for my family.' Now 11,000,-000 cows supply 40,000,000 inhabitants with milk, butter, and cheese, and allow large exports of the latter article. At least 225,000,000 gallons of milk are sold annually. The annual butter product of our country now is more than 500,000,000 pounds, and of cheese, 70,000,000. There are now about 30,000,000 horned cattle in the United States, equal in average quality to those of any country in the world.

"A hundred years ago, mules and asses were chiefly used for farming purposes and ordinary transportation. Carriage horses were imported from Europe. Now, our horses of every kind are equal to those of any other country. It is estimated that there are about 10,000,000 horses in the United States, or one to every four persons.

"Sheep husbandry has greatly improved. The inferior breeds of the last century, raised only in sufficient quantity to supply the table, and the domestic looms in the manufacture of yarns and coarse cloth, have been superseded by some of the finer varieties. Merino sheep were introduced early in this century. The embargo before the war of 1812, and the establishment of manufactures here afterward, stimulated sheep and wool raising, and these have been important items in our national wealth. There are now about 30,000,000 sheep in the United States. California is taking the lead as a wool-producing State. In 1870, the wool product of the United States amounted to 100,000,000 pounds.

"Improvements in the breed of swine during the last fifty years have been very great. They have become a large item in our national commercial statistics. At this time there are about 26,000,000 head of swine in this country. Enormous quantities of pork, packed and in the form of bacon, are exported annually.

"These brief statistics of the principal products of agriculture, show its development in this country and its importance. Daniel Webster said, 'Agriculture feeds us; to a great extent it clothes us; without it we should not have manufactures; we should not have commerce. They all stand together like pillars in the cluster, the largest in the center, and that largest—AGRICULTURE.'

"The great manufacturing interests of our country are the product of the century now closing. The policy of the British government was to suppress manufacturing in the English-American colonies, and cloth-making was confined to the household. When non-importation agreements cut off supplies from Great Britain, the Irish flax-wheel and the Dutch wool-wheel were made active in families. All other kinds of manufacturing were of small account in this country until the concluding decade of the last century. In Great Britain the inventions of Hargreaves, Arkwright, and Crompton, had stimulated the cotton and woolen manufactures, and the effects finally reached the United States. Massachusetts offered a grant of money to promote the establishment of a cotton-mill, and one was built at Beverly in 1787, the first erected in the United States. It had not the improved English machinery. In 1789, Samuel Slater came from England with a full knowledge of that machinery, and in connection with

Messrs. Almy and Brown of Providence, R. I., established a cotton factory there in 1790, with the improved implements. Then was really begun the manufacture of cotton in the United States. Twenty years later, the number of cotton-mills in our country was one hundred and sixty-eight, with 90,000 spindles. The business has greatly expanded. In Massachusetts, the foremost State in the manufacture of cotton, there are now over two hundred mills, employing, in prosperous times, 50,000 persons, and a capital of more than $30,000,000. The city of Lowell was founded by the erection of a cotton-mill there in 1822; and there the printing of calico was first begun in the United States soon afterward.

"With wool, as with cotton, the manufacture into cloth was confined to households, for home use, until near the close of the last century. The wool was carded between two cards held in the hands of the operator, and all the processes were slow and crude. In 1797, Asa Whittemore of Massachusetts invented a carding-machine, and this led to the establishment of woolen manufactures outside of families. In his famous report on manufactures, in 1791, Alexander Hamilton said that of woolen goods, hats only had reached maturity. The business had been carried on with success in colonial times. The wool was felted by hand, and furs were added by the same slow process. This manual labor continued until a little more than thirty years ago, when it was supplanted by machinery. Immense numbers of hats of every kind are now made in our country.

"At the time of Hamilton's report, there was only one woolen-mill in the United States. This was at Hartford, Connecticut. In it were made cloths and cassimeres. Now, woolen factories may be found in almost every State in the Union, turning out annually the finest cloths, cassimeres, flannels, carpets, and every variety of goods made of wool. In this business, as in cotton, Massachusetts has taken the lead. The value of manufactured woolens in the United States, at the close of the civil war, was estimated at about $60,000,000. The supply of wool in the United States has never been equal to the demand.

"The smelting of iron ore and the manufacture of iron has become an immense business in our country. The development of ore deposits and of coal used in smelting, are among the marvels of our history. English navigation laws discouraged iron manufacture in the colonies. Only blast-furnaces for making pig-iron were allowed. This product was nearly all sent to England in exchange for manufactured articles; and the whole amount of such exportation, at the beginning of the old war for independence, was less than 8,000 tons annually. The colonists were wholly dependent upon Great Britain for articles manufactured of iron and steel, excepting rude implements made by blacksmiths for domestic use. During the war, the Continental Congress were compelled to establish manufactures of iron and steel. These were chiefly in Northern New Jersey, the Hudson Highlands, and Western Connecticut, where excellent ore was found, and forests in abundance for making charcoal. The first use of anthracite coal for smelting iron was in the Continental Armory at Carlisle, in Pennsylvania, in 1775. But charcoal was universally used until 1840 for smelting ores.

"Now, iron is manufactured in our country in every form from a nail to a locomotive. A vast number of machines have been invented for carrying on these manufactures; and the products in cutlery, fire-arms, railway materials, and machinery of every kind, employ vast numbers of men and a great amount of capital. Our locomotive builders are regarded as the best in the world; and no nation on the globe can compete with us in the construction of steam-boats of every kind, from the iron-clad war steamer to the harbor tug.

" In the manufacture of copper, silver, and gold, there has been great progress. At the close of the Revolution, no manufactures of the kind existed in our country. Now, the manufacture of copper-ware yearly, of every kind, and jewelry and watches, has become a large item in our commercial tables.

"The manufacture of paper is a very large item in the business of our country. At the close of the Revolution there were only three mills in the United States. At the beginning of the war, a demand sprung up, and Wilcox, in his mill near Philadelphia, made the first writing-paper produced in this country. He manufactured the thick, coarse paper on which the continental money was printed. So early as 1794 the business had so increased that there were in Pennsylvania alone forty-eight paper-mills. There has been a steady increase in the business ever since. Within the last twenty-five years, that increase has been enormous, and yet not sufficient to meet the demand. Improvements in printing-presses have cheapened the production of books and newspapers, and the circulation of these has greatly increased. It is estimated that the amount of paper now manufactured annually in the United States for these, for paper-hangings, and for wrapping-paper is full 800,000,000 pounds. The supply of raw material here has not been equal to the demand, and rags to the value of about $2,000,-000 in a year have been imported.

"The manufacture of ships, carriages, wagons, clocks and watches, pins, leather, glass, Indian rubber, silk, wood, sewing-machines, and a variety of other things wholly unknown or feebly carried on a hundred years ago, now flourish, and form very important items in our domestic commerce. The sewing-machine is an American invention, and the first really practical one was first offered to the public by Elias Howe, Jr., about thirty years ago. A patent had been obtained for one five years before. Great improvements have been made, and now a very extensive business in the manufacture and sale of sewing-machines is carried on by different companies, employing a large amount of capital and costly machinery, and a great number of persons.

A Mining Scene.

"The mining interests of the United States have become an eminent part of the national wealth. The extraction of lead, iron, copper, the precious metals, and coal, from the bosom of the earth, is a business that has almost wholly grown up within the last hundred years. In 1754 a lead mine was worked in Southwestern Virginia; and in 1778, Dubuque, a French miner, worked lead ore deposits on the western bank of the upper Mississippi. The Jesuit missionaries discovered copper in the Lake Superior region more than two hundred years ago, and that remains the chief source of our native copper ore. That metal is produced in smaller quantities in other States, chiefly in the West and Southwest.

"A lust for gold, and the knowledge of its existence in America, was the chief incentive to emigration to these shores. But within the domain of our Republic, very little of it was found, until that domain was extended far toward the Pacific ocean. It was unsuspected until long after the Revolution. Finally, gold was discovered among the mountains of Virginia, North and South Carolina, and in Georgia. North Carolina was the first State in the Union to send gold to the mint in Philadelphia. Its first small contribution was in 1804. From that time until 1823 the average amount produced from North Carolina mines did not exceed $2,500 annually. Virginia's first contribution was in 1829, when that of North Carolina, for that year, was $128,000. Georgia sent its first contribution in 1830. It amounted to $212,000. The product so increased that branch mints were established in North Carolina and Georgia in 1837 and 1838, and another in New Orleans.

"In 1848, gold was discovered on the American fork of the Sacramento River in California, and soon afterward elsewhere in that region. A gold fever seized the people of the United States, and thousands rushed to California in search of the precious metals. Within a year from the discovery, nearly 50,000 people were there. Less than five years afterward, California, in one year, sent to the United States mint full $40,000,-000 in gold. Its entire gold product to this time is estimated at more than $800,000,000. Over all the far Western States and Territories the precious metals, gold and silver, seem to be scattered in profusion, and the amount of mineral wealth yet to be discovered there seems to be incalculable. Our coal fields seem to be inexhaustible; and out of the bosom of the earth, in portions of our country, flow millions of barrels , annually of petroleum, or rock-oil, affording the cheapest illuminating material in the world.

"Mineral coal was first discovered and used in Pennsylvania at the period of the Revolution. A boat load was sent down the Susquehanna from Wilkesbarre for the use of the Continental works at Carlisle. But it was not much used before the war of 1812; and the regular business of mining this fuel did not become a part of the commerce of the country before the year 1820, when 365 tons were sent to Philadelphia. At the present time the amount of coal sent to market from the American mines, of all kinds, is equal to full 15,000,000 tons annually.

"The commerce of the United States has had a wonderful growth. Its most active development was seen in New England. British legislation imposed heavy burdens upon it in colonial times, and like manufactures, it was greatly depressed. The New Englanders built many vessels for their own use, but more for others; and just before the breaking out of the Revolution, there was quite a brisk trade carried on between the English-American colonies and the West Indies, as well as with the mother country. The colonists exported tobacco, lumber, shingles, staves, masts, turpentine, hemp, flax, pot and pearl ashes, salted fish in great quantities, some corn, live stock, pig-iron, and skins and furs procured by traffic with the Indians. Whale and cod-fishing was an important branch of commerce. In the former, there were 160 vessels employed at the beginning of 1775, and sperm candles and whale oil were exported to Great Britain. In exchange for New England products, a large amount of molasses was brought from the West Indies, and made into rum to sell to the Indians and fishermen, and to exchange for slaves on the coast of Africa. The entire exports of the colonies in the year 1770 amounted in value to $14,262,000.

"At the close of the war, the British government refused to enter into commercial relations with the United States government, believing that the weak league of States would soon be dissolved; but when a vigorous national government was formed in 1789, Great Britain, for the first, sent a resident minister to our government, and entered into a commercial arrangement with us. Meanwhile a brisk trade had sprung up between the colonies and Great Britain, as well as with other countries. From 1784 to 1790 the exports from the United States to Great Britain amounted to $33,-

000,000, and the imports from Great Britain to $87,000,000. At the same time several new and important branches of industry had appeared, and flourished with great rapidity.

"From that time the expansion of American commerce was marvelous, in spite of the checks it received from British jealousy, wars, piracies in the Mediterranean Sea and elsewhere, and the effects of embargoes. The tonnage of American ships, which in 1789 was 201,562, was in 1870 more than 7,000,000. The exports from the United States in 1870 amounted to about $464,-000,000, and the imports to about $395,000,000 in gold.

"The domestic commerce of the United States is immense. A vast sea-coast line, great lakes, large rivers, and many canals, afford scope for inter-State commerce and with adjoining countries,

View on the Erie Canal.

not equaled by those of any nation. The canal and railway systems in the United States are the product chiefly of the present century. So also is navigation by steam, on which river commerce chiefly relies for transportation. This was begun in the year 1807. The first canals made in this country were two short ones, for a water passage around the South Hadley and Montague Falls, in Massachusetts. These were constructed in 1792. At about the same time the Inland Lock Navigation Companies in the State of New York began their work. The Middlesex Canal, connecting Lowell with Boston Harbor, was completed in 1808, and the great Erie Canal, 363 miles in length, was finished in 1825, at a cost of almost $8,000,000. The aggregate length of canals built in the United States is 3,200 miles.

"The first railway built in the United States was one three

miles in length, that connected the granite quarries at Quincy, Mass., with the Neponset River. It was completed in 1827; horse power was used. The first use of a locomotive in this country was in 1829, when one was put upon a railway that connected the coal mines of the Delaware and Hudson Canal Company with Honesdale.* Now, railways form a thick net-work all over the United States east of the Mississippi, and are rapidly spreading over the States and Territories beyond, to the Pacific ocean. To these facilities for commercial operations must be added the Electro-Magnetic Telegraph, an American invention, as a method of transmitting intelligence, and giving warning signals to the shipping and agricultural interests concerning the actual and probable state of the weather each day. The first line, forty miles in length, was constructed between Baltimore and Washington in 1844. Now the lines are extended to every part of our Union, and all over the civilized world, traversing oceans and rivers, and bringing Persia and New York within one hour's space of intercommunication.

"Banking institutions and insurance companies are intimately connected with commerce. The first bank in the United States was established in 1781, as a financial aid to the government. It was called the Bank of North America. The Bank of New York and Bank of Massachusetts were established soon afterward. On the recommendation of Hamilton, in 1791, a national bank was established at Philadelphia, with a capital of $10,000,000, of which sum the government subscribed $2,000,000. Various banking systems, under State charters, have since been tried. During the civil war, a system of national banking was established, by which there is a uniform paper currency throughout the Union. The number of national banks at the close of 1863 was 66; the

---

* This was for freight only. The first passenger railway was opened in 1830, as stated on page 27.

number at the close of 1874 was not far from 1,700, involving
capital to the amount of almost $500,000,000.

"Fire, marine, and life insurance companies have flourished
greatly in the United States. The first incorporated company was

An Ordinary Scene.

Our Illustration shows a Train passing over the Kankakee River, on the Illinois Central
Railroad, and gives a good idea of Modern Engineering Skill.

established in 1792, in Philadelphia, and known as the 'Fire Insurance Company of North America.' Another was established
in Providence, Rhode Island, in 1799, and another in New York
in 1806. The first life insurance company was chartered in Mas-

sachusetts in 1825, and the 'New York Life Insurance and **Trust Company**' was established in 1829. All others are of recent **organization**. As a rule, the business of insurance of every kind is **profitable to** the insurers and the insured. The amount of capital engaged in it is enormous. The fire risks alone, at the close of 1874, amounted to about $200,000,000.

"Our growth in population has **been** steadily increased by **immigration from Europe.** It **began very moderately after the Revolution.** From 1784 to 1794 the average number of immigrants a **year was 4,000.** During the last ten years the number of persons who have **immigrated to the United States** from Europe is estimated at over **2,000,000, who brought with them, in** the aggregate, $200,000,000 **in money.** This **capital and the productive labor** of the immigrants have added much **to the wealth of our country.** This immigration and **wealth is less than during the** ten years preceding the **civil war,** during which time **there** came to this country from **Europe 2,814,554** persons, bringing with **them an average** of at least **$100, or an** aggregate of over $281,000,000.

"The **Arts,** Sciences, and Invention have made **a** great progress in our country during the last hundred **years.** These **at the close** of the Revolution, were of little account in estimating the advance of the race. The practitioners **of the Arts of** Design, at that **period,** were **chiefly** Europeans. **Of** native artists, **C. W.** Peale and **J. S.** Copley stood at the **head of** painters. There were no sculptors, and no engravers of any eminence. Architects, in the proper sense, **there were none.** After the Revolution **a** few good painters appeared, **and these have gradually increased** in numbers and excellence, without much encouragement, **except** in portraiture, until within the **last twenty-five years.** We have now good sculptors, architects, **engravers, and lithographers;** and in all of these departments, **as well as in photography, very great** progress has been made **within the last thirty or forty years.** In wood engraving, especially, the improvement **has** been **wonderful.** Forty years ago there were not more than a dozen practitioners of the art in this country; now there are between four and five hundred. At the head of that class of artists stands the name of **Dr.** Alexander Anderson, **who was** the first man who engraved on wood in the United States. He died in 1870 at the **age of** ninety-five years. In bank-note engraving we **have** attained to greater excellence than any other people. It is considered the most perfect branch of the art in design and execution.

"Associations have been formed for improvements in the Arts of Design. The first was organized in Philadelphia in 1791, by C. W. Peale, in connection with Ceracchi, the Italian sculptor. It failed. In 1802 the American Academy of Fine Arts was organized in the city of New York, and in 1807 the Pennsylvania Academy of Fine Arts, yet in existence, was established in Philadelphia. In 1826 the American Academy of Fine Arts was su-

A Wood Engraver plying his Profession.

perseded by the National Academy of Design, in the city of New York, which is now a flourishing institution.

"In education and literature our progress has kept pace with other things. At the very beginning of settlements, the common school was made the special care of the State in New England. Not so much attention was given to this matter elsewhere in the colonies. The need of higher institutions of learning was early felt; and eighteen years after the landing of the Pilgrims from the Mayflower, Harvard College was founded. When the war for independence began, there were nine colleges in the colonies; namely, Harvard, at Cambridge, Mass.; William and

Mary, at Williamsburg, Va.; Yale, at New Haven, Conn.; College of New Jersey, at Princeton; University of Pennsylvania, at Philadelphia; King's (now Columbia), in the city of New York; Brown University, at Providence, R. I.; Dartmouth, at Hanover, N. H.; and Rutgers at New Brunswick, N. J. There are now about 300 colleges in the United States.

"At the period of the Revolution, teaching in the common schools was very meager, and remained so for full thirty years. Only reading, spelling, and arithmetic were regularly taught. The Psalter, the New Testament, and the Bible constituted the reading-books. No history was read; no geography or grammar was taught; and until the putting forth of Webster's spelling-book in 1783, pronunciation was left to the judgment of teachers. That book produced a revolution.

"As the nation advanced in wealth and intelligence, the necessity for correct popular education became more and more manifest, and associated efforts were made for the improvement of the schools by providing for the training of teachers, under the respective phase of Teachers' Associations, Educational Periodicals, Normal Schools, and Teachers' Institutes. The first of these societies in this country was the 'Middlesex County Association for the Improvement of Common Schools,' established at Middletown, Connecticut, in 1799. But little of importance was done in that direction until within the last forty-five years. Now, provision is made in all sections of the Union, not only for the support of common schools, but for training-schools for teachers. Since the civil war, great efforts have been made to establish common-school systems in the late slave-labor States, that should include among the beneficiaries the colored population. Much has been done in that regard.

"Very great improvements have been made in the organization and discipline of the public schools in cities within the last thirty years. Free schools are rapidly spreading their beneficent influence over the whole Union, and in some States laws have been made that compel all children of a certain age to go to school. Institutions for the special culture of young women in all that pertains to college education, have been established within a few years. The pioneer in this work is Vassar College, at Poughkeepsie, N. Y., which was first opened in the year 1865.

"Besides the ordinary means for education, others have been

established for special purposes. There are Law, Scientific, Medical, Theological, Military, Commercial, and Agricultural schools, and seminaries for the deaf, dumb, and blind. In many States school-district libraries have been established. There are continually enlarging means provided for the education of the whole people. Edmund Burke said, 'Education is the cheap defense of nations.'

"Our literature is as varied as the tastes of the people. No subject escapes the attention of our native scholars and authors. At the period of the Revolution, books were few in variety and numbers. The larger portion of them were devoted to theological subjects. Booksellers were few, and were only found in the larger cities. Various subjects were discussed in pamphlets, not generally in newspapers, as now. The editions of books were small, and as stereotyping was unknown, they became rare in a few years, because there was only a costly way of reproduction.

"In the year 1801, a new impetus was given to the book trade by the formation of the 'American Company of Booksellers'—a kind of 'union.' Twenty years later, competition broke up the association. Before the war of 1812, the book trade in the United States was small. Only school books had very large sales. Webster's spelling-book was an example of the increasing demand for such helps to education. During the twenty years he was engaged on his dictionary, the income from his spelling-book supported him and his family. It was published in 1783, and its sales have continually increased to the present time, when they amount to over 1,000,000 copies a year. Other school books of every kind now have an immense annual circulation. The general book trade in this country is now immense in the numbers of volumes issued and the capital and labor employed. Readers are rapidly increasing. An ardent thirst for knowledge or entertainment to be found in books, magazines, and newspapers, makes a very large demand for these vehicles, while, at the same time, they produce wide-spread in-

4

telligence. The magazine literature, now generally healthful, is a powerful conadjutor of books in this popular culture; and the newspaper, not always so healthful, supplies the daily and weekly demand for ephemerals in literature and general knowledge. To meet that demand required great improvements in printing machinery, and these have been supplied.

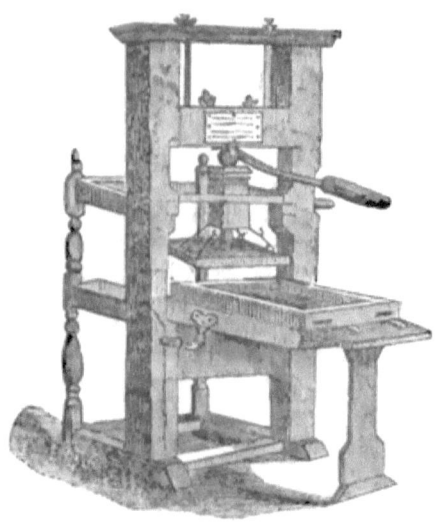

Old Franklin (Ramage) Press.

"The printing-press, at the time of the Revolution, is shown in that used by Franklin, in which the pressure force was obtained by means of a screw. The ink was applied by huge balls; and an expert workman could furnish about fifty impressions an hour. This was improved by Earl Stanhope in 1815, by substituting for the screw a jointed lever. Then came inking machines, and one man could work off 250 copies an hour. Years passed on, and the cylinder press was invented; and in 1847 it was perfected by Richard M. Hoe of New York. This has been further improved lately, and a printing-press is now used which will strike off 15,000 newspapers, printed on both sides, every hour.

"The newspapers printed in the United States at the beginning of the Revolution were few in number, small in size, and very meager in information of any kind. They were issued weekly, semi-weekly, and tri-weekly. The first daily newspaper issued in this country was the *American Daily Advertiser*, established in Philadelphia in 1784. In 1775 there were 37 newspapers and periodicals in the United States, with an aggregate issue that year of 1,200,000 copies. In 1870 the number of daily

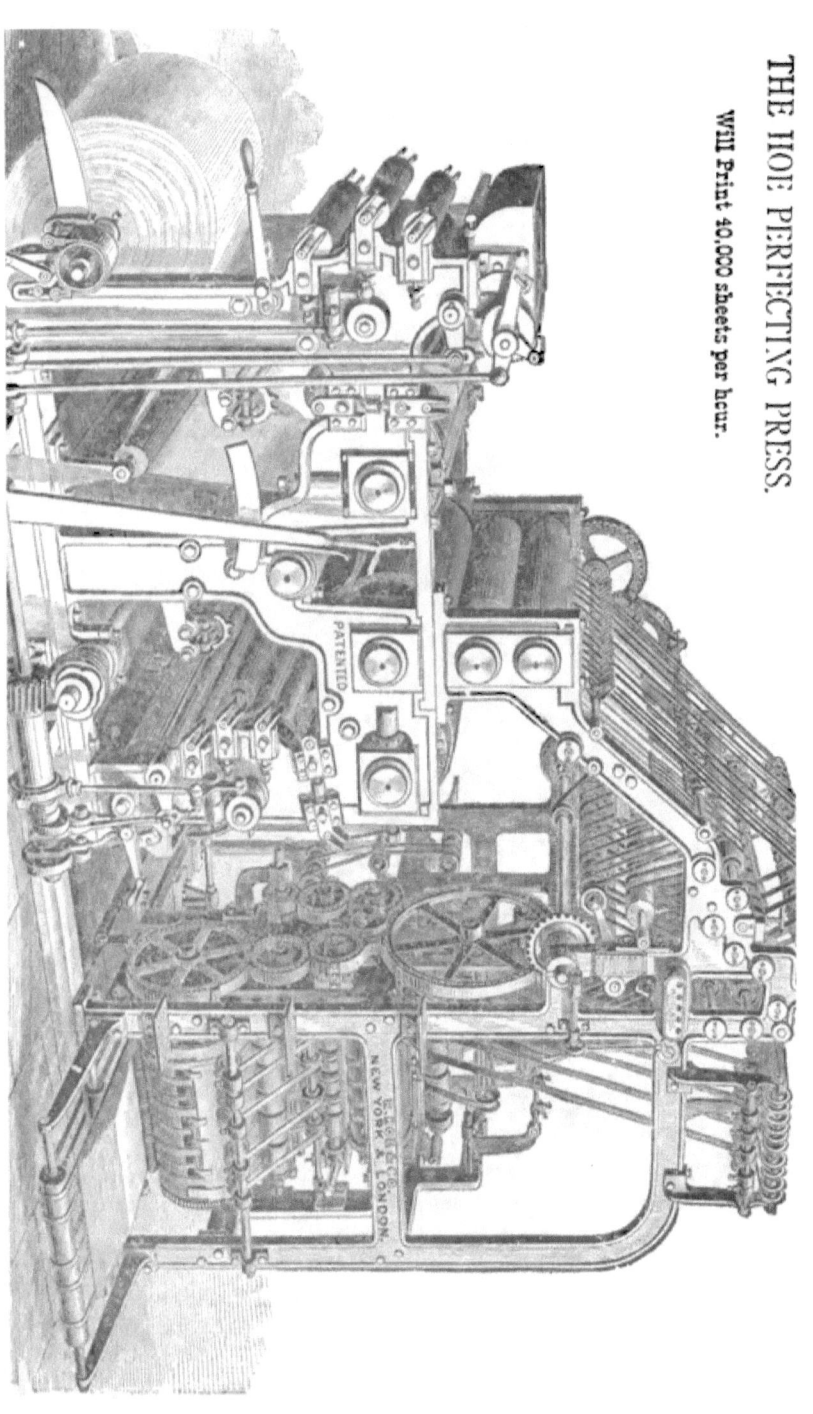

THE HOE PERFECTING PRESS.

Will Print 40,000 sheets per hour.

newspapers in the United States was 542; and of weeklies, 4,425. Of the dailies, 800,000,000 were issued that year; of the weeklies, 600,000,000; and of other serial publications, 100,000,000; making an aggregate of full 1,500,000,000 copies. To these figures should

Battle Creek Tabernacle.

This commodious edifice for divine worship, is 105 by 130 feet, with entrances at each corner, and has a seating capacity for 3,200 persons. It has a gallery on three sides, and three large vestrys, which may become a part of the main auditorium by simply raising the sliding partitions, which are of ground glass. This beautiful structure is especially convenient for Sabbath-school work and General Conferences, and is frequently used for moral lectures and the commencement exercises of the Battle Creek Public Schools.

be made a large addition at the close of 1875. There are now about forty newspapers in the United States which have existed over fifty years.

"In the providing of means for moral and religious culture and benevolent enterprises, there has been great progress in this country during the century now closing. The various religious denominations have in-

Ministering to the Fallen.

creased in membership fully in proportion to the increase of population. Asylums of every kind for the unfortunate and friendless have been multiplied in an equal ratio, and provision is made for all. [The vignettes on this page show common works of philanthropy.]

Home for the Homeless.

"One of the most conspicuous examples of the growth of our Republic is presented by the postal service. Dr. Franklin had been Colonial Postmaster - General, and he was appointed to the same office for one year by the Continental Congress in the summer of 1775. He held the position a little more than a year, and at the end of his official term there were about 50

post-offices in the United States.   All the accounts of the General
Post-Office Department during that period were contained in a
small book consisting of about two quires of foolscap paper,
which is preserved in the Department at Washington City.
Through all the gloomy years of the weak Confederacy, the business of the Department was comparatively light ; and when the
national government began its career in 1789, there were only
about seventy-five post offices, with an aggregate length of post-
roads of about 1,900 miles.   The annual income was $28,000, and
the annual expenditures were $32,000.   The mails were carried
by postmen on horseback, and sometimes on foot.   Now the number of post-offices is over 33,000 ; the aggregate length of post-
routes is 256,000 miles ; the annual revenue, $23,000,000, and the
annual expenditures, $29,000,000.

"We may safely claim for our people and country a progress
in all that constitutes a vigorous and prosperous nation during
the century just passed, equal, if not superior, to that of any
other on the globe.   And to the inventive genius and skill of the
Americans may be fairly awarded a large share of the honor acquired by the construction of machinery, which has so largely
taken the place of manual labor.   In that progress the American
citizen beholds a tangible prophecy of a brilliant future for his
country."

The following paragraphs which went the rounds
of the papers a few years ago, present a good sum-
mary of the success " Brother Jonathan " has achieved
thus far in his career :—

"Brother Jonathan commenced business in 1776, with thirteen
States and 815,615 square miles of territory, which was occupied
by about 3,000,000 of civilized human beings.   He has now a
family of 43,000,000, who occupy thirty-seven States and nine
Territories, which embrace over 3,000,000 square miles.   He
has 65,000 miles of railroad, more than sufficient to reach twice
and a half around the globe.   The value of his annual agricultural productions is $2,500,000,000, and his gold mines are capable
of producing $70,000,000 a year.   He has more than 1,000 cotton
factories, 580 daily newspapers, 4,300 weeklies, and 625 monthly
publications.   He has also many other things too numerous and
too notorious to mention."

"The United States of America issues more newspapers, in number and in aggregate circulation, than all the rest of the world combined. America outnumbers the press of Great Britain, six to one, and has nearly half a dozen daily papers which print more copies every issue than does the London *Times.*"

The rate of growth maintained in this country since the compilation of the foregoing figures in 1876, may be best shown by comparing them with the figures on some of the items named above from the census of 1880. Thus the people of the United States, at this last-named date, possessed, in round numbers, 38,000,000 cattle and 48,000,000 swine. This is a larger number of cattle than any other nation can show, India having but 30,000,000, and Russia 29,000,000. We have 10,500,000 horses, being surpassed in this respect only by Russia, which has 20,000,000. We come fourth in the list of sheep-raising nations, having 36,000,000; but in the food-producing animals, cattle and hogs, our country leads the world.

According to returns for the year 1882, our corn crop amounted to 2,700,000,000 bushels; wheat, 520,-000,000 bushels; hay, 32,000,000 tons; coal, 80,000,-000 tons; petroleum, 27,500,000 barrels; pig iron, 4,000,000 tons; manufactured steel rails, 900,000 tons.

And nature herself, by the physical features she has stamped upon our country, has seemed to lay it out as a field for national development on the most magnificent scale. Here we have the largest lakes, the longest rivers, the mightiest cataracts, the deepest caves, the broadest and most fertile prairies, and the richest mines of gold and iron and coal and copper, to be found upon the globe.

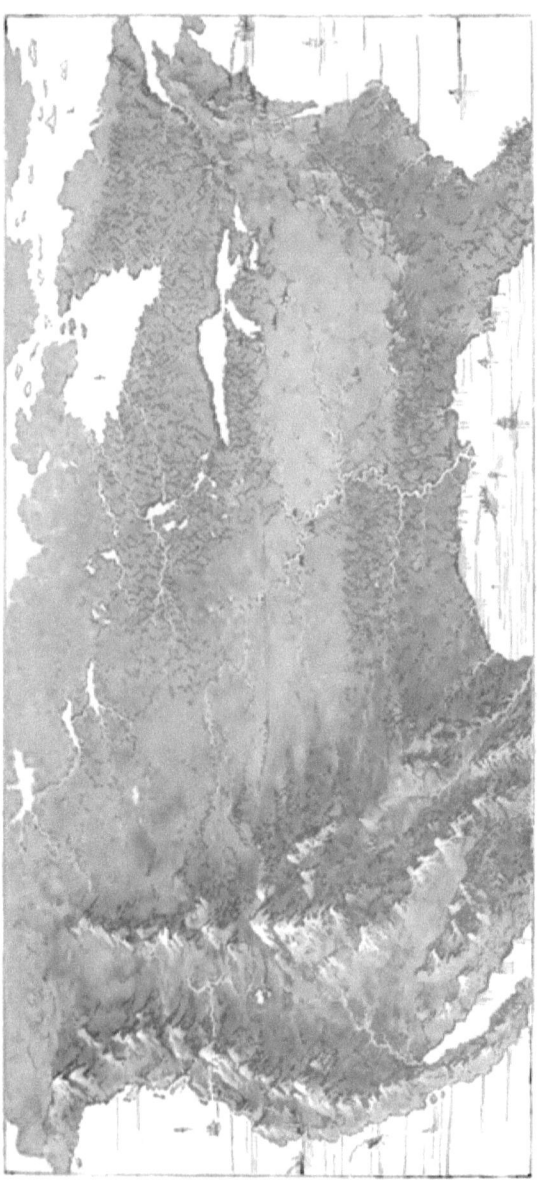

A Bird's-eye View of the United States.

The illustration here given takes in so large a portion of North America, including most of the British dominions on the north, as to show the position of the United States in the heart of the continent, and give a general idea of its physical features. Behold the vast basin drained by the Tennessee, Ohio, Mississippi, and Missouri Rivers; while the lofty mountain ranges on the west furnish unlimited mineral resources; and long ocean coast lines east and west, put the country in easy communication with all the world.

5

One of the most important industries of the world is the lumber business, the traffic in timber for building houses, ships, etc., and manufacturing purposes. The principal nations engaged in this business, outside of the United States, are Norway, Russia, Germany, British North America, and to some extent, France. In our own country immense lumber districts are found in Maine, New York, Pennsylvania, Michigan, Illinois, Wisconsin, Minnesota, Indiana, some portions of the Southern States, California, and Oregon. The more important centers of the trade are Bangor, Me., Boston, Chicago, the lake ports generally, Albany, N. Y., Savannah, and Brunswick, Ga., and Pensacola, Florida. There were in 1870, 26,945 lumber manufactories, employing 163,637 men, using $161,500,273 invested capital, paying $46,231,328 in wages, and producing $252,339,029 worth of lumber. Grave fears are excited by the meteorological effects which are likely to follow this removal of the forests.

"When America was discovered, there were but sixty millions of gold in Europe. California and the Territories around her have produced one thousand millions of dollars in gold in twenty years. Sixty-one million dollars was the largest annual gold yield ever made in Australia. California has several times produced ninety millions of gold in a year."—*Townsend*, p. 384.

"The area of workable coal-beds in all the world outside the United States is estimated at 26,000 square miles. That of the United States, not including Alaska, is estimated at over 200,000 square miles, or *eight times as large as the available coal area of all the rest of the globe!*"—*American* Year *Book for* 1869, p. 655.

"The iron product and manufacture of the United States has increased enormously within the last few years, and the vast beds of iron convenient to coal in various parts of the Union are destined to make America the chief source of supply for the world." "Three mountains of solid iron [in Missouri], known as Iron Mountain, Pilot Knob, and Shepherd's Mountain, are among the most remarkable natural curiosities on our continent."—*Id.*, p. 654.

And the people have taken hold to lay out their work on the grand scale that nature has indicated. Excepting only the Houses of Parliament in London, our national Capitol at Washington is the most spacious and imposing national edifice in the world. By the unparalleled feat of a subterranean tunnel two miles out under the bottom of the lake, Chicago obtains her water. Chicago is the most extensive grain and lumber market in the world; and Philadelphia and New York contain the largest and best-furnished printing establishments now in existence. The submarine cable, running like a thread of light through the depths of the broad Atlantic from the United States to England, a conception of American genius, is the greatest achievement in the telegraphic line. The Pacific Railroad, that iron highway from the Atlantic to the Pacific, stands at the head of all monuments of engineering skill in modern times.

Capitol Building at Washington, D. C.

The entire length of the Capitol is 751½ feet, and its greatest depth, including porticoes and steps, is 348 feet. The ground covered by the entire building is a little over 3½ acres. The walls of the Central Building are of sandstone, painted white. The Extensions are of white marble, slightly variegated with blue. The Dome is of cast-iron, 135½ feet in diameter, and rises to a hight of 287½ feet above the basement floor. On the top of the Dome is a bronze statue of LIBERTY, 19¼ feet high.   [59]

The Washington Monument.

This is the tallest structure yet erected by the hand of man. It was commenced in 1848, completed in 1884, and dedicated on Washington's birthday, Feb. 22, 1885. The shaft rises to a hight of 500 feet 5½ inches. This is surmounted by an apex of 7-inch marble slabs 55 feet high, making the total hight 555 feet 5½ inches, which is 597 feet 3 inches above low-water level in the Potomac. Cost $1,187,710.31.

Following the first Atlantic cable, soon came a second almost as a matter of course ; and following the Central Pacific Railroad, a southern line has been opened, and a northern line has more recently been completed. And what results are expected to flow from these mighty enterprises? The *Scientific American* of Oct. 6, 1866, says :—

"To exaggerate the importance of this transcontinental highway is almost impossible. To a certain extent it will change the relative positions of this country, Europe, and Asia. . . . With the completion of the Pacific Railroad, instead of receiving our goods from India, China, and Japan, and the 'isles of the sea,' by way of London and Liverpool, we shall bring them direct by way of the Sandwich Islands and the railroad, and become the carriers, to a great extent, for Europe. But this is but a portion of the advantage of this work. Our Western mountains are almost literally mountains of gold and silver. In them the Arabian fable of Aladdin is realized. . . . Let the road be completed, and the comforts as well as the necessaries furnished by Asia, the manufactures of Europe, and the productions of the States, can be brought by the iron horse almost to the miner's door ; and in the production and possession of the precious metals, the blood of commerce, we shall be the richest nation on the globe. But the substantial wealth created by the improvement of the soil and the development of the resources of the country, is a still more important element in the result of this vast work."

Thus, with the idea of becoming the carriers of the world, the highway of the nations, and the richest power on the globe, the American heart swells with pride, and mounts up with aspirations to which there is no limit.

And the extent to which we have come up is further shown by the influence which we are exerting on other nations. Speaking of America, Mr. Townsend, in the work above cited, p. 462, says :—

"Out of her discovery grew the European reformation in re-

Bartholdi's Statue of Liberty Enlightening the World.

Erected on Bedloe Island in New York harbor. This monument is over 300 feet high. The statue alone, from the heel to the top of the head, measures 111 feet. The torch is to be lighted with an electric light. This tower is 50 feet higher than the celebrated Colossus of Rhodes, one of the seven wonders of the ancient world. It is the largest statue ever erected.

The Brooklyn Bridge.

The total length of this unequaled structure is 5,989 feet; width, 85 feet; length of river span, 1,595 feet; the hight in the center, above high water mark, is 135 feet; the four large cables are each composed of 6,300 parallel wires, and are 15¾ inches in diameter; the towers are 277 feet in hight; and the cost of the whole structure, was thirteen millions of dollars.

ligion; out of our Revolutionary war grew the revolutionary period of Europe. And out of our rapid development among great States and happy peoples, has come an immigration more wonderful than that which invaded Europe from Asia in the latter centuries of the Roman empire. When we raised our flag on the Atlantic, Europe sent her contributions; it appeared on the Pacific, and all Orientalism felt the signal. They are coming in two endless fleets, eastward and westward, and the highway is swung between the oceans for them to tread upon. We have lightened Ireland of half of her weight, and Germany is coming by the village-load every day. England herself is sending the best of her workingmen now (1869), and in such numbers as to dismay her Jack Bunsbys. What is to be the limit of this mighty immigration?"

J. P. Thompson (United States as a Nation, p. 180) says:—

"History gives examples of the migration of tribes and peoples for the occupation of new territories by settlement or conquest; but there is no precedent for a nation receiving into its bosom millions of foreigners as equal sharers in its political rights and powers. With a magnanimity almost reckless, the United States has done this and has survived. Immigration first assumed proportions worthy of note in the decade from 1830 to 1840, when it reached the figure of 599,000. In the decade from 1840 to 1850, it increased to 1,713,000; and the report of the Bureau of Statistics for 1874, gives for the ten calendar years from Jan. 1, 1864, to Dec. 31, 1873, inclusive, a net immigration of 3,287,994. Compare these figures with the fact that the purchase of Louisiana, over a million square miles, brought with it scarcely twenty thousand white inhabitants, and the nearly a million square miles acquired through Texas and the Mexican cessions, brought only some fifty thousand, and it will be seen how much more formidable has been the problem of immigration than that of territory."

The *American Traveler*, published in Boston, Mass., in its issue of Feb. 24, 1883, says:—

"The growth of immigration is one of the most striking facts of the period. In 1881 the total arrivals were 720,000, and in

Fulton's First Steamboat, 1807.

The "Sound" Steamer "Pilgrim," 1885.

Said to be the most elegantly furnished steamer in the world.

1882 they rose to 735,000. These figures are impressive. They foreshadow an addition to our population, by immigration alone, if this rate is maintained, of seven million persons in the next ten years,"

This would be more than twice the entire population of the country at the beginning of our independence. It is estimated that last year's immigrants brought with them a cash capital of $62,470,000 ; and if each one is worth, as a producing machine, as is claimed from careful estimates, $1,000, Europe has added to our capital stock, the past two years, the handsome sum of $1,455,000,000.

Speaking of our influence and standing in the Pacific, Mr. Townsend, p. 608, says :—

"In the Pacific ocean, these four powers [England, France, Holland, and Russia] are squarely met by the United States, which, without possessions or the wish for them, has paramount influence in Japan, the favor of China, the friendly countenance of Russia, and good feeling with all the great English colonies planted there. The United States is the only power on the Pacific which has not been guilty of intrigue, of double-dealing, of envy, and of bitterness, and it has taken the *front rank* in influence without awakening the dislike of any of its competitors, possibly excepting those English who are never magnanimous."

And Hon. Wm. H. Seward, on his return from his celebrated trip around the world, said, "Americans are now the fashion all over the world."

With one more extract we close the testimony on this point. In the New York *Independent* of July 7, 1870, Hon. Schuyler Colfax, then Vice-President of the United States, glancing briefly at the past history of this country, said :—

"Wonderful, indeed, has been that history. Springing into life from under the heel of tyranny, its progress has been onward, with the firm step of a conqueror. From the rugged clime of

The Great Prairies of the West.

New England, from the banks of the Chesapeake, from the Savannahs of Carolina and Georgia, the descendants of the Puritans, the Cavalier, and the Huguenot, swept over the towering Alleghanies, but a century ago the barrier between civilization on the one side and almost unbroken barbarism on the other; and the banners of the Republic waved from flag-staff and highland, through the broad valleys of the Ohio, the Mississippi, and the Missouri. Nor stopped its progress there. Thence onward poured the tide of American civilization and progress, over the vast regions of the Western plains; and from the snowy crests of the Sierras you look down on American States fronting the calm Pacific, an empire of themselves in resources and wealth, but loyal in our darkest hours to the nation whose authority they acknowledge, and in whose glory they proudly share.

"From a territorial area of less than nine hundred thousand square miles, it has expanded into over three millions and a half, —fifteen times larger than that of Great Britain and France combined,—with a shore-line, including Alaska, equal to the entire circumference of the earth, and with a domain within these lines far wider than that of the Romans in their proudest days of conquest and renown. With a river, lake, and coastwise commerce estimated at over two thousand millions of dollars per year; with railway traffic of from four to six thousand millions per year, and the annual domestic exchanges of the country running up to nearly ten thousand millions per year; with over two thousand millions of dollars invested in manufacturing, mechanical, and mining industry; with over five hundred millions of acres of land in actual occupancy, valued, with their appurtenances, at over seven thousand millions of dollars, and producing annually crops valued at over three thousand millions of dollars; with a realm which, if the density of Belgium's population were possible, would be vast enough to include all the present inhabitants of the world; and with equal rights guaranteed to even the poorest and humblest of over forty millions of people, we can, with a manly pride akin to that which distinguished the palmiest days of Rome, claim, as the noblest title of the world, 'I am an American citizen.'"

And how long a time has it taken for this wonderful transformation? In the language of Edward

Everett, "They are but lately dead who saw the first-born of the Pilgrims;" and Mr. Townsend (p. 21) says, "The memory of one man can swing from that time of primitive government to this—when thirty-eight millions of people [he could now say fifty-five millions] living on two oceans and in two zones, are represented in Washington, and their consuls and ambassadors are in every port and metropolis of the globe."

The Mayflower.

From a model in Pilgrim Hall, at Plymouth, Mass.

The East and the West.

CHAPTER III.

POLITICAL AND RELIGIOUS INFLUENCE OF THE NATION.

THE great instrument which our forefathers set forth as their bill of rights—the Declaration of Independence—contains these words :—

"We hold these truths to be self-evident, that all men are created equal; that they are endowed by their Creator with certain unalienable rights; that among these are life, liberty, and the pursuit of happiness." And in Art. IV., Sec. 4, of the Constitution of the United States, we find these words: "The United States shall guarantee to every State in this Union a republican form of government." A republican form of government is one in which the power rests with the people, and the whole machinery of government is worked by representatives elected by them.

This is a sufficient guarantee of civil liberty. What is said respecting religious freedom? In Art. VI. of the Constitution, we read: "No religious test shall ever be required as a qualification to any office of public trust under the United States." In Art. I. of Amendments of the Constitution, we read: "Congress shall make no law respecting an establishment of religion, or prohibiting the free exercise thereof."

In reply to questions as to the design of the Constitution, from a committee of a Baptist society in Virginia, George Washington wrote, Aug. 4, 1789, as follows :—

"If I had the least idea of any difficulty resulting from the Constitution adopted by the Convention of which I had the honor to be the President when it was formed, so as to endanger the rights of any religious denomination, then I never should have attached my name to that instrument. If I had any idea that the general government was so administered that the liberty of conscience was endangered, I pray you be assured that no man would be more willing than myself to revise and alter that part of it, so as to avoid all religious persecutions. You can, without doubt, remember that I have often expressed my opinion, that every man who conducts himself as a good citizen is accountable to God alone for his religious faith, and should be protected in worshiping God according to the dictates of his own conscience."

In 1830, certain memorials for prohibiting the transportation of the mails and the opening of post-offices on Sunday were referred to the Congressional Committee on Post-offices and Post-roads. The committee reported unfavorably to the prayer of the memorialists. Their report was adopted, and printed by order of the Senate of the United States, and the committee discharged from the further consideration of the subject. Of the Constitution they say :—

"We look in vain to that instrument for authority to say whether the first day, or seventh day, or whether any day, has been made holy by the Almighty.

"The Constitution regards the conscience of the Jew as sacred as that of the Christian, and gives no more authority to adopt a measure affecting the conscience of a solitary individual than of a whole community. That representative who would violate this principle would lose his delegated character, and forfeit the confidence of his constituents. If Congress should declare the first day of the week holy, it would not convince the Jew nor the Sabbatarian. It would dissatisfy both, and consequently convert neither. . . . If a solemn act of legislation shall in one point define the law of God, or point out to the citizen one religious duty, it may with equal propriety define every part of revelation, and enforce every religious obligation, even to the forms and ceremonies of worship, the endowments of the church, and the support of the clergy.

"The framers of the Constitution recognized the eternal principle that man's relation to his God is above human legislation, and his right of conscience inalienable. Reasoning was not necessary to establish this truth ; we are conscious of it in our own bosoms. It is this consciousness, which, in defiance of human laws, has sustained so many martyrs in tortures and flames. They felt that their duty to God was superior to human enactments, and that man could exercise no authority over their consciences. It is an inborn principle which nothing can eradicate.

"It is also a fact that counter memorials, equally respectable, oppose the interference of Congress, on the ground that it would be legislating upon a religious subject, and therefore unconstitutional."

Hon. A. H. Cragin, of New Hampshire, in a speech in the House of Representatives, said :—

"When our forefathers reared the magnificent structure of a free republic in this Western land, they laid its foundations broad and deep in the eternal principles of right. Its materials were all quarried from the mountain of truth ; and as it rose majestically before an astonished world, it rejoiced the hearts and hopes of mankind. Tyrants only cursed the workmen and their workmanship. Its architecture was new. It had no model in Grecian or Roman history. It seemed a paragon let down from Heaven to inspire the hopes of men, and to demonstrate God's favor to the people of the New World. The builders recognized the rights of human nature as universal. Liberty, the great first right of man, they claimed for 'all men,' and claimed it from 'God himself.' Upon this foundation they erected the temple, and dedicated it to Liberty, Humanity, Justice, and Equality. Washington was crowned its patron saint. Liberty was then the national goddess, worshiped by all the people. They sang of liberty, they harangued for liberty, they prayed for liberty. Slavery was then hateful. It was denounced by all. The British king was condemned for foisting it upon the colonies. Southern men were foremost in entering their protest against it. It was then everywhere regarded as an evil, and a crime against humanity."

Again, the Bible, and the Bible alone, is the Protestant rule of faith ; and liberty to worship God according to the dictates of one's own conscience is the standard of religious freedom in this land ; and from the quotations herewith presented, it is evident that while the government pledges to all its citizens the largest amount of civil freedom, outside of license, it has determined to lay upon the people no religious restrictions, but to guarantee to all liberty to worship God according to the Protestant principle.

It is these heaven-born principles,—civil and religious liberty,—so clearly recognized, so openly acknowledged, and so amply guaranteed, that have made this nation the attraction it has been to the people of other lands, and which have drawn them in such multitude to our shores.

Townsend ("Old World and New," p. 341) says :—

"And what attached these people to us ? In part, undoubtedly, our zone, and the natural endowments of this portion of the globe. In part, and of late years, our vindicated national character, and the safety of our institutions. *But the magnet in America is that we are a republic—a republican people!* Cursed with artificial government, however glittering, the people of Europe, like the sick, pine for nature with protection, for open vistas and blue sky, for independence without ceremony, for adventure in their own interest ; and here they find it ! "

Thompson ("United States as a Nation," p. 29) gives this view of the religious element that entered into this organization :—

"In the movements in the colonies that prepared the way for the Revolution, the religious spirit was a vital and earnest element. Some of the colonies were the direct offspring of religious persecution in the old country, or of the desire for a larger freedom of faith and worship ; and so jealous were they of any interference with the rights of conscience, that their religion was fitly described [by Burke in his Speech of Conciliation] as 'a refinement on the principle of resistance, the dissidence of dissent, and the Protestantism of the Protestant religion.' And the colonies that were founded in that spirit of commercial adventure, or for extending the realm of Great Britain, became also an asylum for religious refugees from all nations, and by the prospect of a larger and freer religious life, attracted to themselves the men of different races and beliefs who had learned to do and to suffer for their faith."

On page 31, he further says :—

"Thus it came to pass that the religious wars and persecutions of Europe in the sixteenth and seventeenth centuries, were a training school for the political independence of the United States of America in the eighteenth century. Diverse and seemingly incongruous as were the nationalities represented in the colonies,— Dutch, French, German, Swedish, Scotch, Irish, English,—they had all imbibed, either by experience or by inheritance, something of the spirit of personal independence, and especially of religious liberty. Gustavus Adolphus designed his colony of Swedes for the benefit of 'all oppressed Christendom.' Penn, the Quaker, established Pennsylvania as 'a free colony for all mankind,' where the settlers 'should be governed by laws of their own making.' The first charter of the Jerseys—which were largely peopled by Quakers and Scotch and Irish Presbyterians—declared that 'No person shall at any time, in any way, or on any pretense, be called in question, or in the least punished or hurt, for opinion in religion.' And Oglethorpe's Colony of Georgia was founded to be a refuge for 'the distressed people of Britain, and the persecuted Protestants of Europe;' then the German Moravian settled side by side with the French Huguenot and the Scotch Presbyterian under the motto, 'We toil not for ourselves, but for others.'

"Pere Hyacinthe, after a tour in New England, said he had remarked in every town three institutions that epitomized American society,—the bank, the school, and the church. A true picture. And you see the intellectual and the spiritual are two to one against the material,—the bank, the store-house of gains and savings, the school and the church, the distributing reservoirs of what is freely taken from the bank and given to those educating and spiritualizing forces of society.

" 'The Americans,' says De Tocqueville, 'show by their practice that they feel the high **necessity of imparting** morality **to demo-** cratic communities by **means** of religion. . . . In the **United** States, on the first day of every week, the trading and working life of the nation seems suspended ; **all noises** cease ; a deep tran- quillity, say rather the solemn **calm of meditation,** succeeds the turmoil **of the** week, and **the soul resumes** possession and **con-** templation of itself. Upon **this** day the marts of traffic are de- **serted ;** every member of **the** community, **accompanied by** his **children, goes to church, where** he **listens to strange language,** **which would seem unsuited to his ear.'** This last expression **shows** that even the philosophical acumen **of** De Tocqueville had failed **to** penetrate to **the secret of religious life** in America. That is no 'strange language' **to which the American** banker, merchant, farmer, mechanic, listens **when he goes to church** on Sunday; it is the language he was **accustomed in childhood to** hear from his parents ; **the** language that perhaps **he** himself **has** used in his own family **every** day of the week at morning prayer ; **the lessons** that he inculcates to his children,—'**of** the finer pleasures which **belong to** virtue alone, and **of the** true happiness **which attends it.'** It is **not** on Sunday alone, as De Tocqueville **imagined, 'that the American steals an** hour from himself, and **laying aside for a while the** petty passions which agitate his life **and the** ephemeral interests which **engross it,** strays at once into **an** ideal world, where **all is great, eternal, and pure.'** Thousands upon thousands of **the busiest men in** America do this every day with undeviating regularity. This *is* **their life,**—in that ideal world ; and **they bring from** this springs **and motives to** action in the world of affairs."—*Id.*, pp. 219, 220.

The success of the United States in erecting at once a permanent and stable form of government has been an astonishment to other nations. Edouard Laboulaye, one of the foremost patriots and publicists of France, just after the revolution of 1848 said :—

" **In the last sixty years** we have changed eight or ten times our government and **our** constitution ; have passed from anarchy to despotism ; tried two or three forms of the republic and of **monarchy ;** exhausted **proscription, the** scaffold, civil and **foreign** war; and after so many attempts, and attempts paid with the fortune and the blood of France, we are hardly more advanced than at the outset; The constitution of 1848 took for its model the constitution of 1791, which had no life; and to-day we are agitating the same questions that in 1789 we flattered ourselves we had resolved. How is it that the Americans have organized liberty upon a durable basis, while we, who surely are not inferior to them in civilization—we who have their example before our eyes—have always miscarried?"

Thompson ("United States as Nation," p. 107) quotes the foregoing from "Etudes Morales et Politiques," p. 285, and spends a few moments considering a proper answer to this question which the Frenchman in so much astonishment asks. He makes the answer to consist principally in the fact that the Americans conceived and adopted a superior constitution —a constitution which has sprung from the noble principles which have given this nation its political and religious influence, as noticed in this chapter. He says :—

"But in this point of constitution-making, it will also be seen that the Americans, with a rare felicity, succeeded in incorporating the constitution of the nation, which is its life principle, with the national constitution, which gives to the national life its definitive form and expression. They not only achieved independence, but, in the happy phrase of the French critic, they '*organized* liberty.' This success was due to training, to methods, and to men, or rather to that mysterious conjunction of men and events that make the genius of an epoch akin to inspiration."

The value and influence of this constitution is shown in the fact that "to-day a leading organ of opinion in England pronounces the Constitution of the United States 'the most sacred political document in the world.'"—*Id.* p. 160.

The growing influence of American opinions and

ideas is still further shown in the recognition of American literature abroad. Says Thompson (p. 231), " Many of us can remember the sneer of the Edinburgh *Review*, 'Who reads an American book?' The laugh is turned, now that everywhere in England one sees the railway book-stalls, and the shelves of circulating libraries, crowded with American books in ready demand ; that one can count up scores of American authors reprinted in England (in the catalogue of a single London publisher, I lately saw twelve American names) ; that in ' The International Scientific Series,' published at London and Leipzig, the names of Cooke, Dana, Draper, Flint, Whitney, appear side by side with Bain, Carpenter, Huxley, Lubbock, Spencer, Tyndall, Bernstein, Lisbreich, Lenckart, Steinthal, Virchow ; that every leading English review now has its department of American literature. The *Athenæum* finds much to praise, and even the hypercritical *Saturday Review*, now and then throws us such tidbits as these : ' Hawthorne is one of the most fascinating of novelists. Whittier's " Mabel Martin " is enough to make the reputation of any poet.' True we have given birth to no Shakspeare nor Byron ; but with the list of contemporary English poets, from Tennyson down to Swinburne, we need not hesitate to compare our list from Bryant down to Whitman, each after his kind."

The stability of our government through the changes and vicissitudes which have revolutionized if not overthrown other governments, is a further evidence of the solid political and religious basis on which its foundations are laid. On this point we quote again from the same volume from which the last few extracts are given, p. 148 :—

"Frederic the Great died ; and, twenty years after, the Prussia that he had created lay dismantled, dismembered, disgraced, at the dictation of Napoleon. Napoleon abdicated ; and France has wandered through all forms of government, seeking rest and finding none. Washington twice voluntarily retired from the highest posts of influence and power,—the head of the army, the head of the State ; but the freedom he had won by the sword, the institutions he had organized as president of the Federal Convention, the government he had administered as President of the Union, remained unchanged and have grown in strength and majesty through all the growing years."

American missionaries have gone to all the world, and in numbers and activity hold an equal place with those of any other nation ; while the American Bible Society, in the extent of its operations, sending out millions of copies of the Scriptures in all the leading languages of the world, stands next to the original society of the mother country.

This country has now come to be looked upon as the model, after which other governments may profitably pattern. Under the title of "The Model Republic," Cyrus D. Foss, pastor of St. Paul's Methodist Episcopal Church, New York, preached a sermon, which appeared in the *Methodist*, in December 1867, from which the reader will be pleased to read the following extracts, which may fitly close the present chapter :—

"Let every thoughtful American bless God that he lives in this age of the world, and in this country on the globe ; not in the dark past, where greatness and even goodness could accomplish so little ; not in the oriental world, where everything is stiffened and is hard as cast-iron ; but now where such mighty forces are at work for the uplifting of humanity, and just here at this focal point of power,

" In no vainglorious spirit, but with a sincere desire to awaken your gratitude to Almighty God for his astonishing mercies to us as a people, I propose this inquiry : What is the place of America in history ? God gives each nation a work to do. For that work he bestows adequate and appropriate endowments, and to it he summons the nation by a thousand trumpet calls of providence. If those calls are unheeded, if the nation is hopelessly recreant, he dashes it in pieces like a potter's vessel. Witness Assyria ; witness the Jewish people ; nation after nation—a long procession— has faded away at the blast of the breath of his nostrils.

"I maintain to-day that God has signalized this great American nation, this democratic republican nation, this Protestant Christian nation, above all the nations that are or ever have been upon the face of the globe, by the place and the work he has assigned it. Look at its place on the globe, and its place among the centuries. What a magnificent arena for a young nation to step forth upon and begin its march to a destiny inconceivably glorious : Suppose an angel flying over all the earth two hundred years ago, looking down upon the crowded populations of Europe and Asia, and the weak and wretched tribes of Africa, perceiving that humanity never rises to its noblest development, save in the north temperate zone—turning his flight westward across the Atlantic, there dawns upon him the vision of a new world—a world unpopulated save by a few scattered and wandering tribes of aboriginal savages, and by thirteen sparse colonies of the hardiest and best of immigrants along the Atlantic coast. He beholds a continent marvelously beautiful with unlimited resources to be developed ; its rivers open all parts of the country, and bring all into communication with two great oceans and with the tropic gulf. He sees a soil inexhaustibly fertile ; he sees the mountains (for an angel's eye can search their treasures) full of gold, silver, copper, iron, and coal. He sees a country insulated by three thousand miles of ocean from all the nations, needing contiguity with none —a Cosmos in itself. Would not this angel-gazer say, ' My God has assuredly made and endowed this peerless continent for some glorious end. The rest of the world is occupied, and the most of it cursed by occupation. Here is virgin soil ; here is an arena for a new nation, which, perchance, profiting by the mistakes of the long, dark past, may, by the blessing of God, work out for itself and for humanity a better destiny ' ?

"Note again the place of America in the scale of the centuries. Why was this continent hid from the eye of Europe so long? And why, after its discovery, was it kept unsettled for a century and a quarter longer, the thought of it all that time being only a disturbing leaven in the mind of Europe? Ah! God would not suffer it that tyrannical ideas of government or religion should take root here. He veiled the New World from the vision of the Old, until the Old had cultivated a seed worthy to plant the New. No crowned despots, no hooded monks, were to flourish here. No hoary superstitions, no ancient usurpations, were to take root here. Why was the era of this nation's birth coeval with that of the development of inventive genius? Why was it that this land was comparatively unsettled until the iron horse was ready to career across its plains, leap its rivers, dive through its mountains, and bring its most distant cities into vicinage?—until Leviathan stood waiting to plough the ocean, and bring the nations into brotherhood?—until the fiery steeds of heaven were being harnessed to fly with tidings in a single instant across the continent or under the ocean? Why was the beginning of our national history delayed until the doctrines of civil and religious liberty—a thousand times strenuously asserted and bravely defended—had emerged into prominence and power, so that the American freeman of today stands upon the shoulders of thirty generations of heroic battles for the right? Why—most remarkable coincidence of all—why does it occur that just at the time of the vigorous infancy of this favored nation, the church of God should awake from the slumber of ages, acknowledge the universal bond of brotherhood, and begin in this age, within the lifetime of men here present, those sublime evangelizing agencies which are the chief glory of the century, and which are to bring this world to the feet of Jesus?* No candid man can ponder these thoughts without wondering what God designs for this young giant which he has so located on the surface of this globe, and on the scale of the centuries.

"The thesis I shall defend is this: God designated the United

---

* We should be glad if we could sympathize with the speaker in this view. But we are not able to find in the Scriptures any evidence that the world is all to be brought into obedience to Christianity before the second coming of Christ.

States of America as the *Model Republic and the great evangelizer of the world.* The questions I have just propounded suggest a line of argument which will prove this proposition, and by proving it, devolve upon us here in this country a responsibility, the like of which has never been laid upon any nation. Let me premise two things essential to the argument. America is certainly the observed of all observers. The eyes of all nations are upon her. This free government, this 'experiment at free government,' as European absolutists have sneeringly termed it, fixes the gaze of the whole world. There is no nation, no tribe, civilized or semi-civilized, on the whole earth, that does not look this way, and feel that humanity has a stake in this land. This Hercules, who, when in his cradle, bearded and defeated the British Lion; who, in his callow youth, repeated that feat on those watery plains, where, till then, the foe had ranged acknowledged lord, and who has just now, in his vigorous manhood, throttled and slain the many-headed hydra of rebellion—secession, treason, and slavery— this Hercules, somehow, has come to be gazed upon by all lands, and, somehow, the oppressed of every nation on the face of the earth have reached the conviction that he is their champion.

"The other preliminary thought is this : In stating the mission of America, I have mentioned two things—that God meant it to be a model Republic, and the great evangelizer, and these two are one. We cannot consider them separately, and draw out entirely distinct lines of proof. It is idle for any nation at this age to expect greatness without acknowledging God, and falling into the ranks as an obedient subject of his kingdom. In ancient times, the case was different; but now Christian nations control the world, and depend upon it, brethren, the hands will never go backward on the dial. France tried to get on without a God in the time of her first revolution, but Napoleon, for reasons of State, restored the Catholic religion. His most appreciative historian, M. Thiers, gives us a deeply interesting account of this singular passage in his history. Napoleon said : " For my part, I never hear the sound of the church bell in the neighboring village without emotion." He knew that the hearts of the people were stirred by the same deep yearnings after God which filled his own, and so he proposed to restore the worship of God to infidel France. The savans of Paris ridiculed the proposal, laughed it to scorn, declared it was weakness in him to yield to a superstition that had forever passed, and that he needed no such aid to government, and that he could do what he pleased. ' Yes,' said he, ' but I act only with regard to the real and sensibly-felt wants of France.' Negotiations were opened with the Pope, and the Romish worship was set up, amid the enthusiasm of the nation. The historian utters this reflection : ' Whether true or false, sublime or ridiculous, men must have a religion.' Later, and with deeper meaning, Perrier, successor to Lafayette as prime minister to Louis Philippe, said, on his death-bed : ' France must have religion.' So I say to-day concerning that better faith, which overthrows what Romanism sets up; which breaks the shackles Romanism binds on; which is the only security of national permanence—America must have religion. In order to be the model Republic, she must be the great evangelizer.

"The two evangels of civil and religious liberty are ours. There are two great methods by which God indicates his will concerning a nation—by the providential training he bestows upon it, and by the resources he puts within its reach. Now, in the light of these two criteria, let us look at this country and see if God does not proclaim his will as plainly as though he had written it in letters of fire on the sky over every American sunset, or deeply graven it in rocky characters on the crest of every American mountain : ' My will is, that on this new continent, the nation I plant here shall be the model Republic and the great evangelizer of the world.' I have already indicated in general outline this train of argument ; but let us now look first behind us at our history, and then around us at our resources, and see what are their teachings. While we do not believe in ' manifest destiny,' in the sense of blind fate, or of results absolutely certain without regard to national character and endeavor, we do believe that the breath of God has inspired the heart of America with a sublime idea, and that the hand of God has marvelously led her along toward its realization, and has gifted her with munificent resources for the completion of this great work.

"Glance backward at our history, and keep in mind the question what it all meant. This country was discovered by a religious navigator, sent out by a religious queen, and the ruling motive in the minds of both of them was a religious one. Isabella and Columbus both intended to give the gospel to the natives of any lands that might be discovered. America was discovered just

after the art of printing had begun its marvelous quickening of the
human mind. Now who shall settle it? Papists? They found
it. Spaniards? Frenchmen? Both wanted it. No; God's plan
will be imperiled unless colonists of a certain language, and of a
certain religious faith, shall be the first settlers of the land. The
settlers must have the truest religious faith there is on the earth,
and must speak only that language which, more than any other
language, is full of the inspirations of liberty. They come—and
for what? With the noblest motives that ever inspired the
bosom of an emigrant, see them land from the Mayflower upon
the frozen beach, amid the storms of winter, dropping tears
which freeze as they fall and yet tears of gratitude.

> " ' What sought they thus afar?
>   Bright jewels of the mine?
> The wealth of seas? the spoils of war?
>   They sought a faith's pure shrine.
> Aye, call it holy ground,
>   The spot where first they trod;
> They left unstained what there they found—
>   Freedom to worship God.'

" They had trouble enough from the aborigines to drive them
together, and to drive them to God. They had the utmost sim-
plicity of manners, the utmost reverence for the Bible, and the
utmost detestation of tyranny, whether in the Church or State.
They had not for the love of freedom left their homes in the Old
World to become slaves in the New. The God who instituted the
colonies moulded their history. He kept them connected with the
mother country until they were strong enough to stand alone
among the nations, and then he overruled the manner of their
breaking away so as to inspire them with a perpetual hatred of all
oppression. Why the British Parliament should have passed the
Stamp Act, and why, in repealing it, it should have re-asserted the
false principles underlying it ; why it should have so long persisted
in treating Englishmen here as Englishmen there would never
have submitted to be treated at all, no man can explain on any
other hypothesis than this : that England was judicially blinded,
in order that America might be free.

" And this is not merely the opinion of Americans spoken a
century after. It was the opinion of British statesmen at the
time. The halls of Parliament, the whole realm, rang with notes

of warning at that hour. Lord Chatham said: 'The gentleman tells us that America is obstinate, America is almost in open rebellion. I rejoice that America has resisted. Three millions of people so dead to all the feelings of liberty as voluntarily to submit to be slaves would have been fit instruments to make slaves of the rest.' This was said in Parliament ten years before the Declaration of Independence. Wesley, who is usually represented as having been the foe of our independence, and to whom history has at length done tardy justice, on the very first day after the reception of the news of Lexington and Concord, sat down and wrote to Lord North and the Earl of Dartmouth, each an emphatic letter: 'I am a High-churchman, the son of a High-churchman, brought up from my childhood in the highest notions of passive obedience and non-resistance, and yet, in spite of all my long-rooted prejudices, I cannot avoid thinking these, an oppressed people, asked for nothing more than their legal rights, and that in the most modest and inoffensive manner that the nature of the thing would allow.' 'And if arms were to be resorted to, how could it happen that Great Britain should fail in the contest? How could it be that she should not be able, after overpowering the fleets and armies of the first nations of Europe [and this is an Englishman's question], immediately to discomfit the farmers and merchants of America?' There is but one explanation: 'We got not the land in possession by our own sword, neither did our own arms save us; but thy right hand and thine arm, and the light of thy countenance, because thou hadst a favor unto us.' God released the young giant from the swaddling-bands of colonial dependence. And why should it not be so? Why should a country like this, the most magnificent of any country on the earth, a country in whose lakes England might have been thrown and buried, whose descending seas make her greatest rivers appear, in comparison, like brooks and rivulets, whose cataracts might have drowned out her cities—why should this magnificent country be shackled by the chains put on it by the selfishness of its parent? It was not according to the will of God. He chose that here, in an independent career of unparalleled freedom to man, this country should go forth on its path of progress, and hold its place among the nations unsurpassed by any until human happiness and grandeur this side the grave should be no more.

"The ideal of government is popular government. The divine right of kings is an exploded fancy. The best ends of government can never be realized by the rule of one or of a few. God gave to Israel a king in his wrath. The rights of man, the dignity of man, the direct relation and responsibility of man to God—these ideas stand forth most clearly where there is no king, no noble nor ignoble pedigree, no bar between the poorest boy in the land and the highest post of honor. Many an experiment of republican government had failed for the lack of general intelligence and of a pure religion.

"Absolutists pointed to Rome, to Sparta, to France, and sneered at the democratic idea. For the grandest and final experiment of self-government, God reserved this peerless continent. Such a new work, politically, can be best accomplished on virgin soil, where no old castles, no effete conservatism should bind men subserviently to a blundering past—where all things summon them to hold communion, not with dead men's bones, but with nature, with freedom, and with God.

"A rapid glance at the resources of this country will deepen our conviction of the grandeur of its mission. We shall see that it has ample resources, material and moral, for the great work to which it is summoned. We have the heart of the continent, the north temperate zone. If you will study history, you will find that no great nation has ever existed on the earth except in that zone. There must be the hardening of the muscles and the fiber, and, the quickening of the mind, which can be only where summer's heat gives place to winter's frost.

"We have also a coast-line greater than that of any other nation. The relation of this fact to the theme will quickly appear. Arnot counsels fearful Englishmen to turn for comfort from the newspaper to the map. He bids them notice that the coast-line of Great Britain is three times greater than that of France, and thence argues that the commercial and naval supremacy of Great Britain is forever assured. The argument is sound. Now, our coast-line is several times greater than that of any other nation. We have two oceans, the Gulf of Mexico, and the great lakes; and rivers piercing the land bring all the country right down to the sea. The commercial and the naval greatness of America can easily be all that they need it to be for the accomplishment of those things which we believe God has assigned for this nation to accomplish in the world. Our agricultural and mineral resources, and the rapidly increasing population which is developing them, must have a few words.

"Sir Morton Peto, the great railroad manager, whose travels in our own country excited so much attention in financial circles, went back to his own country amazed at our resources, and wrote a book which you ought to read. It would astound you by its revelations of the greatness of our country, which we ourselves do not begin to understand. Let me give you two or three facts concerning our resources. In 1850 the ten Western States produced 46,000,000, bushels of wheat; in 1860, 102,000,000. The mines of gold and silver are nearly all on public lands, and

Oil Wells and Plant of Pumps and Tanks.

Governor Walker says: 'They are the property of the Federal Government, and their intrinsic value exceeds our public debt.' It wants only the Pacific railroad to make them yield $150,000,-000 annually. In Missouri there is an iron mountain 228 feet high, covering an area of 500 acres, and containing 230,000,000 tons of pure ore, and every foot of descent below the surface will give 3,000,000 tons. The upper seam of the coal-field about Pittsburg contains over 53½ thousand millions tons of coal—that is 2,000 tons for every dollar of our national debt; and the Keystone State, which in other ways contributed so nobly to the national cause, came forward in the hour of our sorest need, and poured into our finances an element of marvelous quickening and strength—oil, which lubricated the machinery of the government, and helped to illuminate the night of our trial. In 1862, 42,000,-000 gallons of petroleum were exported, and its benefits extended far beyond its cash value. It employed labor and rewarded capital; it stimulated internal industry and external commerce. But all our people are employed; how, then, can these immense resources ever be developed?—By the rapidly multiplying millions. In 1800, there were in Indiana 4,875 inhabitants; in 1860, 1,350,-428. In 1849, in Minnesota, 4,000 inhabitants; in 1864, 350,000. In 1850, there were 1,900 acres of land ploughed in Minnesota; in 1860, 433,276 acres.

"Now, what is the bearing of these startling facts upon our argument? A great nation must be materially great. It must have room to stand on, and a field to work in, for only work can make a man or nation great. These amazing resources are to furnish us the machinery for a splendid career of civil, moral, and religious progress."

CHAPTER IV.

IMPORTANT PROBABILITIES CONSIDERED.

OUR country's progress, even under so brief a survey as that contained in the preceding chapters, must strike every one as a marvel of national growth. And when we take into consideration, the convictions expressed by some of the eminent authors from whom we have quoted, that the hand of Providence has been more conspicuous in the development of this nation than in that of any other, it is calculated to intensify greatly our interest in the subject, and hasten us on to an investigation of the query whether this nation is not, as other nations have been, mentioned in that prophetic word which has outlined the great epochs of human history, pointed out the nations, and in some instances the individuals, which were to act a part therein, and described the movements they would make. Certainly if the hand of Providence has been so conspicuously present in our history, as some of the writers already referred to affirm, we could hardly do less than look for some mention of this government in that Book which makes it a special purpose to record the workings of that Providence among mankind. What, then, are the probabilities in the matter? On what conditions might we expect to find mention of it? If the same conditions exist here, as those upon which other nations have been made subjects of prophecy, we should expect to find mention of this also. On what conditions, then, have other

[89]

nations found a place on the prophetic record?—On these conditions: first, if they have acted any prominent part in the world's history; and secondly, and above all, if they have had jurisdiction over the people of God, or have maintained such relations with them that the history of the latter could not be written without mention of the former.   In the prophecies and records of the Bible compared with the records of secular history, we find data from which to deduce the rule here given respecting the prophetic mention of earthly governments; and as it is a very important one, the reader will permit us to state it again: Whenever the relation of God's people to any nation are such that a true history of the former, which is the object of all revelation, could not be given without a notice of the latter, such nation is mentioned in prophecy.

And all these conditions are certainly fulfilled in our government. As regards the first, no nation has ever attracted more attention, excited more profound wonder, or given promise of greater eminence or influence among the nations of the earth; and as touching the second, certainly here, if anywhere on the globe, are to be found a strong array of Christians, such as are the salt of the earth and the light of the world, whose history could not be written without mention of that government under which they live and enjoy their liberty.

With these probabilities in favor of the proposition that this government should be a subject of prophecy, let us now take a brief survey of those symbols found in the word of God which represent earthly governments. These are found chiefly, if not entirely, in the books of Daniel and the Revelation.

In Daniel 2, a symbol is introduced in the form of a great image, consisting of four parts,—gold, silver, brass, and iron,—which is finally dashed to atoms, and a great mountain, taking its place, fills the whole earth, and remains forever. In Daniel 7, the prophet records a vision in which he was shown a lion, a bear, a leopard, and a great and terrible nondescript beast, which after passing through a new and remarkable phase, is cast into a lake of fire, and utterly perishes. In Daniel 8, mention is made of a ram, a he-goat, and a horn little at first, but waxing exceeding great, which is finally broken without hand. Verse 25. In Revelation 9, we have a description of locusts like unto horses. In Revelation 12, we have a great red dragon. In Revelation 13, a blasphemous leopard beast is brought to view, and a beast with two horns like a lamb. In Revelation 17, John gives us a graphic pen-picture of a scarlet-colored beast, upon which a woman sits holding in her hand a golden cup, full of filthiness and abomination.

What governments and what powers are represented by all these? Do any of them symbolize our own? Some of them certainly represent earthly kingdoms, for so the prophecies themselves expressly inform us; and in the application of nearly all of them there is quite a uniform agreement among expositors. The four parts of the great image of Daniel 2 represent four kingdoms. They symbolize respectively, Babylon, or Chaldea, Medo-Persia, Grecia, and Rome. The lion of the seventh chapter also represents Babylon; the bear, Medo-Persia; the leopard, Grecia; and the great and terrible beast, Rome. The horn with human eyes and mouth, which appears in the second phase of this beast, represents the pa-

pacy, and covers its history down to the time when
it was temporarily overthrown by the French in 1798.
In Daniel 8, likewise, the ram represents Medo-Persia ; the he-goat, Grecia ; and the little horn, Rome.
All these have a very clear and definite application
to the governments named.   None of them thus far
can have any reference to the United States.

The symbols brought to view in Revelation 9, all
commentators concur in applying to the Saracens
and Turks.   The dragon of Revelation 12 is the acknowledged symbol of Pagan Rome.   The leopard
beast of the Revelation 13 can be shown to be
identical with the eleventh horn of the fourth beast of
Daniel 7, and hence to symbolize the papacy.   The
scarlet beast and woman of Revelation 17 as evidently apply also to Rome under papal rule, the
symbols having especial reference to the distinction
between the civil power and the ecclesiastical, the
one being represented by the beast, the other by the
woman seated thereon.

There is one symbol left, last but not least, the
youngest of the family, that vigorous and sprightly
fellow with two horns like a lamb, brought to view in
Revelation 13 : 11-17—what nation does that symbolize ?   On this there is more difference of opinion.
Let us, therefore, before seeking for an application,
look at the time and territory covered by those already examined.   Babylon and Medo-Persia covered
all the civilized portion of Asia, in ancient times.
Greece covered Eastern Europe, including Russia.
Rome, with the ten kingdoms into which it was divided before the end of the fifth century A. D., as represented by the ten toes of the image, the ten horns
of the fourth beast of Daniel 7, the ten horns of the

dragon of Revelation 12, and the ten horns of the leopard beast of Revelation 13, covered all Western Europe. In other words, all the civilized portions of the eastern hemisphere from the earliest times to the present are absorbed by the symbols already examined, respecting the application of which there is scarcely any room for doubt.

But there is a mighty nation in this western hemisphere, worthy, as we have seen, of being mentioned in prophecy, which is not yet brought in ; and there is one symbol remaining, the application of which has not yet been made. All the symbols but one are applied, and all the available portions of the earth, with the exception of our own government, are covered by the nations which these symbols represent. Of all the symbols mentioned, one alone—the two-horned beast of Revelation 13—is left ; and of all the countries of the earth respecting which any reason exists why they should be mentioned in the prophecy, one alone—our own government—remains. Do the two-horned beast and the United States belong together? If they do, then all the symbols find an application, and all the ground is covered. If they do not, it follows, first, that the United States is not represented in prophecy by any of the national symbols, as, for the reasons already stated, we should expect it would be ; and secondly, that the symbol of the two-horned beast of Revelation 13 : 11–17 finds no government to which it can apply. But the first of these suppositions is *not probable* ; and the second is *not possible*.

CHAPTER V.

A CHAIN OF PROPHECY.

ET us now enter upon a more particular examination of the second symbol of Revelation 13, with a view to determining its application with greater certainty. What is said respecting this symbol—the beast with two horns like a lamb—is not an isolated and independent prophecy, but is connected with what precedes; and the symbol itself is but one of a series. It is proper, therefore, to examine briefly the preceding symbols, since if we are able to make a satisfactory application of them, it will guide us in the interpretation of this.

The line of prophecy of which this forms a part commences with Revelation 12. The book of the Revelation is evidently not merely one consecutive prophecy of events to transpire from the beginning to the close of the gospel dispensation, but is composed of a series of such consecutive prophecies, each line taking up its own class of events, and tracing them through from the days of the prophet to the end of time; and when one line of prophecy is completed, another is introduced into the narrative, which in order of time goes back into the past, perhaps to the beginning, and follows its own series of events down to the end. That such a new series of prophetic events is introduced in Revelation 12, is evident; since in the preceding chapter a line of prophecy comes to its completion in the great day of God's wrath, the judgment of the dead, and the eternal

[94]

reward of those that fear God and revere his name.
No line of prophecy can go further ; and any events
to transpire in probation, subsequently mentioned,
must of course belong to a new series.

Commencing, then, with chapter 12, how far does
this line of prophecy extend? The first symbol introduced which can be applied to an earthly government, is the great red dragon. The second is the
beast of Revelation 13, which, having the body of a
leopard, may for brevity's sake, be called the leopard
beast. To this beast the dragon gives his seat,
power, and great authority. This beast, then, is connected with the dragon, and belongs to this line of
prophecy. The third symbol is the two-horned beast
of Revelation 13. This beast exercises certain power
in the presence of the leopard beast, and causes the
earth and them that dwell therein to worship him.
This beast, therefore, is connected with the leopard
beast, and hence belongs to the same line of prophecy. The conclusion of the prophecy is not reached
in chapter 13, and hence this line of events does not
end with that chapter, but must be looked for farther
on in the record. Going forward into chapter 14, we
find a company brought to view who are redeemed
from among men (which expression can mean nothing else than translation from among the living at
the second coming of Christ) ; and they sing a song
before the throne which none but themselves can
learn. In chapter 15, we have a company presented
before us who have gotten the victory over the beast,
his image, the mark, and the number of his name, the
very objects brought to view in the concluding portion of Revelation 13. This company also sing a song,
even the song of Moses and the Lamb ; and they

sing it while standing upon the sea of glass, as stated in verse 2. Turning to chapter 4 : 6, we learn that this sea of glass is " before the throne." The conclusion, therefore, follows that those who sing before the throne, in chapter 14, are identical with those who sing on the sea of glass (before the throne), in chapter 15, inasmuch as they stand in the same place, and the song they both sing is the first glad song of actual redemption. But the declarations found in chapter 15 show that the company introduced in the opening of chapter 14 have been in direct conflict . with the powers brought to view in the closing verses of chapter 13, and have gained the victory over them. Being thus connected with these powers, they form a part of the same line of prophecy. But here this line of prophecy must end ; for this company is spoken of as redeemed, and no line of prophecy, as already noticed, can go beyond the eternal state.

The line of prophecy in which the two-horned beast stands, is, therefore, one which is very clearly defined ; it commences with chapter 12, and ends with verse 5 of chapter 14. The student of prophecy finds it one of vast importance ; the humble child of God, one of transcendent interest. It begins with the Church, and ends with the Church,—the Church, at first in humility, trial, and distress ; at last, in victory, exaltation, and glory. This is the one object which ever appears the same in all the scenes here described, and whose history is the leading theme of the prophecy, from first to last. Trampled under the feet of the three colossal persecuting powers here brought to view, the followers of Christ for long ages bow their heads to the pitiless storm of oppression and persecution ; but the end repays them all; for John beholds them at last, the storms all over, their conflicts all ended, waving palm-branches of victory, and striking on harps celestial a song of everlasting triumph within the precincts of the heavenly land.

Having found the line of prophecy of which the symbol before us forms a part thus definitely located and defined, we now enter upon its examination. The first inquiry is, What power is designated by the great red dragon of chapter 12? The chapter first speaks of a woman clothed with the sun, the moon under her feet, and upon her head a crown of twelve stars. A woman is the symbol of the Church, a lewd woman representing a corrupt or apostate Church, as in Eze. 23: 2–4, etc., which refers to the Jewish Church in a state of backsliding, and in Rev. 17: 3–6, 15, 18, which refers to the apostate Romish Church; and a virtuous woman representing the true Church, as in the verse under consideration. At what period in her history could the Church of Christ be properly represented as here described? Ans. At the opening of the gospel dispensation, and at no other time; for then the glory of this dispensation, like the light of the sun, had just risen upon her; the former or Mosaic dispensation, which, like the moon, shone with a borrowed light, had just passed, and lay beneath her feet: and twelve inspired apostles, like a crown of twelve stars, graced the first organization of the gospel Church. To this period these representations can apply, but to no other. The prophet antedates this period a little by referring to the time when the Church, with long expectation, was awaiting the advent into this world of the glorious Redeemer, and represents the new dispensation as al-

7

ready opened, and the Christian Church organized, as this was the condition in which Christ was to leave it at the conclusion of his brief earthly ministry.

A man child, here represented as the offspring of this woman, appears upon the scene. Verse 5. This child was to rule all nations with a rod of iron, and was caught up to God and his throne. These declarations are true of our Lord Jesus Christ, but of no one else. See Ps. 2 : 7-9 ; Eph. 1 : 20, 21 ; Heb. 8 : 1 ; Rev. 3 : 21. There is therefore no mistaking the time when, nor the place where, the opening of this prophecy is located. We mention these facts for the purpose of identifying the power symbolized by the dragon, which is the point we are seeking to ascertain ; for the dragon stood before the woman to devour her child as soon as it should be born. Who attempted the destruction of our Lord when he appeared as a babe in Bethlehem ?—Herod. And who was Herod ?—A Roman governor. Rome, which then ruled over all the earth (Luke 2 : 1), was the responsible party in this transaction. Rome was the only power which at this time could be symbolized in prophecy, as its dominion was universal. It is not without good reason, therefore, that Pagan Rome is considered among Protestant commentators to be the power indicated by the great red dragon. And it may be a fact worth mentioning that during the second, third, fourth, and fifth centuries of the Christian era, next to the eagle, the *dragon* was the principal standard of the Roman legions ; and that dragon was painted *red*.

There is but one objection we need pause to answer before passing to the next symbol. Is not the dragon plainly called the Devil and Satan, in verse

9 ? How, then, can the term "dragon" be applied to Pagan Rome? That it is primarily applied to the Devil, there seems to be no doubt ; but that it should be applied also to some of his chief agents, would seem to be appropriate and unobjectionable. Now Rome, being at this time pagan, and the supreme empire of the world, was the great and sole agent in the hands of the Devil for carrying out his purposes, so far as they pertained to national affairs. Hence the use of that symbol to designate, and the application of that term to describe, the Roman power.

Having identified the power symbolized by the dragon, it is not necessary here to enter into other particulars concerning it, the object being to hasten on to the second symbol of chapter 13. We therefore pass on to an examination of the next symbol, which is the leopard beast of the first part of chapter 13. To this beast the dragon gives his seat, his power, and great authority. Verse 2. It would be sufficient on this point simply to show to what power the dragon, Pagan Rome, transferred its seat and gave its power. The seat of any government is certainly its capital city. The city of Rome was the dragon's seat. But in A. D. 330 Constantine transferred the seat of empire from Rome to Constantinople ; and Rome was given up—to what? to decay, desolation, and ruin ?—No ; but to a power which would render it far more celebrated than it had ever before been, not as the seat of pagan emperors, but as the city of St. Peter's pretended successors, the seat of a spiritual kingdom which was not only to become more powerful than any secular government, but which, through the magic of its fatal sorcery, was to exercise dominion over the kings of the earth. Thus was Rome—the seat of the dragon—given to the papacy by the transfer of the throne of the emperors to Constantinople by Constantine in A. D. 330 ; and the decree of Justinian, issued in 533, and carried into effect in 538, constituting the pope the head of all the churches and the corrector of heretics, was the investing of the papacy with that power and authority which the prophet foresaw. See Croly on the Apocalypse, pp. 114, 115.

It is very evident, therefore, that this leopard beast is a symbol of the papacy. But there are other considerations which prove this. This beast has the body of a leopard, the mouth of a lion, and the feet of a bear. In Daniel's vision of chapter 7, he was shown a lion, bear, and leopard ; and the fact that this beast has the features of each of these, shows it to be some power which succeeded the kingdoms symbolized by those three beasts of Daniel's prophecy, and one which retained some of the characteristics of them all ; and that was Rome. But this is not the first, or pagan form of the Roman government ; for that is represented by the dragon ; and this is the form which next succeeded that, which was the papal.

But what most clearly shows that this beast represents the papacy, is its identity with the little horn of the fourth beast of Daniel 7, which all Protestants agree in applying to the papal power.

1. *Their Chronology.* (1.) After the great and terrible beast of Daniel 7, which represents Rome in its first, or pagan form, is fully developed, even to the existence of the ten horns, or the division of the Roman empire into ten parts, the little horn arises. Verse 24. (2.) This leopard beast likewise succeeds the dragon, which also represents Rome in its pagan

form. These powers—the little horn and the leopard beast—appear, therefore, upon the stage of action at the *same time; i. e.,* next after the decadal division of the Roman empire, as shown by the ten horns of Daniel's fourth beast, and after the same division into ten parts, as symbolized by the ten horns of the dragon.

2. *Their Location.* (1.) The little horn plucked up three horns to make way for itself. The last of these, the Gothic horn, was plucked up when the Goths were driven from Rome in 538, and the city was left in the hands of the little horn, which has ever since held it as the seat of its power. (2.) To the leopard beast, also, the dragon gave its seat, the city of Rome. They therefore occupy the *same location.*

3. *Their Character.* (1.) The little horn is a blasphemous power; for it speaks great words against the Most High. Dan. 7 : 25. (2.) The leopard beast is also a blasphemous power; for it bears upon its head the name of blasphemy; it has a mouth speaking great things and blasphemies; and he opens his mouth in blasphemy against God to blaspheme his name, and his tabernacle, and them that dwell in heaven. Rev. 13 : 1, 5, 6. Therefore, they both maintain exactly the *same character.*

4. *Their Work.* (1.) The little horn, by a long and heartless course of oppression against the saints of the Most High, wears them out; and they are given into his hand. Dan. 7 : 25. He makes war against them, and prevails. Verse 21. (2.) The leopard beast also makes war upon the saints, and overcomes them. Rev. 13 : 7. This shows that they do the *same work,* and against the same class of people.

5. *The Time of Their Continuance.* (1.) Power was

given to the little horn to continue a "time and
times and the dividing of time." Dan. 7 : 25. A
time in Scripture phraseology is one *year.* Dan. 4 :
25. (The "seven times" of Nebuchadnezzar's hu-
miliation, Josephus informs us, were *seven years.*)
Times, that is two times, the least that can be expressed by the plural, would be two years more ; and
the dividing of time, or half a time, half a year more,
making in all three and a half years. (2.) To the
leopard beast, power was also given to continue forty-
two months. There being twelve months to the
year, this period gives us again just three and a half
years. And this being prophetic time, a day for a
year (Num. 14 : 34 ; Eze. 4 : 6), and there being, according to Scripture reckoning, thirty days to a
month, or three hundred and sixty days to the ordinary Bible year (Gen. 7 : 11, 24 ; 8 : 4), we have in
each case twelve hundred and sixty years for the
continuance of the little horn and the leopard beast.
Thus we see that they continue the *same length of
time.*

6. *Their Overthrow.* (1.) At the end of the "time,
times, and a half," the dominion of the little horn was
to be taken away. Dan. 7 : 26. (2.) At the end of
the forty-two months, the same length of time, the
leopard beast was also to be slain, politically, with
the sword, and go into captivity. Rev. 13 : 3, 10.

These are points which prove not merely similar-
ity, but identity. For whenever two symbols, as in
this instance, represent powers that,—

1. Come upon the stage of action at the *same
time,*

2. Occupy the *same territory,*

3. Maintain the *same character,*

4. Do the *same work,*

5. Continue the *same length of time,* and

6. Meet the *same fate,*—

Those two symbols must represent one and the same power.

And in all these particulars there is, as we have seen, the most exact coincidence between the little horn of the fourth beast of Daniel 7 and the leopard beast of Revelation 13 ; and all are fulfilled by one power ; and that is the papacy. For 1. The papacy succeeded to the pagan form of the Roman empire ; 2. It has, ever since it was first established, occupied the seat of the dragon, the city of Rome, building for itself such a sanctuary—St Peter's—as the world nowhere else beholds ; 3. It is a blasphemous power, speaking the most presumptuous words it is possible for mortal lips to utter against the Most High ; 4. It has worn out the saints, the "Religious Encyclopedia" estimating that the lives of fifty millions of Christians have been quenched in blood by its merciless implements of torture ; 5. It has continued a "time, times, and a half," or "forty-two months," or twelve hundred and sixty years. Commencing in 538, when the decree of Justinian in behalf of papal supremacy was first made effectual by the overthrow of the Goths, the papacy enjoyed a period of uninterrupted supremacy for just twelve hundred and sixty years, to 1798 ; and 6. Then its power was temporarily overthrown, and its influence permanently crippled, when the French, under Berthier, entered Rome in triumph, and the pope was taken prisoner, and died in exile.

Can any one doubt that the papacy is the power in question, and that the interpretation of this symbol brings us down within eighty-seven years of our own time? We regard the exposition of the prophecy thus far as clear beyond the possibility of refutation ; and if this is so, our future field of inquiry lies within a very narrow compass, as we shall presently see.

CHAPTER VI.

LOCATION OF THE GOVERNMENT REPRESENTED BY THE SECOND SYMBOL OF REVELATION 13.

FOLLOWING the leopard, or papal beast of Revelation 13 in consecutive order, comes another symbol whose appearance the prophet delineates, and whose work he describes, in the following language :—

VERSE 11. And I beheld another beast coming up out of the earth ; and he had two horns like a lamb, and he spake as a dragon. 12. And he exerciseth all the power of the first beast before him, and causeth the earth and them which dwell therein to worship the first beast, whose deadly wound was healed. 13. And he doeth great wonders, so that he maketh fire come down from heaven on the earth in the sight of men, 14, and deceiveth them that dwell on the earth by the means of those miracles which he had power to do in the sight of the beast ; saying to them that dwell on the earth, that they should make an image to the beast which had the wound by a sword, and did live. 15. And he had power to give life unto the image of the beast, that the image of the beast should both speak, and cause that as many as would not worship the image of the beast should be killed. 16. And he causeth all, both small and great, rich and poor, free and bond, to receive a mark in their right hand, or in their foreheads ; 17 · and that no man might buy or sell, save he that had the mark, or the name of the beast, or the number of his name.

These few verses, with an allusion to the same power under the name of "the false prophet" in Rev. 16 : 13 and 19 : 20, furnish all the testimony we have respecting the two-horned beast ; but brief as it is, it gives sufficient data for a very certain appli-

cation of the symbol in question. As an example of
the world of meaning which prophecy can condense
into a few words, a portion of the first verse of the
foregoing quotation may be instanced. Here, within
a compass of nineteen words, only three of which are
words of more than one syllable, six grand points are
made, which, taken together, are sufficient to determine accurately the application of this symbol. The
prophet says, first, that it is "another beast;" secondly, that when his attention was turned to it, it
was "coming up;" thirdly, that it came up "out of
the earth;" fourthly, that it had "two horns;" fifthly,
that these horns were like those of "a lamb;" and
sixthly, this symbol is introduced after the preceding
beast went into captivity.

The two-horned beast, then, is "another beast," in
addition to, and different from, the papal beast which
the prophet had just had under consideration; that
is, it symbolizes a power separate and distinct from
that which is denoted by the preceding beast. This
which John calls "another beast" is certainly no
part of the first beast; and the power symbolized by
it is likewise no part of that which is intended by
that beast. This is fatal to the claim of those, who,
to avoid the application of this symbol to our own
government, say that it denotes some phase of the
papacy; for in that case it would be a part of the
preceding or leopard beast.

To avoid this difficulty, it is claimed that the two-
horned beast represents the religious or ecclesiastical,
and the leopard beast the civil, power of Rome under
papal rule, and that these symbols correspond to the
beast and woman in Rev. 17, the one representing
the civil power, the other the ecclesiastical. But this

claim also falls to the ground just as soon as it is shown that the leopard beast represents the religious as well as the civil element of that power. And nothing is easier than to show this.

Take the first symbol, the dragon. What does it represent?—Rome. But this is not enough; for Rome has presented two great phases to the world, and the inquirer wants to know which one is intended by this symbol. The answer then is, Pagan Rome; but just as soon as we add "pagan," we introduce a religious element; for paganism is one of the mighties' systems of false religion ever devised by the archenemy of truth. It was, then, the religious element in the empire that determined what symbol should be used to represent it; and the dragon represented Rome while under the control of a particular form of religion.

But the time comes when another symbol is introduced upon the scene—the leopard beast arises out of the sea. What power is symbolized by this? The answer is still, Rome. But the dragon symbolized Rome, and why not let that symbol continue to represent it? Whoever attempts to answer this question must say that it is because a change had taken place in the power. What change? Two kinds of changes are conspicuous in the history of Rome,—changes in the form of government, and a change in religion. But this cannot denote any change in the form of government; for the seven different forms of government that Rome consecutively assumed are represented by the seven heads of the dragon and the seven heads of the leopard beast. The religious change alone must therefore be denoted by this change of symbols. Paganism and

Christianity coalesced, and the mongrel production was the papacy ; and this new religion, and this alone, made a change in the symbol necessary. Every candid mind must assent to this ; and this assent is an admission of the utter absurdity of trying to limit this symbol to the civil power alone. So far from its representing the civil power alone, it is to the ecclesiastical element that it owes its very existence. The ecclesiastical is therefore the essential element, and without it the symbol could not exist.

That the leopard beast represents ecclesiastical as well as civil power is further shown in the arguments already presented to prove that this beast is identical with the little horn of the fourth beast of Daniel 7, which symbolizes the papacy in all its component parts and through all its history. It is the leopard beast alone that is identical with this little horn, not the leopard beast and the two-horned beast taken together.

Again, Pagan Rome gave its seat to the papacy. The dragon gave his seat to the leopard beast. If it takes both the leopard beast and the two-horned beast to constitute the papacy, the prophet should have said that the dragon gave his seat and power to these two beasts combined. The fact that this transfer was to the leopard beast alone, is proof positive that that beast alone symbolizes the papacy in its entirety.

When, therefore, John calls the two-horned beast "another beast," it is certain that he does not mean any particular phase, or any part, of the papal power.

It is claimed by others that the two-horned beast represents England ; by still others, France ; and by some, Russia, etc. The first, among many other fatal objections to all these applications, is, that the territory occupied by all these powers is already appropriated by preceding symbols. The prophecy does not read that the lion, the bear, or the leopard re-appeared under a new phase; or that one of the ten horns of the leopard beast became another beast. If the two-horned beast symbolized any of these, it would be a part of other beasts instead of "another beast," separate and distinct as it must be from all the rest. It is a law of symbols that each one occupies territory peculiarly its own, that is, the territory which constituted the original government was no part of that which had been occupied by the previous powers. Thus, Babylon had its territory; and Medo-Persia rose on the territory not occupied by Babylon; and Medo-Persia and Babylon together covered all that portion of Asia known to ancient civilization. The Grecian, or Macedonian, kingdom arose to the west of them, occupying all Eastern Europe, so far as it was then known to the ancients. Rome rose still to the west, in territory unoccupied by Grecia. Rome was divided into ten kingdoms; but though Rome conquered the world, we look for these ten kingdoms only in that territory which had never been included in other kingdoms. We look not to Eastern Europe, for that was included in the dominion of the third beast; nor to Asia, for that constituted the empires of the first and second beasts; but to Western Europe, which territory was unoccupied until taken by Rome and its divisions.

The ten kingdoms which rose out of the old Roman empire are enumerated as follows by Machiavel, indorsed by Bishop Newton, Faber, and Dr.

Hales: 1. The Huns; 2. The Ostrogoths; 3. The Visigoths; 4. The Franks; 5. The Vandals; 6. The Suevi; 7. The Burgundians; 8. The Heruli; 9. The Anglo-Saxons; and 10. The Lombards. These kingdoms have since been known, says Scott, as the "ten kingdoms of the Western empire," and they are distinguishable at the present day, some of them even by their modern names; as, Hungary from the Huns, Lombardy from the Lombards, France from the Franks, and England from the Anglo-Saxons. These ten kingdoms being denoted by the ten horns of the leopard beast, it is evident that all the territory included in these ten kingdoms is to be considered as covered by that symbol. England is one of these ten kingdoms; France is another. If, therefore, we say that either of these is the one represented by the two-horned beast, we make one of the horns of the leopard beast constitute the two-horned beast. But this the prophecy forbids; for while John sees the leopard beast fully developed, with his horns all complete and distinct, he beholds the two-horned beast coming up, and calls it "another beast." We are therefore to look for the government which this beast symbolizes in some country outside the territory occupied by the four beasts and the ten horns already referred to. But these, as we have seen, cover all the available portions of the eastern hemisphere.

Another consideration pointing to the locality of this power is drawn from the fact that John saw it arising from the earth. If the sea from which the leopard beast arose (Rev. 13 : 1) denotes peoples, nations, and multitudes, as John expressly affirms that it does in Rev. 17 : 15, his use of the word "earth" here would suggest, by contrast, a new and previously-unoccupied territory.

Being thus excluded from eastern continents and impressed with the idea of looking to territory not previously known to civilization, we turn of necessity to the western hemisphere. And this is in full harmony with the ideas already quoted, and more which might be presented, that the progress of empire is with the sun around the earth from east to west. Commencing in Asia, the cradle of the race, it would end on this continent, which completes the circuit. Bishop Berkeley, in his celebrated poem on America, written more than one hundred years ago, in the following forcible lines, pointed out the then future position of America, and its connection with preceding empires :—

> " Westward the course of empire takes its way,
>   The first four acts already past,
>   A fifth shall close the drama with the day ;
>   Time's noblest offspring is the last."

By the " first four acts already past," the bishop had undoubted reference to the four universal kingdoms of Daniel's prophecy. A fifth great power, the noblest and the last, was, according to his poem, to arise this side the Atlantic, and here close the drama of time, as the day here ends its circuit.

To what part of the American continent shall we look for the power in question ?—To the most powerful and prominent nation, certainly. This is so self-evident that we need not stop to pass in review the frozen fragments of humanity on the north of us, nor the weak, superstitious, semi-barbarous, revolutionary, and uninfluential kingdoms to the south of us. No ; we come to the United States, and here we are held. To this nation the question of the location of the two-horned beast undeviatingly leads us.

As an objection to this view, it may occur to some minds that the two-horned beast exercises all the power of the first beast before him (Greek, ἐνώπιον, literally, in his eyes, or before his face), and does wonders in his sight; and how can the United States, separated by an ocean from European kingdoms, hold such an intimate relation to them? We answer, Space and time are annihilated by the telegraph. Through the Atlantic cable (an enterprise which, by the way, owes its origin to the United States), the lightnings are continually picturing to European beholders the affairs of America. Any important event occurring here is described the next hour in the journals of Europe. So far as the transmission of an account of our proceedings to the people of the Old World is concerned, it is as if America lay at the mouth of the English Channel.

And the eyes of all Europe are intently watching our movements. Says Mr. Townsend (New World and Old, p, 583) :—

"All the great peoples of Europe are curiously interested and amazed in the rise of America, and their rulers at present compete for our friendship. 'Europe,' said the prince Talleyrand long ago, 'must have an eye on America, and take care not to offer any pretext for recrimination or retaliation. America is growing every day. She will become a colossal power, and the time will come when (discoveries enabling her to communicate more easily with Europe) she will want to say a word in our affairs, and have a hand in them.' "

The time has come, and the discoveries have been made, to which Talleyrand referred. It is almost as easy now to communicate with Europe as with our nearest town. By these things the attention of the world is drawn still more strongly toward us; and thus whatever the United States does, it is done in the sight—yes, even before the eyes—of all Europe.

One strong pillar in the argument is thus firmly set. The terms of the prophecy absolutely fix the location of the power symbolized by the two-horned beast; and that location is in this western hemisphere. It can be nowhere else. And the conclusion is just as unavoidable that our own nation is the power in question.

8

CHAPTER VII.

WHEN MUST THE GOVERNMENT INDICATED BY THIS SYMBOL ARISE?

HAVING become satisfied *where* the power symbolized by the two-horned beast must be located, we now inquire respecting the *time when* we may look for its development. At what period in this world's history is the rise of this power placed in the prophecy? On this point, as on the preceding, the foundation for the conclusions at which we must arrive is already laid in the facts elicited in reference to the preceding, or leopard beast. It was at the time when this beast went into captivity, or was killed (politically) with the sword (verse 10), or (which we suppose to be the same thing) had one of its heads wounded to death (verse 3), that John saw the two-horned beast coming up. If the leopard beast, as we have conclusively proved, signifies the papacy, and the going into captivity met its fulfillment in the temporary overthrow of the popedom by the French in 1798, then we have the epoch definitely specified when we are to look for the rising of this power. The expression, "coming up," must signify that the power to which it applies was but newly organized, and was then just rising into prominence and influence. The power represented by this symbol must, then, be some power which in 1798 stood in this position before the world.

That the leopard beast is a symbol of the papacy,

[114]

there can be no question ; but some may want more
evidence that the wounding of one of its heads, or
its going into captivity, was the overthrow of the papacy in 1798. This can easily be given. A nation
being represented by a wild beast, the government
of that nation, that by which it is controlled, must,
as a very clear matter of course, be considered as answering to the head of the beast. The seven heads
of this beast would therefore denote seven different
governments ; but all the heads pertain to one beast,
and hence all these seven different forms of government pertain to one empire. But only one form of
government can exist in a nation at one time ; hence
the seven heads must denote seven forms of government to appear, not simultaneously, but succes-
sively. But these heads pertain alike to the dragon
and the leopard beast, from which this one conclusion only can be drawn ; namely, that Rome, during
its whole history, embracing both its pagan and papal phases, would change its government six times,
presenting to the world seven different forms in all.
And the historian records just that number as per-
taining to Rome. Rome was ruled first by Kings ;
secondly, by Consuls ; thirdly, by Decemvirs ; fourthly,
by Dictators ; fifthly, by Triumvirs ; sixthly, by Emperors ; and seventhly, by Popes. See " American
Encyclopedia."

John saw one of these heads wounded as it were
to death. Which one ?—Can we tell ? Let it be
noticed, first, that it is one of the heads of the beast
which is wounded to death, and not one of the heads
of the dragon ; that is, it is some form of government which existed in Rome after the change of
symbols from the dragon to the leopard beast. We

then inquire, How many of the different forms of Roman government belonged absolutely to the dragon, or existed in Rome while it maintained its dragonic, or pagan form? These same seven heads are again presented to John in Rev. 17; and the angel there explains that they are seven kings, or forms of government (verse 10); and he informs John that five are fallen, and one is; that is, five of these forms of government were already past in John's day, and he was living under the sixth. Under what form did John live?—The imperial, it being the cruel decree of the emperor Domitian which banished him to the Isle of Patmos, where this vision was given. Kings, Consuls, Decemvirs, Dictators, and Triumvirs were all in the past in John's day. Emperors were then ruling the Roman world; and the empire was still pagan. Six of these heads, therefore,—Kings, Consuls, Decemvirs, Dictators, Triumvirs, and Emperors, —belonged to the dragon; for they all existed while Rome was pagan; and it was no one of these that was wounded to death; for had it been, John would have said, I saw one of the heads of the dragon wounded to death. The wound was inflicted after the empire had so changed in respect to its religion that it became necessary to represent it by the leopard beast. But the beast had only seven heads, and if six of them pertain to the dragon, only one remained to have an existence after this change in the empire took place. After the Emperors, the sixth and last head that existed in Rome in its dragonic form, came the Popes, the only head that existed after the empire had nominally become Christian. The "Exarch of Ravenna" existed so "short a space" (Rev.

17 : 10) that it has no place in the general enumeration of the heads of this power.

From these considerations it is evident that the head which received the mortal wound was none other than the papal head. This conclusion cannot be shaken. We have now only to inquire when the papal head was wounded to death. It could not certainly be till after the papacy had reached that degree of development that caused it to be mentioned on the prophetic page. But after it was once established, the prophecy marked out for it an uninterrupted rule of 1260 years, which dating from its rise in 538, would extend to 1798. And right there the papacy was, for the time being, overthrown. General Berthier, by order of the French Directory, moved against the dominions of the pope in January, 1798. February 10, he effected an entrance into the self-styled "Eternal City," and on the 15th of the same month proclaimed the establishment of the Roman Republic. The pope, after this deprivation of his authority, was conveyed to France as a prisoner, and died at Valence, Aug. 29, 1799.

This would have been the end of the papacy had this overthrow been made permanent. The wound would have proved fatal had it not been healed. But, though the wound was healed, the scar (to extend the figure a little) has ever since remained. A new pope was elected in 1800, and the papacy was restored, but only to a partial possession of its former privileges.

Rev. Geo. Croly, A. M., speaking upon this point, says :—

"The extinction of *torture* and *secrecy* is the virtual extinction of the tribunal. The power of the pope, as a *systematic* persecutor, has thus been annulled by the events growing out of the Republican era of 1793."—*Croly on the Apocalypse*, p. 257.

Let the reader look carefully at this event. It furnishes a complete fulfillment of the prophecy; and it is the only event in all Roman history which does this; for, though the first six heads were each in turn exterminated, or gave place to a succeeding head, of no one of them could it be said that it received a deadly wound, which was afterward healed. And as this overthrow of the papacy by the French military must be the wounding of the head mentioned in Rev. 13 : 3, so, likewise, must it be the going into captivity and the killing with the sword mentioned in verse 10; for it is an event of the right nature to fulfill the prophecy, and one which occurred at the right time; namely, at the end of the time, times, and a half, the forty-two months, or the 1260 years; and no other event can be found answering to the record in these respects. We are not left, therefore, with any discretionary power in the application of this prophecy; for God, by his providence, has marked the era of its accomplishment in as plain a manner as though he had proclaimed with an audible voice, "Behold here the accomplishment of my prophetic word!"

Thus clearly is the exact time when we are to look for the rise of the two-horned beast indicated in the prophecy; for John, as soon as he beholds the captivity of the first or leopard beast, says, "And I beheld another beast coming up." And his use of the present participle, "coming" up, clearly connects this view with the preceding verse, and shows it to be an event transpiring simultaneously with the going into captivity of the previous beast. If he had

said, " And I had seen another beast coming up," it
would prove that when he saw it, it was coming up,
but that the time when he beheld it was indefinitely
in the past. If he had said, " And I beheld another
beast which had come up," it would prove that although his attention was called to it at the time
when the first beast went into captivity, yet its rise
was still indefinitely in the past. But when he says,
" I beheld another beast *coming up*," it proves that
when he turned his eyes from the captivity of the
first beast, he saw another power just then in the
process of rapid development among the nations of
the earth. So, then, about the year 1798, the star of
that power which is symbolized by the two-horned
beast must be seen rising over the horizon of the nations, and claiming its place in the political heavens.
In view of these considerations, it is useless to speak
of this power as having arisen ages in the past. To
attempt such an application is to show one's self utterly reckless in regard to the plainest statements of
inspiration.

Again, the work of the two-horned beast is plainly
located, by verse 12, this side the captivity of the
first beast. It is there stated, in direct terms, that
the two-horned beast causes "the earth and them
which dwell therein to worship the first beast, whose
deadly wound was healed." But worship could not
be rendered to a beast whose deadly wound was
healed, till after that healing was accomplished.
This · brings the worship which this two-horned
beast enforces unmistakably within the present century.

Says Eld. J. Litch (Restitution, p. 131) :—

"The two-horned beast is represented as a power existing and
performing his part after the death and revival of the first beast."

Mr. Wesley, in his notes on Rev. 14, written in
1754, says of the two-horned beast :—

"He has not yet come, though he cannot be far off; for he is
to appear at the end of the forty-two months of the first beast."

We find three additional declarations in the book
of Revelation which prove, in a general sense, that
the two-horned beast performs his work with that
generation of men who are to behold the closing up
of all earthly scenes, and the second coming of our
Lord Jesus Christ; and these will complete the argument on this point.

1. The first is the message of the third angel,
brought to view in the 14th of Revelation. It is not
our purpose to enter into an exposition of the three
messages of that chapter. We call the attention of
the reader to only one fact, which must be apparent
to all; and that is, that the third of these messages
is the last warning of danger and the last offer of
mercy before the close of human probation; for the
event which immediately follows is the appearance
of one like the Son of man, on a white cloud, coming to reap the harvest of the earth (verse 14), which
can represent nothing else but the second advent of
the Lord from heaven. Whatever views, therefore,
a person may take of the first and second messages,
and at whatever time he may apply them, it is very
certain that the third and last one covers the closing
hours of time, and reaches down to the second coming of Christ. And what is the burden of this message? It is a denunciation of the unmingled wrath
of God against those who worship the beast and his

image. But this worship of the beast and his image is the very practice which the two-horned beast endeavors to enforce upon the people. The third message, then, is a warning against the work of the two-horned beast. And as there would be no propriety in supposing this warning to be given after that work was performed, since it could appropriately be given only when the two-horned beast was about to enforce that worship, and while he was endeavoring to enforce it, and since the second coming of Christ immediately succeeds the proclamation of this message, it follows that the duties enjoined by this message, and the decrees enforced by the two-horned beast, constitute the last test to be brought to bear upon the world ; and hence the two-horned beast performs his work, not ages in the past, but among the last generation of men.

2. The second passage showing that the work of the two-horned beast is performed just before the close of time, is found in Rev. 15 : 2, which we have shown to refer to the same company spoken of in chapter 14 : 1–5. Here is a company who have gained the victory over the beast and his image, and the mark and the number of his name ; in other words, they have been in direct conflict with the two-horned beast, which endeavors to enforce the worship of the beast and the reception of his mark. And these are " redeemed from among men " (14 : 4), or are translated from among the living at the second coming of Christ. 1 Cor. 15 : 51, 52 ; 1 Thess. 4 : 16, 17. This, again, shows conclusively that it is the last generation which witnesses the work of this power.

3. The third passage is Rev. 19 : 20, which speaks

of the two-horned beast under the title of the false
prophet, and mentions a point not given in Rev. 13;
namely, the doom he is to meet.   In the battle of the
great day, which takes place in connection with the
second coming of Christ (verses 11–19), the false
prophet, or two-horned beast, is cast alive into a lake
of fire burning with brimstone ; and the word "alive"
signifies that this power will be at that time a living
power, performing its part in all its strength and
vigor.   This power is not to pass off the stage of action and be succeeded by another, but is to be a
ruling power till destroyed by the King of kings and
Lord of lords when he comes to dash the nations
in pieces with a rod of iron.   Ps. 2 : 9.

The sum of the argument, then, on this matter of
chronology, is this : That the two-horned beast does
not come into the field of this vision previous to the
year 1798 ; that it performs its work while the last
generation of men is living on the earth ; and that
it comes up to the battle of the great day a living
power in the full vigor of its strength.

As it was shown in the argument on the location
of the two-horned beast that we are limited in our
application to the Western Continent, so we are limited still further by its chronology ; for it must not
only be some power which arises this side of the Atlantic, but one which is seen coming up here at a
particular time.   Taking our stand, then, in the year
1798, the time indicated in the prophecy, we invite
the careful attention of the reader to this question :
What independent power in either North or South
America was at that time "coming up" in a manner
to answer to the conditions of the prophecy ?   All
that part of North America lying to the north of us

was under the dominion of Russia and Great Britain. Mexico, to the southwest, was a Spanish colony. Passing to South America, Brazil belonged to Portugal; and most of other South American States were under Spanish control. In short, there was not then a single civilized, independent government in the New World, except our own United States. This nation, therefore, must be the one represented in the prophecy; for no other answers the specifications in the least degree. It has always taken the lead of all European settlements in this hemisphere. It was "coming up" at the exact time indicated in the prophecy. Like a lofty monument in a field all its own, we here behold the United States grandly overtowering all the continent. So far as God's providence works among the nations for the accomplishment of his purposes, it is visible in the development of this country as an agent to fulfill his word. On these two vital points of LOCATION and CHRONOLOGY, the arguments which show that OUR COUNTRY IS THE ONE represented by the symbol of the two-horned beast are ABSOLUTELY CONCLUSIVE.

CHAPTER VIII.

THE UNITED STATES HAS ARISEN IN THE EXACT MANNER INDICATED BY THE SYMBOL.

THE manner in which the two-horned beast was seen coming up shows, equally with its location and its chronology, that it is a symbol of the United States. John says he saw the beast coming up "out of the earth." And this expression must have been designedly used to point out the contrast between the rise of this beast and that of other national prophetic symbols. The four beasts of Dan. 7 and the leopard beast of Rev. 13 all arose out of the sea. Says Daniel, "The four winds of the heaven strove upon the great sea; and four beast came up from the sea." The sea denotes peoples, nations, and tongues (Rev. 17 : 15), and the winds denote political strife and commotion. Jer. 25 : 32, 33. There was, then, in this scene, the dire commotion of nature's mightiest elements,—the wind above, the waters beneath, the fury of the gale, the roaring and dashing of the waves, and the tumult of the raging storm; and in the midst of this war of elements, as if aroused from the depths of the sea by the fearful commotion, these beasts one after another appeared. In other words, the governments of which these beasts were symbols owed their origin to movements among the people which would be well represented by the sea lashed into foam by the sweeping gale; they arose

[124]

by the upheavals of revolution, and through the strife of war.

But when the prophet beholds the rising of the two-horned beast, how different the scene! No political tempest sweeps the horizon, no armies clash together like the waves of the sea. He does not behold the troubled and restless surface of the waters, but a calm and immovable expanse of earth. And out of this earth, like a plant growing up in a quiet and sheltered spot, he sees this beast, bearing on his head the horns of a lamb, those eloquent symbols of youth and innocence, daily augmenting in bodily proportions, and daily increasing in physical strength.

If any one should here point to the war of the Revolution as an event which destroys the force of this application, it would be sufficient to reply: 1. That war was at least fifteen years in the past when the two-horned beast was introduced into the field of this vision ; and 2. The war of the Revolution was not a war of conquest. It was not waged to overthrow any other kingdom and build this government on its ruins, but only to defend the just rights of the American people. An act of resistance against continual attempts of injustice and tyranny cannot certainly be placed in the same catalogue with wars of aggression and conquest. The same may be said of the war of 1812. Hence, these conflicts do not even partake of the nature of objections to the application here set forth.

The same view of this point is taken by eminent statesmen here and elsewhere. In a speech at the "Centennial Dinner," at the Westminster Palace Hotel, London, July 4, 1876, J. P. Thompson, LL. D., said :—

"I thank God that this birthday of the United States as a nation does not commemorate a victory of arms. War preceded it, gave occasion to it, followed it; but the figure of Independence shaped on the Fourth of July, 1776, wears no helmet, brandishes no sword, and carries no stain of slaughter and blood. I recognize all that war has done for the emancipation of the race, the progress of society, the assertion and maintenance of liberty itself; I honor the heroes who have braved the fury of battle for country and right, I appreciate the virtues to which war at times has trained nations as well as leaders and armies; yet I confess myself utterly wearied and sated with these monuments of victory in every capital of Europe, made of captured cannon, and sculptured over with scenes of carnage. I am sick of that type of history that teaches our youth that the Alexanders and Cæsars, the Frederics and Napoleons, are the great men who have made the world; and it is with a sense of relief and refreshment that I turn to a nation whose birthday commemorates a great moral idea, a principle of ethics applied to political society,—that government represents the whole people, for the equal good of all. No tide of battle marks this day; but itself marks the high water line of heaving, surging humanity."—*United States as a Nation,* pp. xiii, xiv.

Hon. Wm. M. Evarts quotes with approval a saying of Burke, respecting our Revolution, as follows :—

"A great revolution has happened—a revolution made, not by chopping and changing of power in any of the existing States, but by the appearance of a new State, of a new species in a new part of the globe. It has made as great a change in all the relations and balances and gravitations of power, as the appearance of a new planet would in the system of the solar world.'

The word which John uses to describe the manner in which this beast comes up is very expressive. It is ἀναβαῖνον (*anabainon*), one of the prominent definitions of which is, "To grow or spring up as a plant." And it is a remarkable fact that this very figure has been chosen by political writers as the one conveying the best idea of the manner in which this government has arisen. Mr. G. A. Townsend, in his work entitled, " The New World Compared with the Old," p. 462, says :—

"Since America was discovered, she has been a subject of revolutionary thought in Europe. The mystery of *her coming forth from vacancy,* the marvel of her wealth in gold and silver, the spectacle of her captives led through European capitals, filled the minds of men with unrest ; and unrest is the first stage of revolution."

On p. 635, he further says :—

"In this web of islands—the West Indies—began the life of both [North and South] Americas. There Columbus saw land, there Spain began her baneful and brilliant Western Empire ; thence Cortez departed for Mexico, De Soto for the Mississippi, Balboa for the Pacific, and Pizarro for Peru. The history of the United States was separated by a beneficent Providence far from this wild and cruel history of the rest of the continent, and *like a silent seed we grew into empire* [italics ours] ; while empire itself, beginning in the South, was swept by so interminable a hurricane that what of its history we can ascertain is read by the very lightnings that devastated it. The growth of English America may be likened to a series of lyrics sung by separate singers, which, coalescing, at last make a vigorous chorus, and this, attracting many from afar, swells and is prolonged, until presently it assumes the dignity and proportions of epic song."

A writer in the Dublin *Nation*, about the year 1850, spoke of the United States as a wonderful empire which was " *emerging,*" and " *amid the silence of the earth* daily adding to its power and pride."

In Martyn's " History of the Great Reformation," Vol. iv. p. 238, is an extract from an oration delivered by Edward Everett on the English exiles who founded this government, in which he says :—

"Did they look for a retired spot, inoffensive from its obscurity, safe in its remoteness from the haunts of despots, where the little church of Leyden might enjoy freedom of conscience ? Behold the mighty regions over which in *peaceful conquest—victoria sine clade* — they have borne the banners of the cross."

We now ask the reader to look at these expressions side by side,—" coming up out of the earth," " coming forth from vacancy," " emerging amid the silence of the earth," " like a silent seed we grew into empire," " mighty regions " secured by " peaceful conquest." The first is from the prophet, stating what *would be* when the two-horned beast should arise ; the others are from political writers, telling what *has been* in the history of *our own government.* Can any one fail to see that the last four are exactly synonymous with the first, and that they record a complete accomplishment of the prediction ? And what is not a little remarkable, those who have thus recorded the fulfillment have, without any reference to the prophecy, used the very figure which the prophet employed. These men, therefore, being judges,— men of large and cultivated minds, whose powers of discernment all will acknowledge to be sufficiently clear,—it is certain that the particular manner in which the United States has arisen, so far as it concerns its relation to other nations, answers most strikingly to the development of the symbol under consideration.

We now extend the inquiry a step further : Has the United States "come up" in a manner to fulfill the prophecy in respect to the achievements this government has accomplished ? Has the progress made been sufficiently great and sufficiently rapid to correspond to that visible and perceptible growth which John saw in the two-horned beast ?

In view of what has already been presented in Chapter II., this question need not be asked. To

show how the development of our country answers
to the "coming up" of the symbol, would be but to
repeat the evidence there given. *When* was the
wonderful national development indicated by the
two-horned beast to appear?—In the very era of the
world's history where our own government has appeared. *Where* was it to be witnessed?—In that
territory which our own government occupies. We
call the attention of the reader again to the wonderful facts stated in Chapter II. Their significance is
greatly enhanced by the representations of that portion of the prophecy we are now considering. Read
again the statement from Macmillan & Co., on p. 26,
showing that during the half century ending in 1867,
the United States added to its domain over fourteen
hundred thousand square miles of territory more
than any other single nation added to its area, and
over eight hundred thousand more than was added
to their respective kingdoms by all the other nations
of the earth put together. Its increase in population
and all the resources of national strength during the
same time were equally noteworthy. And this marvelous exhibition has occurred, be it remembered, at
that very epoch when the prophecy of the two-horned
beast bids us look for a new government just then
arising to prominence and power among the nations
of the earth. According to the argument on the
chronology of this symbol, we cannot go back of the
present century for its fulfillment ; and we submit to
the candid reader that to apply this to any other government in the world but our own during this time,
would be contrary to fact, and utterly illogical. It
follows, then, that our own government is the one in
question ; for this is the one which, at the right time

9

and in the right place, has been emphatically "coming up."

The only objection we can anticipate is that this nation has progressed too fast and too far,—that the government has already outgrown the symbol. But what shall be thought of those who deny that it has any place in prophecy at all? No; this prodigy has its place on the prophetic page; and the path which has thus far led us to the conclusion that the two-horned beast is the prophetic symbol of the United States, is hedged in on either side by walls of adamant that reach to heaven. To make any other application is an utter impossibility. The thought would be folly, and the attempt, abortion.

CHAPTER IX.

THE TWO GREAT PRINCIPLES OF THIS GOVERNMENT.

HAVING given us data by which to determine the location, chronology, and rapid rise of this power, John now proceeds to describe the appearance of the two-horned beast, and speak of his acts in such a manner as clearly to indicate his character, both apparent and real. Every specification thus far examined has held the application imperatively to the United States, and we shall find this one no less strong in the same direction.

This symbol has "two horns like a lamb." To those who have studied the prophecies of Daniel and John, horns upon a beast are no unfamiliar features. The ram (Dan. 8:3) had two horns. The he-goat that came up against him had at first one notable horn between his eyes. Verse 5. This was broken, and four came up in its place toward the four winds of heaven. Verse 8. From one of these came forth another horn, which waxed exceeding great. Verse 9. The fourth beast of Dan. 7 had ten horns. Among these, a little horn with eyes and mouth, far-seeing, crafty, and blasphemous, arose. Dan. 7:8. The dragon and leopard beast of Rev. 12 and 13, denoting the same as the fourth beast of Dan. 7 in its two phases, have each the same number of horns, signifying the same thing. And the symbol under consideration has two horns like a lamb. From the use of the horns on the other symbols, some facts are apparent which may guide us to an understanding of their use on this last one.

[131]

A horn is used in the Scriptures as a symbol of
strength and power, as in Deut. 33 : 17, and of glory
and honor, as in Job 16 : 15.

A horn is sometimes used to denote a nation as a
whole, as the four horns of the goat, the little horn of
Dan. 8, and the ten horns of the fourth beast of Dan.
7 ; and sometimes some particular feature of the government ; as the first horn of the goat, which denoted
not the nation as a whole, but the civil power, as cen-
tered in the first king, Alexander the Great.

Horns do not always denote division, as in the case
of the four horns of the goat, etc. ; for the two horns
of the ram denote the *union* of Media and Persia in
one government.

A horn is not used exclusively to represent civil
power ; for the little horn of Daniel's fourth beast, the
papacy, was a horn when it plucked up three other
horns, and established itself in 538. But it was then
purely an ecclesiastical power, and so remained for
two hundred and seventeen years from that time,
when Pepin, in the year 755, made the Roman pontiff
a grant of some rich provinces in Italy, which first
constituted him a temporal monarch. (Goodrich's
History of the Church, p. 98 ; Bower's History of
the Popes, vol. ii, p. 108.)

With these facts before us, we are prepared to inquire into the significance of the two horns which
pertain to this beast. Why does John say that he
has "two horns like a lamb" ? Why not simply "two
horns"? It must be because these horns possess pe-
culiarities which indicate the character of the power
to which they belong. The horns of a lamb indicate,
first, youthfulness, and secondly, innocence and gen-
tleness. As a power which has but recently arisen,

the United States answers to the symbol admirably in respect to age; while no other power, as has already abundantly been proved, can be found to do this. And considered as an index of power and character, it can be decided what constitutes the two horns of the government, if it can be ascertained what is the secret of its strength and power, and what reveals its apparent character, or constitutes its outward profession. The Hon. J. A. Bingham gives us the clue to the whole matter when he states that the object of those who first sought these shores was to found "what the world had not seen for ages; viz., a Church without a pope, and a State without a king." Expressed in other words, this would be a government in which the church should be free from the civil power, and civil and religious liberty reign supreme.

And what is the profession of this government in these respects? As already noticed, that great instrument which our forefathers set forth as their bill of rights—the Declaration of Independence—affirms that all men are created on a plane of perfect equality; that their Creator has endowed them all alike with certain rights which cannot be alienated from them; that among these are life, of which no man can rightfully deprive another, and liberty, to which every one is alike entitled, and the pursuit of happiness, in any way and every way which does not infringe upon the rights of others.

So much for the department of civil liberty. In the domain of spiritual things the position of this government is no less explicit and no less broad and liberal. In the Old World what multitudes have been deprived of "life, liberty, and the pursuit of happiness," on account of a peculiarity of belief in religious matters! What woes have been inflicted upon humanity by the efforts of spiritual tyrants to fetter men's consciences! What a grand safeguard is erected against these evils in the noble provisions of our Constitution, that no person shall be prohibited from freely exercising his religion (on the implied condition, of course, that no other person's rights are infringed upon) ; that Congress shall make no law in regard to any religious establishment ; and that no religious profession shall qualify, and no lack of it debar, a person from any office of public trust under the United States. Thus the right of worshiping God according to the dictates of his own conscience is guaranteed to every man.

In the chapter on the political and religious influence of this nation, these points are brought out more fully. And to the matter of that chapter the reader is again referred.

Here, then, are two great principles standing prominently before the people,—*Republicanism* and *Protestantism*. And what can be more just, and innocent, and lamb-like than these? And here, also, is the secret of our strength and power. Had some Caligula or Nero ruled this land, we should look in vain for what we behold to-day. Immigration would not have flowed to our shores, and this country would never have presented to the world so unparalleled an example of national growth.

One of these two lamb-like horns may therefore represent the great principle of civil liberty in this government ; and the other, the equally great principle of religious liberty, which men so highly prize, and have so earnestly sought. As says Mr. Foss in his sermon before quoted, "The two evangels of civil and religious liberty are ours." How better could these two great principles be symbolized than by the horns of a lamb? This application is warranted by the facts already set forth respecting the horns of the other powers. For (1.) the two horns may belong to one beast, and denote union instead of division, as in the case of the ram (Dan. 8); (2.) a horn may denote a purely ecclesiastical element, as the little horn of Daniel's fourth beast; and (3.) a horn may denote the civil power alone, as in the case of the first horn of the Grecian goat. On the basis of these facts, we have these two elements, Republicanism and Protestantism, here united in one government, and represented by two horns like the horns of a lamb. And these are nowhere else to be found; nor have they appeared, since the time when we could consistently look for the rise of the two-horned beast, in any nation upon the face of the earth except our own.

And with these horns there is no objection to be found. They are like those of a lamb, the Bible symbol of purity and innocence. The principles are all right. The outward appearance is unqualifiedly good. But, alas for our country! its acts are to give the lie to its profession. The lamb-like features are first developed, but the dragon voice is to be heard hereafter.

CHAPTER X.

INCONSISTENT UTTERANCES.

FROM the facts thus far elicited in this argument, we have seen that the government symbolized by the two-horned beast must be,—

1. Some government distinct from the powers of the Old World, whether civil or ecclesiastical ;

2. That it must arise this side the Atlantic ;

3. That it must be seen coming into influence and notoriety about the year 1798 ;

4. That it must rise in a peaceful manner ;

5. That its progress must be so rapid as to strike the beholder with as much wonder as the perceptible growth of an animal before his eyes ;

6. That it must be a republic ;

7. That it must exhibit before the world, as an index of its character and of the motives by which it is governed, two great principles, in themselves perfectly just, innocent, and lamb-like ; and

8. That it must perform its work in the present century.

And we have seen that of these eight specifications just two things can be said : First, that they are all perfectly met in the history of the United States thus far ; and secondly, that they are not met in the history of any other government on the face of the earth. Behind these eight lines of defense, therefore, the argument lies impregnably intrenched.

And the American patriot, the man who loves his country, and takes a just pride in her thus-far glorious record and noble achievements (and who does

not ?), needs an argument no less ponderous and immovable, and an array of evidence no less clear, to
enable him to accept the painful sequel which the remainder of the prophecy also applies to this government, hitherto the best the world has ever seen ; for
the prophet immediately turns to a part of the picture which is dark with injustice, and marred by oppression, deception, intolerance, and wrong.

After describing the lamb-like appearance of this
symbol, John immediately adds, " And he spake as a
dragon." The dragon (Pagan Rome), the first link
in this chain of prophecy, was a relentless persecutor
of the church of God. The leopard beast (the Papacy)
which follows, was likewise a persecuting power,
grinding out for 1260 years the lives of millions of the
followers of Christ. The third actor in the scene, the
two-horned beast, speaks like the first, and thus shows
himself to be a dragon at heart; "for out of the
abundance of the heart the mouth speaketh," and in
the heart actions are conceived. This, then, like the
others, is a persecuting power ; and the reason that
any of them are mentioned in prophecy, is simply because they are persecuting powers. God's care for
the church, his little flock, is what has led him to give
a revelation of his will, and point out the foes with
whom they would have to contend. To his church,
all the actions recorded of the dragon and leopard
beast relate ; and in reference to the church, therefore, we conclude that the dragon voice of this power
is uttered.

The "speaking" of any government must be the
public promulgation of its will on the part of its law-
making and executive powers. Is this nation, then,
to issue unjust and oppressive enactments against the

people of God? Are the fires of persecution, which in other ages have devastated other lands, to be lighted here also? We would fain believe otherwise; but notwithstanding the pure intentions of the noble founders of this government, notwithstanding the worthy motives and objects of thousands of Christian patriots to-day, we can but take the prophecy as it reads, and expect nothing less than what it predicts. John heard this power speak, and the voice was that of a dragon.

Nor is this so improbable an issue as might at first appear. The people'of the United States are not all saints. The masses, notwithstanding all our gospel light and gospel privileges, are still in a position for Satan to suddenly fire their hearts with the basest of impulses. This nation, as we have seen, is to exist to the coming of Christ; and the Bible very fully sets forth the moral condition of the people in the days that immediately precede that event. Iniquity is to abound, and the love of many to wax cold. Matt. 24:12. Evil men and seducers are to wax worse and worse. 2 Tim. 3:13. Scoffers are to arise, saying, "Where is the promise of his coming?" 2 Pet. 3:3, 4. The whole land is to be full of violence, as it was in the days of Noah, and full of licentiousness, as was Sodom in the days of Lot. Luke 17:26-30. And when the Lord appears, faith will scarcely be found upon the earth (Luke 18:8); and those who are ready for his coming will be but a "little flock." Luke 12:32. Can the people of God think to go through this period, and not suffer persecution?—No; this would be contrary to the lessons taught by all past experience, and just the reverse of what we are warranted by the word of God to expect. "All that will live godly in Christ Jesus shall suffer persecution." If ever this was true in the history of the church, we may expect it to be emphatically so when, in the last days, the world is in its aphelion as related to God, and the wicked touch their lowest depths of iniquity and sin.

Let, then, such a general spirit of persecution arise as the foregoing scriptures declare will in the last days exist, and what is more probable than that it should assume an organized form? In this country the will of the people is law. And let there be a general desire on the part of the people for certain oppressive enactments against believers in unpopular doctrines, and what would be more easy and natural than that such desire should immediately crystallize into systematic action, and oppressive measures take the form of law? Then we should have just what the prophecy indicates. Then would be heard the voice or the dragon.

And there are elements already in existence which furnish a luxuriant soil for a baleful crop of future evil. Our nation has grown so rapidly in wealth that it stands to-day as the richest nation in the world. Wealth leads to luxury, luxury to corruption, corruption to the breaking down of all moral barriers; and then the way is open for the worst passions to come to the front, and for the worst principles to bear rule. The prevailing condition of things is graphically described by the late distinguished and devoted J. H. Merle D'Aubigne, author of the "History of the Reformation." Just previous to his death he prepared a paper for the Evangelical Alliance, in which he gave utterance to the following weighty and startling words :—

"If the meeting for which you are assembled is an important
one, the period at which it is held is equally so, not only on account of the great things which God is accomplishing in the world,
but also by reason of the great evils which the spirit of darkness
is spreading throughout Christendom. The despotic and arrogant
pretensions of Rome have reached in our days their highest pitch,
and we are consequently more than ever called upon to contend
against that power which dares to usurp the divine attributes.
But that is not all. While superstition has increased, unbelief has
done so still more. Until now the eighteenth century—the age
of Voltaire—was regarded as the epoch of most decided infidelity;
but how far does the present time surpass it in this respect! . . .
But there is a still sadder feature of our times. Unbelief has
reached even the ministry of the word."

Political corruption is preparing the way for deeper
sin. It pervades all parties. Look at the dishonest
means resorted to to obtain office,—the bribery, the
deceptions, the ballot-stuffing. Look at the stupendous revelations of municipal corruption lately dis-
closed in New York City,—millions upon millions
stolen directly and barefacedly from the city treasury
by its corrupt officials. Look at the civil service of
this government. Speaking on this point, *The Nation*
of Nov. 17, 1870, said :—

"The newspapers are generally believed to exaggerate most of
the abuses they denounce ; but we say deliberately, that no denunciation of the civil service of the United States which has ever appeared in print has come up, as a picture of selfishness, greed,
fraud, corruption, falsehood, and cruelty, to the accounts which
are given privately by those who have seen the real workings of
the machine."

Revelations are continually coming to light, going
beyond the worst fears of those who are even the most
apprehensive of wrongs committed among all classes
of society at the present time. The nation stands
aghast to-day at the evidence of corruption in high

places which is thrust before its face. Yet a popular ministry, in their softest and most soothing tones, declare that the world is growing better, and sing of a good time coming.

The Detroit *Evening News* of March 4, 1876, referring to Secretary Belknap's fall, said :—

"The revelations of corruption in connection with the administration of the Federal government have gone further than anybody's worst fears, in the humiliating intelligence of Secretary Belknap's disgrace. That among the underlings there were to be found rascals, might have been expected in such times as these, but that a minister of the Cabinet should have turned out to be nothing better than a vulgar thief is something which must fill this nation with dismay, and the civilized world with contempt. Where is all this to stop? Are we so utterly rotten as a people that nothing but vileness can come uppermost,—that we cannot preserve even the great offices of the Cabinet from the possession of rascals?"

Again the *News* says :—

"Washington seems to be ingulfed in iniquity and steeped in corruption. Disclosures of fraud in high places are pushing one another toward the light. Belknap, Logan, Delano, Ingalls—and where the black list will stop, Heaven only knows."

Since the foregoing was written, who will say that there has been any real improvement in the tone of public morals? And further enumeration is here unnecessary. Enough crops out in every day's history to show that moral principle, the only guarantee for justice and honesty in a government like ours, is sadly wanting.

And evil is also threatening from another quarter. Creeping up from the darkness of the Dark Ages, a hideous monster is intently watching to seize the throat of liberty in our land. It thrusts itself up into the noonday of the nineteenth century, not that it may be benefited by its light and freedom, but that it may suppress and obscure them. The name of this monster is Popery ; and it has fixed its rapacious and blood-thirsty eyes on this land, determined to make it its helpless prey. It already decides the elections in some of our largest cities. It controls the revenues of the most populous State in the Union, and appropriates annually hundreds of thousands of dollars raised from Protestant taxes, to the support of its own ecclesiastical organizations, and to the furtherance of its own religious and political ends. It has attained such a degree of influence that it is only by a mighty effort of Protestant patriotism that any measures against which the Romish element combines its strength can now be carried. And corrupt and unscrupulous politicians stand ready to concede its demands, in order to secure its support for the advancement of their own ambitious aims. Look at the so-called "Freedom of Worship" bill, by which Papists would compel the general public to support in public institutions its own peculiar form of worship and priestly influence,—a bill which has been, and in all probability is destined more fully to be, an occasion of wrangling in the New York Legislature. Rome is in the field, with the basest and most fatal intentions, and with the most watchful and tireless energy. It is destined to play an important part in our future troubles ; for it is symbolized by the very beast which the two-horned beast is to cause the earth and them that dwell therein to worship, and before whose eyes it is to perform its wonders. Rev. 14 : 12.

And in our own better Protestant churches there is that which threatens to lead to most serious evils. On this point one of their own popular ministers, who is well qualified to speak, may testify. A sermon by Charles Beecher contains the following statements :—

"Our best, most humble, most devoted servants of Christ, are fostering in their midst what will one day, not long hence, show itself to be the spawn of the dragon. They shrink from any rude word against creeds with the same sensitiveness with which those holy fathers would have shrunk from a rude word against the rising veneration of saints and martyrs which they were fostering. . . . The Protestant evangelical denominations have so tied up one another's hands, and their own, that, between them all, a man cannot become a preacher at all, anywhere, without accepting some book besides the Bible. . . . And is not the Protestant Church apostate ? Oh ! remember, the final form of apostasy shall rise, not by crosses, processions, baubles. We understand all that. Apostasy never comes on the outside. It develops. It is an apostasy that shall spring into life within us,—an apostasy that shall martyr a man who believes his Bible ever so holily ; yea, who may even believe what the creed contains, but who may happen to agree with the Westminster Assembly, that, proposed as a test, it is an unwarrantable imposition. That is the apostasy we have to fear, and is it not already formed ? . . . Will it be said that our fears are imaginary ? Imaginary ! Did not the Rev. John M. Duncan, in the years 1825–6, or thereabouts, sincerely believe the Bible ? Did he not even believe substantially the Confession of Faith ? And was he not, for daring to say what the Westminster Assembly said, that to require the reception of that creed as a test of ministerial qualification was an unwarrantable imposition, brought to trial, condemned, excommunicated, and his pulpit declared vacant ? There is nothing imaginary in the statement that the creed-power is now beginning to prohibit the Bible as really as Rome did, though in a subtler way.

"Oh, woful day ! Oh, unhappy Church of Christ, fast rushing round and round the fatal circle of absorbing ruin ! . . . Daily does every one see that things are going wrong. With sighs does every true heart confess that rottenness is somewhere, but, ah ! it is hopeless of reform. We all pass on, and the tide rolls down to night. The waves of the coming conflict which is to convulse Christendom to her center are beginning to be felt. The deep heavings begin to swell beneath us. 'All the old signs fail.' 'God answers no more by Urim and Thummim, nor by dream, nor

by prophet.' Men's hearts are failing them for fear, and for looking after those things that are coming on the earth. Thunders
mutter in the distance. Winds moan across the surging bosom of
the deep. All things betide the rising of that fatal storm of divine indignation which shall sweep away the vain refuge of lies."

In addition to this, we have spiritualism, infidelity,
socialism, free-love, the trades unions, or labor against
capital, and communism,—all assiduously spreading
their principles among the masses. These are the
very principles that worked among the people, as the
exciting cause, just prior to the terrible French Revolution of 1789–1800. Human nature is the same in
all ages, and like causes will surely produce like effects. These causes are now all in active operation ;
and how soon they will culminate in a state of anarchy, and a reign of terror as much more frightful than
the French Revolution as they are now more widely
extended, no man can say.

Such are some of the elements already at work ;
such is the direction in which events are moving.
And how much further is it necessary that they should
progress in this manner before an open war-cry from
the masses of persecution against those whose simple
adherence to the Bible shall put to shame their man-
made theology, and whose godly lives shall condemn
their wicked practices, would seem in nowise startling or incongruous ?

But some may say, through an all-absorbing faith
in the increasing virtue of the American people, that
they do not believe that the United States will ever
raise the hand of persecution against any class. Very
well. This is not a matter over which we need to in-
dulge in any controversy. No process of reasoning
nor any amount of argument can ever show that it

will *not* be so.   We think we have shown good ground ·
for strong probabilities that this government may yet
commit itself to the work of religious persecution ;
and we shall present more forcible evidence, and
speak of more significant movements hereafter.   As
we interpret the prophecy, we look upon it as inevitable.   But the decision of the question must be left
to time ; we can neither help nor hinder its work.
Time will soon correct all errors, and solve all doubts,
on this question.

10

CHAPTER XI.

HE DOETH GREAT WONDERS.

IN further predicting the work of the two-horned beast, the prophet says, "And he exerciseth all the power of the first beast before him, and causeth the earth and them which dwell therein to worship the first beast, whose deadly wound was healed." This language is urged by some to prove that the two-horned beast must be some power which holds the reins of government in the very territory occupied by the first, or preceding beast, which is the papacy; for, otherwise, how could he exercise his power?

If the word "before" denoted precedence in time, and the first (or papal) beast passed off the stage of action when the two-horned beast came on, just as Babylon gave place to Persia, which then exercised all the power of Babylon before it, there would be some plausibility in the claim. But the word rendered "before" is ἐνώπιον *(cnopion)*, which means, literally, "in the presence of." And so the language, instead of proving what is claimed, becomes a most positive proof that these two beasts—the leopard papal beast and the two-horned beast—are distinct and contemporary powers.

The first beast is in existence, having all its symbolic vitality, at the very time the two-horned beast is exercising power in his presence. But this could not be, if his dominion had passed into the hands of the two-horned beast; for a beast, in prophecy, ceases to exist when his dominion is taken away. What

[146]

caused the change in the symbols, as given in the seventh chapter of Daniel, from the lion, representing Babylon, to the bear, representing Persia?—Simply a transfer of dominion from Babylon to Persia. And so the prophecy explains the successive passing away of these beasts, by saying that their "lives were prolonged," but their "dominion was taken away" (verse 12) ; that is, the territory of the kingdom was not blotted from the map, nor the lives of the people destroyed, but there was a transfer of power from one nationality to another. So the fact that the leopard beast, here in Rev. 13, is spoken of as still an existing power, when the two-horned beast works in his presence, is proof that he is, at that time, in possession of all the dominion that was ever necessary to constitute him a symbol in prophecy.

What power, then, does the two-horned beast exercise? Not the power which belongs to, and is in the hands of, the leopard, or papal beast, surely ; but he exercises, or essays to exercise, in his presence, power of the same kind and to the same extent. The power which the first beast exercised,—that alone with which the prophecy is concerned,—was a terrible power of oppression against the people of God (verse 7) ; and this is a further indication of the character which the two-horned beast is finally to sustain in this respect.

The latter part of the verse, "And causeth the earth and them which dwell therein to worship the first beast, whose deadly wound was healed," is still further proof that the two-horned beast is no phase nor feature of the papacy ; for the papal beast is certainly competent to enforce his own worship in his own country, and from his own subjects. But it is the two-horned beast which causeth the earth (the territory out of which it arose, and over which it rules), and them which dwell therein, to worship the first beast. This shows that this beast occupies territory over which the first beast has no jurisdiction.

"And he doeth great wonders, so that he maketh fire come down from heaven on the earth in the sight of men." In this specification we have still further proof that our own government is the one represented by the two-horned beast. That we are living in an age of wonders, none can deny. Time was, and that not twoscore of years ago, when the bare mention of achievements which now constitute the warp and woof of every-day life, was considered the wildest chimera of a diseased imagination. Now, nothing is too wonderful to be believed, nor too strange to happen. Go back only a little more than half a century, and the world, with respect to those things which tend to domestic convenience and comfort,—the means of illumination, the production and application of heat, and the performance of various household operations; with respect to methods of rapid locomotion from place to place, and the transmission of intelligence from point to point, stood about where it did in the days of the patriarchs. Suddenly the waters of that long stream over whose drowsy surface scarcely a ripple of improvement had passed for three thousand years, broke into the white foam of violent agitation. The world awoke from the slumber and darkness of ages. The divine finger lifted the seal from the prophetic books, and brought that predicted period when men should run to and fro, and knowledge should be increased. Then men bound the elements to their chariots, and, reaching up, laid hold

upon the very lightning, and made it their message-bearer around the world. Nahum foretold that at a certain time the chariots should be with flaming torches and run like the lightnings. Nahum 2 : 3, 4. Who can behold, in the darkness of the night, the locomotive dashing over its iron track, the fiery glare of its great lidless eye driving the shadows from its path, and torrents of smoke and sparks and flame pouring from its burning throat, and not realize that ours are the eyes that are privileged to look upon a fulfillment of Nahum's prophecy? But when this should take place, the prophet said that the times would be burdened with the solemn work of God's "preparation."

"Canst thou send lightnings," said God to Job, "that they may go, and say unto thee, Here we are?" Job. 38 : 35. If Job were living to-day, he could answer, Yes. It is one of the current sayings of our time that "Franklin tamed the lightning, and Prof. Morse taught it the English language."

So in every department of the arts and sciences, the advancement that has been made within the last half century is without precedent in the world's history. And in all these the United States takes the lead. These facts are not, indeed, to be taken as a fulfillment of the prophecy, but they show the spirit of the age in which we live, and point to this time as a period when we may look for wonders of every kind.

The wonders to which the prophecy (Rev. 13) refers are evidently wrought for the purpose of deceiving the people; for verse 14 reads, "And deceiveth them that dwell on the earth by means of those miracles which he had power to do in the sight of the beast."

THE TWO-HORNED BEAST THE SAME AS THE FALSE PROPHET OF CHAPTER 19.

The work attributed in verse 14, just quoted, to the two-horned beast, identifies this power with the false prophet of Rev. 19 : 20 ; for this false prophet is the agency that works miracles before the beast, " with which," says John, "*he deceived them that had received the mark of the beast, and them that worshiped his image*,"—the very actions which the two-horned beast is to cause men to perform. We can now ascertain by what means the miracles in question are wrought ; for Rev. 16 : 13, 14, speaks of *spirits of devils* working miracles, which go forth unto the kings of the earth and of the whole world, to gather them to the battle of the great day of God Almighty ; and these miracle-working spirits go forth out of the mouths of certain powers, one of which is *this very false prophet*, or two-horned beast.

Miracles are of two kinds—true and false, just as we have a true Christ and false christs, true prophets and false prophets, and true apostles and false apostles. By a false miracle we mean, not a pretended miracle, which is no miracle at all, but a real miracle, a supernatural performance, wrought *in the interest of falschood*, for the purpose of deceiving the people, or of proving a lie. The miracles of this power are real miracles, but are wrought for the purpose of deception. The prophecy does not read that he deceived the people by means of the miracles which he *claimed* that he was able to perform, or which he pretended to do, but which he *had power* to do.

They, therefore, fall far short of the real intent of

the prophecy, who suppose that the great wonders wrought by this power were fulfilled by Napoleon when he told the Mussulmans that he could command a fiery chariot to come down from heaven, but never did it ; or by the pretended miracles of the Romish Church, which are only shams, mere tricks played off by unscrupulous and designing priests upon their ignorant and superstitious dupes.

Miracles, or wonders, such as are to be wrought by the two-horned beast, and, withal, as we think, the very ones referred to in the prophecy, are mentioned by Paul in 2 Thess. 2 : 9, 10. Speaking of the second coming of Christ, he says, " Whose coming is after [κατὰ, at the time of, 2 Tim. 4 : 1]* the working of Sa-

---

* The one whose coming is referred to in 2 Thess, 2 : 9, is shown by the connection to be the same as the one whose coming is spoken of in verse 8; and that is Christ. In the original the connection is very direct; thus, καταργήσει τῇ ἐπιφανείᾳ τῆς παρουσίας αὐτοῦ, οὗ ἐστιν ἡ παρουσία κατ' ἐνέργειαν τοῦ Σαρανᾶ, etc. There would seem to be no question but that the relative οὗ must refer to the preceding αὐτοῦ as its antecedent; for the sentence literally reads, "And shall destroy with the brightness of *his* coming, *of whom* the coming is after the working of Satan," etc. In this case we cannot give to κατὰ the definition of "through," "by means of " or "according to," as it frequently means; for the coming of Christ is not "by means of," or "according to," the working of Satan. But κατὰ has another definition when used with an accusative, and when referring to time. It then means, "within the range of, during, in the course of, at, about." (Bagster's Analytical Greek Lexicon.) It is here used with the accusative,—ἐνέργειαν,—and although the word is not directly a noun of time, it is a word which necessarily involves the idea of duration; for the working of Satan must occupy time. We submit, therefore, that it may here receive one of the definitions last mentioned, and be rendered "at the time of." The whole passage would then read: " Whom the Lord shall consume with the spirit of his mouth, and shall destroy with the brightness of his coming; whose coming is *at the time of* the working of Satan with all power," etc. Thus rendered, the passage becomes parallel to that of 2 Tim. 4 : 1, where κατὰ is properly rendered "at," meaning "at the time of;" thus, "I charge thee therefore before God, and the Lord Jesus Christ, who shall judge the quick and the dead at his appearing [κατὰ τὴν ἐπιφάνειαν αὐτοῖ] and his kingdom."

tan with all power and signs and lying wonders, and
with all deceivableness of unrighteousness in. them
that perish, because they received not the love of the
truth, that they might be saved." These are no
sleight-of-hand performances, but such a working of
Satan as the world has never before seen. To work
with *all* power and signs and lying wonders, is certainly to do a real and an astounding work, but one
which is designed to prove a lie.

Again, the Saviour, predicting events to occur just
before his second coming, says, " For there shall arise
false christs and false prophets, and shall show great
signs and wonders ; insomuch that if it were possible,
they shall deceive the very elect." Here, again, are
wonders foretold, wrought for the purpose of deception, so powerful that were it possible even the very
elect would be deceived by them.

Thus we have a series of prophecies setting forth
the development, in the last days, of a wonder-working power, manifested to a startling and unprece-
dented degree, in the interest of falsehood and error.
All refer to one and the same thing. The earthly
government with which it was to be especially connected, is that represented by the two-horned beast,
or false prophet. The agency lying back of the outward manifestations was to be Satanic, " the spirit of
devils." The prophecy, according to the application
made of it in this book, calls for such a work as this
in our own country at the present time. Do we behold anything like it ? Read the answer in the lam-
entation of the prophet : " Woe to the inhabiters of
the earth and of the sea ! for the Devil is come down
unto you, having great wrath, because he knoweth
that he hath but a short time." Rev. 12 : 12. Stand

aghast, O Earth! tremble, ye people, but be not deceived! The huge specter of evil confronts us, as the prophet declared. Satan is loosed. From the depth of Tartarus myriads of demons swarm over the land. The prince of darkness manifests himself as never before, and, stealing a word from the vocabulary of heaven to designate his work, he calls it—*Spiritualism.*

1. Does Spiritualism, then, bear these marks of Satanic agency?

(1.) The spirits which communicate claim to be the spirits of our departed friends. But the Bible, in the most explicit terms, assures us that the dead are wholly inactive and unconscious till the resurrection; that the dead know not anything (Eccl. 9:5); that every operation of the mind has ceased (Ps. 146:4); that every emotion of the heart is suspended (Eccl. 9:6); and that there is neither work, nor device, nor knowledge, nor wisdom, in the grave, where they lie. Eccl. 9:10. Whatever intelligence, therefore, comes to us professing to be one of our dead friends, comes claiming to be what, from the word of God, we know he is not. But angels of God do not lie; therefore these are not the good angels. Spirits of devils will lie; this is their work; and these are the credentials which at the very outset they hand us.

(2.) The doctrines which they teach are from the lowest and foulest depths of the pit of lies. They deny God. They deny Christ. They deny the atonement. They deny the Bible. They deny the existence of sin, and all distinction between right and wrong. They deny the sacredness of the marriage relataion; and, interspersing their utterances with the most horrid blasphemies against God and his Son, and everything that is lovely, and good, and pure, they give the freest license to every propensity to sin, and to every carnal and fleshly lust. Tell us not that these things, openly taught under the garb of religion, and backed up by supernatural sights and sounds, are anything less than Satan's masterpiece.

2. Spiritualism answers accurately to the prophecy in the exhibition of great signs and wonders. Among its many achievements these may be mentioned: Various articles have been transported from place to place by spirits alone. Beautiful music has been produced independently of human agency, with and without the aid of visible instruments. Many well-attested cases of healing have been presented. Persons have been carried through the air by the spirits in the presence of many others. Tables have been suspended in the air with several persons upon them. And finally, spirits have presented themselves in bodily form, and talked with an audible voice.

Experiments conducted by the great German philosopher, Prof. Zöllner, demonstrated the following facts, as related by him to Joseph Cook during the late visit of the latter to Europe; namely, abnormal knots were tied in cords; messages were written between doubly and trebly sealed slates; coin passed through a table in a manner to illustrate the suspension of the laws of the impenetrability of matter; straps of leather were knotted under Prof. Zöllner's hands; the impression of two feet was given on sooted paper pasted inside two sealed slates; whole and uninjured wooden rings were placed around the standard of a card-table, over either end of which they could by no possibility be slipped; and finally, the table itself, a heavy beechen structure, wholly disappeared, and then fell down from the top of the room in which Prof. Zöllner and his friends were sitting.

A writer in the *Spiritual Clarion* speaks as follows of the manner in which Spiritualism has arisen, and the astounding progress it has made :—

> "This revelation has been with a power and a might, that, if divested of its almost universal benevolence, had been a terror to the very soul ; the hair of the very bravest had stood on end, and his chilled blood had crept back upon his heart at the sights and sounds of its inexplicable phenomena. It comes with foretokening, with warning. It has been, from the very first, its own best prophet, and step by step it has foretold the progress it would make. It comes, too, most triumphant. No faith before it ever took so victorious a stand in its infancy. It has swept like a hurricane of fire through the land, compelling faith from the baffled scoffer and the most determined doubter."

3. Spiritualism answers to the prophecy in that it had its origin in our own country, thus connecting its wonders with the work of the two-horned beast. Commencing in Hydesville,* N. Y., in the family of Mr. John D. Fox, in the latter part of March, 1848, it spread with incredible rapidity through all the States. It would be impossible to state the number of Spiritualists in this country at the present time. In 1876, only twenty-eight years from the commencement of this remarkable movement, estimates of the number of its adherents were made by different ones, which, though differing somewhat from one another, are nevertheless such as to show that the progress of Spiritualism has been without a parallel. Thus, Judge Edmonds puts the number at five or six millions (5,000,-000 or 6,000,000) ; Hepworth Dixon, three millions (3,000,000) ; A. J. Davis, four million two hundred and

---

* This place is near Rochester, N. Y ; hence the phenomenon was known at first as the "Rochester Knockings."

thirty thousand (4,230,000) ; Warren Chase, eight
millions (8,000,000) ; and the Roman Catholic Council at Baltimore, between ten and eleven millions (10,-
000,000 to 11,000,000). Of those who have become
its devotees, Judge Edmonds said as long ago as
1853 :—

'Besides the undistinguished multitude, there are many now of
high standing and talent ranked among them,—doctors, lawyers,
and clergymen in great numbers, a Protestant bishop, the learned
and reverend president of a college, judges of our higher courts,
members of Congress, foreign ambassadors, and ex-members of the
United States Senate."

This statement was written about thirty-two years
ago ; and from that time to this the work of the spirits
has been steadily progressing and spreading among
all classes of people.

One reason why it is now difficult to estimate the
number of those who might properly be denominated
Spiritualists, is that the more prominent and respectable of the adherents of this movement, are drawing
under cover the obnoxious and immoral features of
the system, heretofore so prominent, and assuming a
Christian garb. By this move they bring themselves
and a multitude of church members upon common
ground, where there is no distinction between them
in fact, though there still may be in name.

And from this nation Spiritualism has gone abroad
into all the earth. Queen Victoria is said to be a
devotee of the new philosophy. See Townsend's
" New World and Old," p. 201. The late rulers, the
Emperor and Empress of France, the Queen of Spain,
Pius IX., and Alexander II., are all said to have sought
to these spirits for knowledge. The same is said of
the present Emperor of Russia, Alexander III., who

is reported to have followed the direction of the spirits in regard to the time and manner of his coronation. Thus it is working its way to the potentates of the earth, and is fast preparing to accomplish its real mission, which is, by deceiving the world with its miracles, to gather the nations to the battle of the great day of God Almighty. Rev. 16 : 13, 14.

Here we pause. Let this work go on a little longer, as it has been going, and as it is still going, and what a scene is before us! Having seen so much fulfilled, we cannot now draw back and deny the remainder. And so we look for the onward march of this last great wonder-working deception, till that is accomplished which in the days of Elijah was a test between Jehovah and Baal, and fire is brought down from heaven to earth in the sight of men. Rev. 13 : 13. Then will be the hour of the powers of darkness,—the hour of temptation that is coming upon all the world to try them that dwell upon the earth. Rev. 3 : 10. Then all will be swept from their anchorage by the strong current of delusion, except those whom it is not possible to deceive—the elect of God. Matt. 24 : 24.

And still the world sleeps on, while Satan, with lightning fingers and hellish energy, weaves over them his last fatal snare. It is time some mighty move was made to waken the world, and arouse the church to the dangers we are in. It is time every honest heart should learn that the only safeguard against the great deception, whose incipient, and even well-advanced workings we already behold before our eyes, is to make the truths of God's holy and immutable word our shield and buckler.

CHAPTER XII.

CHURCH AND STATE.

THE imposing miracles wrought before the people having riveted upon them the chains of a fatal deception, leading them to suppose they have witnessed the great power of God, and must therefore be doing him service, when they have only been dazed with a mighty display of Satanic wonders, and are led captive by the Devil at his will, they are prepared to do the further bidding of the two-horned beast, which is to make an image to the beast which had the wound by a sword, and did live. Rev. 13 : 14.

Once more we remind the reader of the impregnable strength of the argument already presented in previous chapters, fixing the application of this symbol to the United States. This is an established proposition, and needs no further support. An exposition of the remainder of the prophecy will therefore consist chiefly of an effort to determine what acts are to be performed by this government, and a search for indications, if any exist, that they are about to be accomplished. If we shall find evidences springing up on all sides that this government is now moving as rapidly as possible in the very direction marked out by the prophet, these indications, though not necessary to establish the application of the symbol to this government, will serve to stifle the last excuse of skepticism, and become to the believer an impressive evidence of our proximity to the end ; for the acts ascribed to this symbol are but few, and while yet in mid-career, he is ingulfed in the lake of fire of the last great day. [159]

We may, however, notice in passing, another evidence that the government symbolized by the two-horned beast is certainly a republic. This is proved by the language used respecting the formation of the image. It does not read that this power, as an act of imperial or kingly authority, makes an image to the beast; but it *says to them that dwell on the earth*, that is, the people occupying the territory where it arises, that *they* should make an image to the beast. Appeal is made to the people, showing conclusively that the power is in their hands. But just as surely as the government symbolized is a republic, so surely it is none other than the United States of America.

We have seen that the wonder-working Satanic agencies, which are to perform the foretold miracles, and prepare the people for the next step in the prophecy—the formation of the image—are already in the field, and have even now wrought out a work of vast proportions in our country; and we now hasten forward to the very important inquiry, What will constitute the image, and what steps are necessary to its formation?

The people are to be called upon to make an image *to* the beast, which expression doubtless involves the idea of some deferential action toward, or concessions to, that power; and the image, when made, is an image, likeness, or representation *of* the beast. Verse 15. The beast after which the image is modeled is the one which had a wound by a sword and did live; that is, the papacy. From this point is seen the collusion of the two-horned beast with the leopard or papal beast. He does great wonders in the sight of that beast; he causes men to worship that beast; he leads them to make an image to that beast; and he causes all to receive a mark, which is the mark of that beast. These palpable evidences of co-operation with the papal power led Eld. J. Litch, about 1842, to write concerning the two-horned beast thus :—

"I think it is a power yet to be developed, or made manifest, as an accomplice of the papacy in subjecting the world."

To understand what would be an image of the papacy, we must first gain some definite idea of what constitutes the papacy itself. Papal supremacy dates from the time when the decree of Justinian constituting the pope the head of the Church and the corrector of heretics, was carried into effect in A. D. 538. The papacy, then, was a Church clothed with civil power, —an ecclesiastical body having authority to punish all dissenters with confiscation of goods, imprisonment, torture, and death. What would be an image of the papacy? Another ecclesiastical establishment clothed with similar power. How could such an image be formed in this country? It is not difficult to conceive a state of things—a state of things by no means impossible, and according to present prospects not even improbable—which would meet the prophecy precisely. Let the Protestant churches in our land be clothed with power to define and punish heresy, to enforce their dogmas under the pains and penalties of the civil law, and should we not have an exact representation of the papacy during the days of its supremacy?

It may be objected that whereas the papal Church was comparatively a unit, and hence could act in harmony in all its departments in enforcing its dogmas, the Protestant Church is so divided as to be unable to agree in regard to what doctrines shall be made im-

11

perative on the people. We answer, There are certain points which they hold in common, and which are sufficient to form a basis of co-operation. Chief among these may be mentioned the doctrine of "the conscious state of the dead" and "the immortality of the soul," which is both the foundation and superstructure of spiritualism, and also the doctrine that "the first day of the week is the Christian Sabbath."

It may be objected, again, that this view makes one of the horns of this two-horned beast, the Protestant Church, finally constitute the image of the papal beast. If the reader supposes that the Protestant Church constitutes one of the horns of the two-horned beast, we reply that this is a conception of his own. No such idea is here taught; and we mention this objection only because it has been actually urged as a legitimate consequence of the positions here taken. The question is also asked, If the Protestant Church constitutes one horn, may not the Catholic Church constitute the other? Under the shadow of that hypothetical "if," perhaps it might. But neither the one nor the other performs such an office. In Chapter IX. of this work it has been shown that the two great principles—Republicanism and Protestantism—were the proper objects to be symbolized by these two lamb-like horns. But there is the plainest distinction between Protestantism as an embodiment of the great principle of religious liberty, and the different religious bodies that have grown up under its fostering influence,—just as plain as there is between Republicanism, or civil liberty, and the individual who lives in the enjoyment of such liberty. The supposition, therefore, that the Protestant Church is to furnish the material for the image, involves no violation of the symbolic harmony of this prophecy.

Let us look a moment at the fitness of the material. We are not unmindful of the noble service the Protestant churches have rendered to the world, to humanity, and to religion, by introducing and defending, so far as they have, the great principles of Protestantism. But they have made a fatal mistake in stereotyping their doctrines into creeds, and thus taking the first step backward toward the spiritual tyranny of Rome. Thus the good promise they gave of a free religion and an unfettered conscience is already broken ; for if the right of private judgment is allowed by the Protestant Church, why are men condemned and expelled from that Church for no other crime than honestly attempting to obey the word of God, in some particulars not in accordance with her creed? This is the beginning of apostasy. Read Chas. Beecher's work, "The Bible a Sufficient Creed." "Is not the Protestant Church," he asks, "apostate?" Is not the apostasy which we have reason to fear "already formed?" But apostasy in principle always leads to corruption in practice. And so Paul, in 2 Tim. 3 : 1–5, sets forth the condition of the professed Church of Christ in the last days. A rank growth of twenty heinous sins, with no redeeming virtues, shows that the fruits of the Spirit will be choked and rooted out by the works of the flesh. We can look nowhere else for this picture of Paul's to be fulfilled, except to the Protestant Church ; for the class of which he speaks maintain a "form of godliness," or the outward services of a true Christian worship. And is not the Church of our day beginning to manifest to an alarming degree the very characteristics which the apostle has specified ?   Fifteen clergymen of the city of Rochester, N. Y., on Sunday, Feb. 5, 1871, distributed a circular entitled " A Testimony," to fifteen congregations of that city. To this circular the Rochester *Democrat* of Feb. 7 made reference as follows :—

"The 'Testimony' sets out by stating that the foregoing pastors are constrained to bear witness to what they 'conceive to be a fact of our time ; viz., that the prevailing standard of piety among the professed people of God is alarmingly low ; that a tide of worldliness is setting in upon us, indicating the rapid approach of an era such as is foretold by Paul in his second letter to Timothy, in the words, "In the last days perilous times shall come."' These conclusions are reached, not by comparison with former times, but by applying the tests found in the Scriptures. They instance, as proof, 'the spirit of lawlessness which prevails.' The circular then explains how this lawlessness (religious) is shown. Men have the name of religion, but they obey none of its injunctions. There is also a growing disposition to practice, in religious circles, what is agreeable to the natural inclinations, rather than the duties prescribed by the word of God. The tendency to adopt worldly amusements, by professed Christians, is further stated in evidence."

This testimony is very explicit.   When men "have the name of religion, but obey none of its injunctions," they certainly may be said to have "a form of godliness," but to "deny the power ;" and when they "practice in religious circles what is agreeable to the natural inclinations, rather than the duties prescribed by the word of God," they may truthfully be said to be "lovers of pleasures more than lovers of God." And Rochester is not an exception in this respect. It is so all over the land, as the candid everywhere, by a sad array of facts, are compelled to admit.

That the majority of the Christians in our land are still to be found in connection with these churches, is undoubtedly true.   But a change in this respect is also approaching ; for Paul, in his words to Timothy, above referred to, exhorts all true Christians to "turn away" from those who have a form of godliness, but deny the power thereof; and those who desire to live pure and holy lives, who mourn over the desolations of their Zion, and sigh for the abominations done in the land, will certainly heed this injunction of the apostle. There is another prophecy which also shows that when the spirit of worldliness and apostasy has so far taken possession of the professed churches of Christ as to place them beyond the reach of reform, God's true children are every one to be called out, that they become not partakers of their sins, and so receive not of their plagues. Rev. 18 : 4.

From the course which church members are everywhere pursuing, it is plain to be seen in what direction the Protestant churches are drifting ; and from the declarations of God's word it is evident that all whose hearts are touched by God's grace, and molded by his love, will soon come out from a connection in which, while they can do no good to others, they will receive only evil to themselves.

And now we ask the reader to consider seriously for a moment what the state of the religious world will be when this change shall have taken place. We shall then have an array of proud and popular churches, from whose communion all the good have departed, from whom the Holy Spirit is withdrawn, and who are in a state of hopeless departure from God. God is no respecter of persons nor of churches ; and if the Protestant churches apostatize from him, will they not be just as efficient agents in the hand of the enemy as ever pagans or papists have been ? Will they not then be ready for any desperate measure of bigotry and oppression in which he may wish to enlist them? After the Jewish Church had finally rejected Christ, how soon they were ready to imbrue their hands in the blood of his crucifixion! And is it not the testimony of all history that just in proportion as any popular and extensive ecclesiastical organization loses the Spirit and power of God, it clamors for the support of the civil arm?

Let, now, an ecclesiastical organization be formed by these churches; let the government legalize such organization, and give it power (a power which it will not have till the government does grant it) to enforce upon the people the dogmas which the different denominations can all adopt as the basis of union, and what do we have? Just what the prophecy represents,—an image to the papal beast, endowed with life by the two-horned beast, to speak and act with power.

And are there any indications of such a movement? The preliminary question, that of the grand union of all the churches, is now profoundly agitating the religious world.

In May, 1869, S. M. Manning, D. D., in a sermon in Broadway Tabernacle, New York, spoke of the recent efforts to unite all the churches in the land into co-operation on the common points of their faith, as a "*prominent and noteworthy sign of the times.*"

Dr. Lyman Beecher is quoted as saying:—

"There is a state of society to be formed by an extended combination of institutions, religious, civil, and literary, which never exists without the co-operation of an educated ministry."

Chas. Beecher, in his sermon at the dedication of the Second Presbyterian Church, Ft. Wayne, Ind., Feb. 22, 1846, said:—

"Thus are the ministry of the evangelical Protestant denominations not only formed all the way up under a tremendous pressure of merely human fear, but they live, and move, and breathe in a state of things radically corrupt, and appealing every hour to every baser element of their nature to hush up the truth, and bow the knee to the power of apostasy. Was not this the way things went with Rome? Are we not living her life over again? And what do we see just ahead?—Another general council! a world's convention! Evangelical Alliance and Universal Creed!"

The *Banner of Light* of July 30, 1864, said:—

"A system will be unfolded sooner or later that will embrace in its folds Church and State; for the object of the two should be one and the same. The time is rapidly approaching when the world will be startled by a voice that shall say to every form of oppression and wrong, 'Thus far shalt thou go, and no farther.' Old things are rapidly passing away in the religious and social, as well as in the political world. Behold, all things must be formed anew."

The *Church Advocate*, in March, 1870, speaking of the formation of an "Independent American Catholic Church," a movement now agitated in this country, said:—

"There is evidently some secret power at work which may be preparing the world for great events in the near future."

A Mr. Havens, in a speech delivered in New York a few years ago, said:—

"For my own part, I wait to see the day when a Luther shall spring up in this country, who shall found a great American Catholic Church, instead of a great Roman Catholic Church; and who shall teach men that they can be good Catholics without professing allegiance to a pontiff on the other side of the Atlantic."

There are indications, as will be shown in a subsequent chapter, that at no distant day such a Church will be seen, not, indeed, raised up through the instrumentality of a Luther, but rather through the operation of the same spirit that inspired a Fernando Nunez or a Torquemada.

CHAPTER XIII.

THE SUNDAY QUESTION.

THE principal acts ascribed to the two-horned beast, which seem to be performed with special reference to the papal beast, are, causing men to "worship" that beast, causing them to "make an image" to that beast, and enforcing upon them "the mark" of the beast. The image, after it is created and endowed with life, undertakes to enforce the worship of itself. To avoid confusion, we must keep these parties distinct in our minds. There are three here brought before us :—

1. *The Papal Beast.* This power is designated as "the beast," "the first beast," "the beast which had the wound by a sword, and did live," and the "beast whose deadly wound was healed." These expressions all refer to the same power ; and wherever they occur in this prophecy, they have exclusive reference to the papacy.

2. *The Two-Horned Beast.* This power, after its introduction in verse 11 of Rev. 13, is represented through the remainder of the prophecy by the pronoun "he ;" and wherever this pronoun occurs, down to the 17th verse (with possibly the exception of the 16th verse, which perhaps may refer to the image), it refers invariably to the two-horned beast.

3. *The Image of the Beast.* This is, every time, with the exception just stated, called the image ; so that there is no danger of confounding this with any other agent.

The acts ascribed to the image are, speaking, and enforcing the worship of itself under the penalty of death ; and this is the only enactment which the prophecy mentions as enforced under the death penalty. Just what will constitute this worship, it will perhaps be impossible to determine till the image itself shall have an existence. It will evidently be some act or acts by which men will be required to acknowledge the authority of that image, and yield obedience to its mandates.

The "mark of the beast" is enforced by the two-horned beast, either directly or through the image. The penalty attached to a refusal to receive this mark is a forfeiture of all social privileges, a deprivation of the right to buy and sell. Verse 17. The mark is the mark of the papal beast. Against this worship of the beast and his image, and the reception of his mark, the third angel's message of Rev. 14 : 9-12, is a most solemn and thrilling warning.

Here, then, is the issue before us. Human organizations, controlled and inspired by the spirit of the dragon, are to command men to do those acts which are, in reality, the worshiping of an apostate religious power, and the receiving of his mark, or lose the rights of citizenship, and become outlaws in the land,—to do that which constitutes the worship of the image of the beast, or forfeit their lives. On the other hand, God says, by a message mercifully sent out a little before the fearful crisis is upon us, Do any of these things, and you "shall drink of the wine of the wrath of God, which is poured out without mixture into the cup of his indignation." Rev. 14 : 9-11. He who refuses to comply with these demands of earthly powers exposes himself to the severest penalties which human beings

can inflict ; and he who does comply, exposes himself
to the most terrible threatening of divine wrath to be
found in the word of God.   The question whether we
will obey God or man is to be decided by the people
of the present age, under the heaviest pressure, from
either side, that has ever been brought to bear upon
any generation.

The worship of the beast and his image, and the
reception of his mark, must be something that involves the greatest offense that can be committed
against God, to call down so severe a denunciation of
wrath against it.   This is a work, as was shown in
Chapter VII., which takes place in the last days ;
and as God has given us in his word most abundant
evidence to show when we are in the last days, that
no one need be overtaken by the day of the Lord as
by a thief, so, likewise, it must be that he has given
us the means whereby we may determine what this
great latter-day sin is which he has so strongly condemned, that we may not incur the fearful penalty so
sure to follow its commission.   God does not so trifle
with human hopes and human destinies as to denounce
a most fearful doom against a certain sin, and then
place it beyond our power to understand what that
sin is, so that we have no means of guarding against it.

That we are now living in the last days, the volumes of both revelation and nature bear ample and
harmonious testimony.   Evidence on this point we
need not here stop to introduce ; for the testimony
already presented in the foregoing chapters of this
work, showing that the two-horned beast is now on
the stage of action, is in itself conclusive proof of this
great fact, inasmuch as this power exists and performs
its work in the very closing period of human history.

All these things tell us that the time has now come for the proclamation of the third message of Rev. 14 to be given, and for men to understand the terms it uses, and the warning it gives.

We therefore now call attention to the very important inquiry, What constitutes the mark of the beast? The figure of a mark is borrowed from an ancient custom. Says Bishop Newton (Dissertations on the Prophecies, London, one volume edition, p. 546):—

"It was customary among the ancients for servants to receive the mark of their master, and soldiers of their general, and those who were devoted to any particular deity, of the particular deity to whom they were devoted. These marks were usually impressed *on their right hand* or *on their foreheads,* and consisted of some hieroglyphic character, or of the name expressed in vulgar letters, or of the name disguised in numerical letters, according to the fancy of the imposer."

Prideaux says that Ptolemy Philopater ordered all the Jews who applied to be enrolled as citizens of Alexandria to have the form of an ivy leaf (the badge of his god, Bacchus) impressed upon them with a hot iron, under pain of death. (Connection, vol. ii., p. 78.)

The word used for mark in this prophecy is χάραγμα (*charagma*), and is defined to mean, "a graving, sculpture; a mark cut in or stamped." It occurs nine times in the New Testament, and with the single exception of Acts 17:29, refers every time to the mark of the beast. We are not, of course, to understand in this symbolic prophecy that a literal mark is intended; but the giving of the literal mark, as practiced in ancient times, is used as a figure to illustrate certain acts that will be performed in the fulfillment of this prophecy. And from the literal mark as formerly employed, we learn something of its meaning as used in the prophecy; for between the symbol and the thing symbolized there must be some resemblance. The mark, as literally used, signified that the person receiving it was the servant of, acknowledged the authority of, or professed allegiance to, the person whose mark he bore. So the mark of the beast, or of the papacy, must be some act or profession by which the authority of that power is acknowledged. What is it?

It would naturally be looked for in some of the special characteristics of the papal power. Daniel, describing that power under the symbol of a little horn, speaks of it as waging a special warfare against God, wearing out the saints of the Most High, and thinking to change times and laws. The prophet expressly specifies on this point: "He shall *think* to change times and laws." These laws must certainly be the laws of the Most High. To apply it to human laws, and make the prophecy read, "And he shall speak great words against the Most High, and shall wear out the saints of the Most High, and think to change human laws," would be doing evident violence to the language of the prophet. But apply it to the laws of God, and let it read, "And he shall speak great words against the Most High, and shall wear out the saints of the Most High, and shall think to change the times and laws *of the Most High*," and all is consistent and forcible. The Hebrew has דָּת *(dâth)* law, and the Septuagint reads, νόμος *(nomos)*, in the singular, "the law," which more directly suggests the law of God. The papacy has been able to do more than merely "think" to change human laws. It has changed them at pleasure. It has annulled the decrees of kings and emperors, and absolved subjects from allegiance to their rightful sovereigns. It has thrust its long arm into the affairs of nations, and brought rulers to its feet in the most abject humility. But the prophet beholds greater acts of presumption than these. He sees it endeavor to do what it was not able to do, but could only think to do; he sees it attempt an act which no man, nor any combination of men, can ever accomplish; and that is, to change the law of the Most High. Bear this in mind while we look at the testimony of another sacred writer on this very point.

Paul speaks of the same power in 2 Thess. 2; and he describes it, in the person of the pope, as "the man of sin," and as sitting as God in the temple of God (that is, the Church), and as exalting himself "above all that is called God, or that is worshiped." According to this, the pope sets himself up as the one for all the Church to look to for authority, in the place of God. And now we ask the reader to ponder carefully the question how he can exalt himself *above* God. Search through the whole range of human devices, go to the extent of human effort; by what plan, by what move, by what claim, could this usurper exalt himself above God? He might institute any number of ceremonies, he might prescribe any form of worship, he might exhibit any degree of power; but so long as God had requirements which the people felt bound to regard in preference to his own, so long he would not be above God. He might enact a law, and teach the people that they were under as great obligations to that as to the law of God; then he would only make himself equal with God. But he is to do more than this; he is to attempt to raise himself above him. Then he must promulgate a law which *conflicts* with the law of God, and demand obedience to his own law in preference to that of God. There is no other possible way in which he could place himself in the position assigned in the prophecy. But to do this is simply to endeavor to change the law of God; and if he can cause this change to be adopted by the people in place of the original enactment, then he, the law-changer, is above God, the law-maker. And this is the very work that Daniel said he should think to do.

Such a work as this, then, the papacy must accomplish according to the prophecy; and the prophecy cannot fail. And when this is done, what do the people of the world have? They have two laws demanding obedience,—one, the law of God as originally enacted by him, an embodiment of his will, and expressing his claims upon his creatures; the other, a revised edition of that law, emanating from the pope of Rome, and expressing his will. And how is it to be determined which of these powers the people honor and worship? It is determined by the law which they keep. If they keep the law of God as given by him, they worship and obey God. If they keep the law as changed by the papacy, they worship that power. But further: the prophecy does not say that the little horn should set aside the law of God, and give one entirely different. This would not be to change the law, but simply to give a new one. He was only to attempt a change, so that the law that comes from God, and the law that comes from the papacy, are precisely alike, excepting the change which the papacy has made in the former. They have many points in common. But none of the precepts which they contain in common can distinguish a person as the worshiper of either power in preference to the other. If God's law says, "Thou shalt not kill," and the law as given by the papacy says the same, no one can tell by a person's observance of that precept whether he designed to obey God rather than the pope, or the pope rather than God. But when a precept that has been changed is the subject of action,—as, for instance, if God says that the seventh day is the Sabbath on which we must rest, but the pope says that the first day is the Sabbath, and that we should keep this day and not the seventh,—then whoever observes that precept as originally given by God, is thereby distinguished as a worshiper of God ; and he who keeps it as changed, is thereby marked as a follower of the power that made the change. In no other way can the two classes of worshipers be distinguished. From this conclusion, no candid mind can dissent ; but in this conclusion we have a general answer to the question, "What constitutes the mark of the beast ?" namely, THE MARK OF THE BEAST IS THE CHANGE THE BEAST HAS MADE IN THE LAW OF GOD.

We now inquire if the Catholic power has attempted any change in the law of God, and if so, what that change is. By the law of God we mean the moral law, the only law in the universe of immutable and perpetual obligation,—the law of which Webster says, defining the terms according to the sense in which they are almost universally used in Christendom, "The moral law is summarily contained in the decalogue, written by the finger of God on two tables of stone, and delivered to Moses on Mount Sinai."

If, now, the reader will compare the ten commandments as found in Roman Catholic catechisms with those commandments as found in the Bible, he will see that in the catechisms the second commandment is left out, the tenth is divided into two to make up

the lack caused by leaving out the second, thus keeping
good the number ten, and the fourth commandment
(called the third in their enumeration) is made to en-
join the observance of Sunday as the Sabbath, and
prescribe that the day shall be spent in "hearing mass
devoutly, attending vespers, and reading moral and
pious books." Here are several variations from the
decalogue as found in the Bible. Here are some
marked changes. How have they come about? Are
they authorized in the Scriptures? or has the papacy
made them of its own will? Do any of these constitute the change contemplated in the prophecy? and
if so, which? or are they all included in that change?
Let it be borne in mind, that, according to the prophecy, he was to *think* to change times and laws. This
plainly conveys the idea of *intention* and *design*, and
makes these qualities essential to the change in question. But respecting the omission of the second commandment, Catholics argue that it is included in the
first, and hence should not be numbered as a separate
commandment. And on the tenth they claim that
there is so plain a distinction of ideas as to require
two commandments. So they make the coveting of
a neighbor's wife the ninth command, and the coveting of his goods the tenth.

In all this they claim that they are giving the commandments exactly as God intended to have them
understood. So, while we may regard them as errors
in their interpretation of the commandments, we cannot set them down as *intentional changes*. Not so,
however, with the fourth commandment. Respecting
this commandment they do not claim that their ver-
sion is like that given by God. They expressly claim
a change here, and also that the change has been

made by the Church. A few quotations from standard Catholic works will make this matter plain. In a work entitled "Treatise of Thirty Controversies," we find these words:—

"The word of God commandeth the seventh day to be the Sabbath of our Lord, and to be kept holy ; you [Protestants], without any precept of Scripture, change it to the first day of the week, only authorized by our traditions. Divers English Puritans oppose, against this point, that the observation of the first day is proved out of Scripture, where it is said, the first day of the week. Acts 20: 7 ; 1 Cor. 16: 2 ; Rev. 1: 10. Have they not spun a fair thread in quoting these places ? If we should produce no better for purgatory and prayers for the dead, invocation of the saints, and the like, they might have good cause, indeed, to laugh us to scorn ; for where is it written that these were Sabbath days in which those meetings were kept ? Or where is it ordained they should be always observed ? Or, which is the sum of all, where is it decreed that the observation of the first day should abrogate, or abolish, the sanctifying of the seventh day, which God commanded everlastingly to be kept holy ? Not one of these is expressed in the written word of God."

In the "Catholic Catechism of Christian Religion," on the subject of the third (fourth) commandment, we find these questions and answers :—

" *Ques.* What does God ordain by this commandment ?

"*Ans.* He ordains that we sanctify, in a special manner, this day on which he rested from the labor of creation.

" *Q.* What is this day of rest ?

" *A.* The seventh day of the week, or Saturday ; for he employed six days in creation, and rested on the seventh, Gen. 2: 2; Heb. 4: 1; etc.

" *Q.* Is it, then, Saturday we should sanctify in order to obey the ordinance of God ?

" *A.* During the old law, Saturday was the day sanctified ; but *the Church*, instructed by Jesus Christ, and directed by the Spirit of God, has substituted Sunday for Saturday ; so now we sanctify the first, not the seventh day. Sunday means, and now is, the day of the Lord."

12

In the "Catholic Christian Instructed," we read :—

"*Ques.* What are the days which the Church commands to be kept holy ?

"*Ans.* 1st. The Sunday, or the Lord's day, which we observe by apostolic tradition, instead of the Sabbath. 2dly. The feasts of our Lord's Nativity, or Christmas-day ; his Circumcision, or New-Year's day ; the Epiphany, or Twelfth-day ; Easter-day, or the day of our Lord's Resurrection ; the day of our Lord's Ascension ; Whitsunday, or the day of the coming of the Holy Ghost ; Trinity Sunday ; Corpus Christi, or the feast of the Blessed Sacrament. 3dly. We keep the day of the Annunciation, and Assumption of the Blessed Virgin Mary. 4thly. We observe the feast of All-Saints.

"*Q.* What warrant have you for keeping the Sunday preferable to the ancient Sabbath, which was the Saturday ?

"*A.* We have for it the authority of the Catholic Church, and apostolic tradition.

"*Q.* Does the Scripture anywhere command the Sunday to be kept for the Sabbath ?

"*A.* The Scripture commands us to hear the church (Matt. 18: 17; Luke 10: 16), and to hold fast the traditions of the apostles. 2 Thess. 2: 15. But the Scriptures do not in particular mention this change of the Sabbath. St. John speaks of the Lord's day (Rev. 1: 10); but he does not tell us what day of the week this was, much less does he tell us that this day was to take the place of the Sabbath ordained in the commandments. St. Luke also speaks of the disciples meeting together to break bread on the first day of the week. Acts 20: 7. And St. Paul (1 Cor. 16: 2) orders that on the first day of the week the Corinthians should lay by in store what they designed to bestow in charity on the faithful in Judea ; but neither the one nor the other tells us that this first day of the week was to be henceforward the day of worship, and the Christian Sabbath ; so that truly, the best authority we have for this is the testimony and ordinance of the Church. And, therefore, those who pretend to be so religious of the Sunday, whilst they take no notice of other festivals ordained by the same Church authority, show that they act by humor, and not by reason and religion ; since Sundays and holy days all stand upon the same foundation, viz., the ordinance of the Church."—*Catholic Christian Instructed, published by P. J. Kenedy, 5 Barclay St., New York, edition of 1884, pp. 202, 203.*

In the "Doctrinal Catechism" we find further testimony to the same point :—

> "*Ques.* Have you any other way of proving that the Church has power to institute festivals of precept ?
>
> "*Ans.* Had she not such power, she could not have done that in which all modern religionists agree with her—she could not have substituted the observance of Sunday, the first day of the week, for the observance of Saturday, the seventh day, a change for which there is no Scriptural authority."—*Doctrinal Catechism, P. J. Kenedy, New York*, p. 174.

From the article on "Obedience to the Church," Chapter VI., in the same work, p. 181, we take the following :—

> "*Ques.* In what manner can we show a Protestant that he speaks unreasonably against fasts and abstinences ?
>
> "*Ans.* Ask him why he keeps Sunday, and not Saturday, as his day of rest, since he is unwilling either to fast or to abstain. If he reply that the Scripture orders him to keep the Sunday, but says nothing as to fasting and abstinence, tell him the Scripture speaks of Saturday, or the Sabbath, but gives no command anywhere regarding Sunday, or the first day of the week. If, then, he neglects Saturday as a day of rest and holiness, and substitutes Sunday in its place, and this merely because such was the usage of the ancient Church, should he not, if he wishes to act consistently, observe fasting and abstinence, because the ancient Church so ordained ?"

The "Doctrinal Catechism" also attacks the practice of Protestants in not adhering to their platform that the Bible alone is a rule of faith and practice. Among the things not contained in the Scriptures which nevertheless Protestants generally believe, it mentions the following :—

> "It [the Scripture] does not tell us whether infants should be baptized ; whether the obligation of keeping Saturday holy has been done away with ; whether Sunday should be kept in its place," etc.—*Id.*, pp. 87, 88.

In "Abridgment of Christian Doctrine," we find
this testimony :—

> "*Ques.* How prove you that the Church hath power to com-
> mand feasts and holy days ?
>
> "*Ans.* By the very act of changing the Sabbath into Sunday,
> which Protestants allow of ; and therefore they fondly contradict
> themselves by keeping Sunday strictly, and breaking most other
> feasts commanded by the same Church.
>
> "*Q.* How prove you that ?
>
> "*A.* Because by keeping Sunday they acknowledge the Church's
> power to ordain feasts, and to command them under sin."

And finally, W. Lockhart, late B. A. of Oxford, in
the Toronto (Catholic) *Mirror*, offered the following
"challenge" to all the Protestants of Ireland,—a
challenge as well calculated for this latitude as that.
He says :—

> "I do, therefore, solemnly challenge the Protestants of Ireland
> to prove, by plain texts of Scripture, these questions concerning
> the obligations of the Christian Sabbath : 1. That Christians may
> work on Saturday, the old seventh day ; 2. That they are bound
> to keep holy the first day, namely, Sunday; 3. That they are not
> bound to keep holy the seventh day also."

This is what the papal power claims to have done
respecting the fourth (in their enumeration, the third)
commandment. Catholics plainly acknowledge that
there is no Scriptural authority for the change they
have made in this commandment, but that it rests
wholly upon the authority of the Church ; and they
claim this change as a "token," or "mark" of the authority of that Church, appealing in the most explicit
language to the "*very act of changing the Sabbath
into Sunday*" as proof of its power in this respect.
For further testimony on this point, the reader is referred to a tract published at the REVIEW Office, Battle Creek, Mich., entitled, "Who Changed the Sab-

bath?" in which are also extracts from Catholic writers refuting the arguments usually relied upon to prove the Sunday Sabbath, and showing that its only authority is the Catholic Church.

"But," says one, "I supposed that Christ changed the Sabbath." A great many suppose so; and it is natural that they should; for they have been so taught. And while we have no words of denunciation to utter against any such persons for so believing, we would have them at once understand that it is, in reality, one of the most enormous of all errors. We would therefore remind such persons that, according to the prophecy, the only change ever to be made in the law of God, was to be made by the little horn of Daniel 7, the man of sin of 2 Thessalonians 2; and the only change that has been made in it, is the change of the Sabbath. Now, if Christ made this change, he filled the office of the blasphemous power spoken of by both Daniel and Paul,—a conclusion sufficiently hideous to drive any Christian from the view which leads thereto.

Why should any one labor to prove that Christ changed the Sabbath? Whoever does this is performing a thankless task. The pope will not thank him; for if it is proved that Christ wrought this change, then the pope is robbed of his badge of authority and power. And no truly enlightened Protestant will thank him; for if he succeeds, he only shows that the papacy has not done the work which it was predicted that it should do, and therefore that the prophecy has failed, and the Scriptures are unreliable. The matter had better stand as the prophecy has placed it, and the claim which the pope unwittingly puts forth had better be granted. When a person is charged with any work, and abundant evidence is at hand to show that he did it, and the jury bring in a verdict of "Guilty," and finally the person himself steps forth and confesses that he has done the work,—that is usually considered sufficient to settle the matter. So, when the prophecy affirms that a certain power shall change the law of God, and in due time that very power arises, and does the work foretold, and indisputable evidence is presented to show that it has done the work, and finally that power openly claims that it has done it,—what need have we of further evidence?

The world should not forget that the great apostasy foretold by Paul has taken place; that the "man of sin" for long ages held almost a monopoly of what he styled Christian teaching in the world; that the mystery of iniquity has cast the darkness of its shadow and the errors of its doctrines over almost all Christendom; and that out of this era of error and darkness and corruption, the theology of our day has come. Would it, then, be anything strange to find that there are yet some relics of popery to be discarded ere the Reformation will be complete? A. Campbell (Baptism, p. 15), speaking of the Protestant sects, says:—

"All of them retain in their bosom—in their ecclesiastical organizations, worship, doctrines, and observances—various relics of popery. They are at best a reformation of popery, and only reformations in part. The doctrines and traditions of men yet impair the power and progress of the gospel in their hands."

The nature of the change which the little horn has attempted to effect in the law of God is worthy of notice. With true Satanic instinct, he undertakes to change that commandment which, of all others, is the fundamental commandment of the law, the one which makes known who the lawgiver is, and contains his signature of royalty. The fourth commandment does this ; no other one does. Four others, it is true, contain the word "God," and three of them the word "Lord," also. But who is this Lord God of whom they speak ? Without the fourth commandment, it is impossible to tell ; for idolaters of every grade might apply these terms to the multitudinous objects of their adoration. But when we have the fourth commandment to point out the Author of the decalogue, the claims of every false god are annulled at one stroke ; for it is at once seen that the God who here demands our worship is not any created being, but the one who created all things. The maker of the earth and sea, the sun and moon, and all the starry host, the upholder and governor of the universe, is the one who claims, and who, from his position, has a right to claim, our supreme regard in preference to every other object. The commandment which makes known these facts is, therefore, the very one we might suppose that power which designed to exalt itself above God (2 Thess. 2 : 3, 4) would undertake to change. God gave the Sabbath as a memorial of himself, a weekly reminder to the sons of men of his work in creating the heavens and the earth, a great barrier against atheism and idolatry. It is the signature and seal of the law. This the papacy has torn from its place, and erected in its stead, on its own authority, another institution, designed to serve another purpose.

This change of the fourth commandment must therefore be the change to which the prophecy points, and Sunday-keeping must be the "mark of the beast" ! Some who have long been taught to

regard this institution with reverence will perhaps
start back with little less than feelings of horror at this
conclusion. We have not space, nor is this perhaps
the place, to enter into an extended argument on the
Sabbath question, and an exposition of the origin
and nature of the observance of the first day of the
week. Let us submit this one proposition: If the
seventh day is still the Sabbath enjoined in the fourth
commandment; if the observance of the first day of
the week has no foundation whatever in the Scriptures; if this observance has been brought in as a .
Christian institution, and designedly put in place of
the Sabbath of the decalogue by that power which is
symbolized by the beast, and placed there as a badge
and token of its power to legislate for the Church, is
it not inevitably the mark of the beast? The answer
must be in the affirmative. But all these hypotheses
can easily be shown to be certainties. See "History
of the Sabbath," and other works on the subject, published at the REVIEW Office. To these we can only
refer the reader, in passing.

It will be said again, Then all Sunday-keepers have
the mark of the beast; then all the good of past ages
who kept this day, had the mark of the beast; then
Luther, Whitefield, the Wesleys, and all who have
done a good and noble work of reformation, had the
mark of the beast; then all the blessings that have
been poured upon the reformed churches have been
poured upon those who had the mark of the beast.
We answer, *No!* And we are sorry to say that some
professedly religious teachers, though many times
corrected, persist in misrepresenting us on this point.
We have never so held; we have never so taught.
Our premises lead to no such conclusions. Give ear:

The mark and worship of the beast are enforced by
the two-horned beast. The receiving of the mark of
the beast is a specific act which the two-horned beast
is to cause to be done. The third message of Rev.
14 is a warning mercifully sent out in advance to prepare the people for the coming danger. There can,
therefore, be no worship of the beast, nor reception
of his mark, such as is contemplated in the prophecy,
till it is enforced by the two-horned beast. We have
seen that *intention* was essential to the change which
the papacy has made in the law of God, to constitute
it the mark of that power. So *intention* is necessary
in the adoption of that change to make it, on the part
of any individual, the reception of that mark. In
other words, a person must adopt the change know-
ing it to be the work of the beast, and receive it on
the authority of that power, in opposition to the requirement of God.

But how with those referred to above, who have
kept Sunday in the past, and the majority of those
who are keeping it to-day? Do they keep it as an
institution of the papacy?—No. Have they decided
between this and the Sabbath of our Lord, understanding the claims of each?—No. On what ground
have they kept it, and do they still keep it?—They
suppose they are keeping a commandment of God.
Have such the mark of the beast?—By no means.
Their course is attributable to an error unwittingly
received from the Church of Rome, not to an act of
worship rendered to it.

But how is it to be in the future?—The Church
which is to be prepared for the second coming of
Christ must be entirely free from papal errors and
corruptions. A reform must hence be made on the

Sabbath question. The third angel (Rev. 14 : 9–12) proclaims the commandments of God, leading men to the true in the place of the counterfeit. The dragon is stirred, and so controls the wicked governments of the earth that all the authority of human power shall be exerted to enforce the claims of the man of sin. Then the issue is fairly before the people. On the one hand, they are required to keep the true Sabbath ; on the other, a counterfeit. For refusing to keep the true, the message denounces the unmingled wrath of God ; for refusing the false, earthly governments threaten them with persecution and death. With this issue before the people, what does he do who yields to the human requirement? —He virtually says to God, I know your claims, but I will not heed them. I know that the power I am required to worship is anti-Christian, but I yield to it to save my life. I renounce your allegiance, and bow to the usurper. The beast is henceforth the object of my adoration ; under his banner, in opposition to your authority, I henceforth array myself; to him, in defiance of your claims, I henceforth yield the obedience of my heart and life. In comparison with the fear of his punishments, I despise your wrath.

Such is the spirit which will actuate the hearts of the beast-worshipers,—a spirit which insults the God of the universe to his face, and is prevented only by lack of power from overthrowing his government and annihilating his throne. Is it any wonder that Jehovah denounces against so Heaven-daring a course the threatening brought to view in the scripture last referred to—the most terrible threatening that his word contains? Rev. 14 : 9–12.

CHAPTER XIV.

INDICATIONS OF COMING CHANGES.

WE have now found what, according to the prophecy, will constitute the image which the two-horned beast is to cause to be made, and the mark which it will attempt to enforce. The movement which is to fulfill this portion of the prophecy is to be looked for among those classes which constitute the professedly religious portion of the people. First, some degree of union must be effected between the various Protestant churches, with some degree of coalition, also, between these bodies and the beast power, or Roman Catholicism; and secondly, steps must be taken to bring the law of the land to the support of the Sunday Sabbath. These movements the prophecy calls for; and the line of argument leading to these conclusions is so direct and well-defined that there is no avoiding them. They are a clear and logical sequence from the premises given us.

When the application of Rev. 13:11-17 to the United States was first made, over thirty-five years ago, these positions respecting a union of the churches and a grand Sunday movement were taken. But at that time no sign appeared above or beneath, at home or abroad,—no token was seen, no indication existed, that such an issue would ever be made. But there was the prophecy, and that must stand. The United States government had given abundant evidence, by its location, the time of its rise, the manner of its rise, and its apparent character, that it was the power sym-

bolized by the two-horned beast. There could be no
mistake in the conclusion that it was the very nation
intended by that symbol. This being so, it must take
the course, and perform the acts foretold. But here
were predictions which could be fulfilled by nothing
less than the above-named religious movements, resulting in a virtual union of Church and State, and
the enforcement of the papal Sabbath as a mark of
the beast.

To take the position at that time that this government was to pursue such a policy and engage in such
a work, without any apparent probability in its favor,
was no small act of faith. On the other hand, to deny
or ignore it, while admitting the application of the
symbol to this government, would be in accordance
with neither Scripture nor logic. The only course
for the humble, confiding student of prophecy to pursue in such cases, is to take the light as it is given,
and believe the prophecy in all its parts. So the
stand was boldly taken ; and open proclamation has
been made from that day to this, that such a work
would be seen in the United States. With every review of the argument, new features of strength have
been discovered in the application ; and amid a storm
of scornful incredulity, we have watched the progress
of events, and awaited the hour of fulfillment.

Meanwhile, Spiritualism has astonished the world
with its terrible progress, and shown itself to be the
wonder-working element which was to exist in connection with this power. This has mightily strength-
ened the evidence of the application. And now, within
a few years past, what have we further seen ?—No
less than the commencement of that very movement
respecting the formation of the image and the enact-

ment of Sunday laws, which we have so long expected, and which is to complete the prophecy, and close the scene.

Reference was made in Chapter XI. to the movement now on foot for a grand union of all the Churches ; not a union which rises from the putting away of error and uniting upon the harmonious principles of truth, but simply a combination of sects, each retaining its own particular creed, but confederated for the purpose of carrying out more extensively the common points of their faith. This movement finds a strong undercurrent of favor in all the Churches ; and men are engaged to carry it through who are not easily turned from their purpose.

And there has suddenly arisen a class of men whose souls are absorbed with the cognate idea of Sunday reform, and who have dedicated every energy of their being to the carrying forward of this kindred movement. The New York Sabbath Committee have labored zealously, by means of books, tracts, speeches, and sermons, to create a strong public sentiment in behalf of Sunday. Making slow progress through moral suasion, they seek a shorter path to the accomplishment of their purposes through political power. And why not? Christianity has become popular, and her professed adherents are numerous. Why not avail themselves of the power of the ballot to secure their ends? Rev. J. S. Smart (Methodist), in a published sermon on the "Political Duties of Christian Men and Ministers," expresses a largely prevailing sentiment on this question, when he says :—

"I claim that we have, and ought to have, just as much concern in the government of this country as any other men. . . . We are the mass of the people. Virtue in this country is not weak ; her ranks are strong in numbers, and invincible from the righteousness of her cause—invincible if united. Let not her ranks be broken by party names."

A National Association has been in existence for a number of years, which has for its object the securing of such amendments to the national Constitution as shall express the religious views of the majority of the people, and make it an instrument under which the keeping of Sunday can be enforced as the Christian Sabbath. This Association already embraces within its organization a long array of eminent and honorable names,—Governors of States, Presidents of colleges, Bishops, Doctors of Divinity, Doctors of Law, and men who occupy high positions in all the walks of life.

In the Address issued by the officers of this Association, they say :—

"Men of high standing, in every walk of life, of every section of the country, and of every shade of political sentiment and religious belief, have concurred in the measure."

In their appeal, they most earnestly request every lover of his country to join in forming auxiliary associations, to circulate documents, attend conventions, sign the memorial to Congress, etc., etc.

In their plea for an amended Constitution, they ask the people to—

"Consider that God is not once named in our national Constitution. There is nothing in it which requires an 'oath of God,' as the Bible styles it (which, after all, is the great bond both of loyalty in the citizen and of fidelity in the magistrate),—nothing which requires the observance of the day of rest and worship, or which respects its sanctity. If we do not have the mails carried and the post-offices open on Sunday, it is because we have a Postmaster-General who respects the day. If our Supreme Courts are not held, and if Congress does not sit on that day, it is custom, and not law, that makes it so. Nothing in the Constitution gives Sunday quiet to the custom-house, the navy-yard, the barracks, or any of the departments of government.

"Consider that they fairly express the mind of the great body of the American people. This is a Christian people. These amendments agree with the faith, the feelings, and the forms of every Christian church or sect. The Catholic and the Protestant, the Unitarian and the Trinitarian, profess and approve all that is here proposed. Why should their wishes not become law ? Why should not the Constitution be made to suit and to represent a constituency so overwhelmingly in the majority ? . . .

"This great majority are becoming daily more conscious not only of their rights, but of their power. Their number grows, and their column becomes more solid. They have quietly, steadily, opposed infidelity, until it has at least become politically unpopular. They have asserted the rights of man and the rights of the government, until the nation's faith has become measurably fixed and declared on these points. And now that the close of the war gives us occasion to amend our Constitution, that it may clearly and fully represent the mind of the people on these points, they feel that it should also be so amended as to recognize the rights of God in man and in government. Is it anything but due to their long patience that they be at length allowed to speak out the great facts and principles which give to all government its dignity, stability, and beneficence ?"

Thus for several years a movement has been on foot, daily growing in extent, importance, and power, to fulfill that portion of the prophecy of Rev. 13 : 11–17 which first calls forth the dissent of the objector, and which appears from every point of view the most improbable of all the specifications ; namely, the making of an image to the beast and the enforcing of the mark. Beyond this, nothing remains but the sharp conflict of the people of God with this earthly power, and the eternal triumph of the overcomer.

An association, even now national in its character, as already noticed, and endeavoring, as is appropriate for those who have such objects in view, to secure their purposes under the sanction of the highest authority of the land, the national Constitution, already has this matter in hand.   In the interest of this Association there is published, in Philadelphia, a weekly paper called the *Christian Statesman*, in advocacy of this movement.   Every issue of that paper goes forth filled with arguments and appeals from some of the ablest pens in our land, in favor of the desired Constitutional Amendment.   These are the very methods by which, in a country like ours, great revolutions are accomplished ; and no movement has ever arisen in so short a space of time as this to so high a position in public esteem with certain classes, and taken so strong a hold upon their hearts.

Says Mr. G. A. Townsend (New World and Old, p. 212) :—

"Church and State has several times crept into American politics, as in the contentions over the Bible in the public schools, the anti-Catholic party of 1854, etc.   Our people have been wise enough heretofore to respect the clergy in all religious questions, and to entertain a wholesome jealousy of them in politics.   The latest *politico-theological movement* [italics ours] is to insert the name of the Deity in the Constitution."

The present movements of this National Reform Association, and the progress it has made, may be gathered somewhat from the following sketch of its history, and the reports of the proceedings of some of the conventions which have thus far been held.

From the Pittsburg (Pa.) *Commercial* of Feb. 6, 1874, we take the following :—

"The present movement to secure the religious amendment of the Constitution originated at Xenia, Ohio, in February, 1863, in a convention composed of eleven different religious denominations, who assembled for prayer and conference, not in regard to the amendment of the Constitution, but the state of religion.   Meetings (small in numbers) were held shortly after in Pittsburg and elsewhere. At first the Association was called a 'Religious Council;' now it is known as the 'National Association to Secure the Religious Amendment of the Constitution of the United States,' and is becoming more popular, and increasing largely in numbers.

"The first National Convention of the Association was held in the First United Presbyterian Church, Allegheny, Pa., Jan. 27, 1864, at which a large delegation was appointed to present the matter to the consideration of Hon. Abraham Lincoln, President of the United States. An adjourned meeting was held in the Eighth Street Methodist Episcopal Church, Philadelphia, on the 7th and 8th of July of the same year; and another in the same city, in the West Arch Street Presbyterian Church, Nov. 29, 1864.

"Conventions were held in New York in 1868; in Columbus, Ohio, February, 1869; and in Monmouth, Ill., April, 1871.

"National Conventions were held in Pittsburg, 1870; Philadelphia, 1871; Cincinnati, 1872; and New York, 1873. The National Convention which meets this afternoon [Feb. 4, 1874] in Library Hall [in Pittsburg, Pa.], is, we believe, the fifth in order."

From the report of the executive committee at the Cincinnati Convention, Jan. 31, 1872, it appeared that ten thousand copies of the proceedings of the Philadelphia Convention had been gratuitously distributed, and a general secretary had been appointed. Nearly $1,800 was raised at this Convention.

The business committee recommended that the delegates to this Convention hold meetings in their respective localities to ratify the resolutions adopted at Cincinnati; that twenty thousand copies of the proceedings of this Convention be published in tract form; and that the friends of the Association be urged to form auxiliary associations. All these recommendations were adopted.

Among the resolutions passed were the following :—

"*Resolved*, That it is the right and duty of the United States, as a nation settled by Christians,—a nation with Christian laws and usages, and with Christianity as its greatest social force,—to ac-

13

knowledge itself in its written Constitution to be a Christian nation.

"*Resolved*, That the proposed religious amendment, so far from tending to a union of Church and State, is directly opposed to such union, inasmuch as it recognizes the nation's own relations to God, and insists that the nation should acknowledge these relations for itself, and not through the medium of any church establishment."

Of the fifth annual Convention at Pittsburg, Feb. 4, 1874, Eld. J. H. Waggoner, who went as a correspondent from the S. D. Adventists, says, in the *Advent Review* of Feb. 17, 1874 :—

"This was a meeting of delegates, but was largely attended. The number of delegates holding certificates was 641 ; non-certified, 432 ; total, 1,073, representing 18 States. Petitions to Congress, partially returned, as I understood, footed up over 54,000 names.

"It has been strongly impressed upon my mind that we have underestimated, rather than overestimated, the rapid growth and power of this movement. Those who think we have been deluded in confidently looking for a great change in the nature and policy of our government, could but be convinced that we are right in this if they would attend such a meeting as this, or by other means become acquainted with what is actually taking place in this respect. The reason assigned for calling a delegated convention is that no place could be found large enough to accommodate a mass-meeting of the friends of the cause. But it is proposed to hold mass-meetings in the several States, and have a general grand rally in 1876, the centennial anniversary of our independence.

"The animus of this meeting cannot be understood nor appreciated by any one who did not attend it. It was a large gathering of delegates and others, and for enthusiasm and unanimity, is rarely equaled. This feature can be but feebly described in any published report ; and I notice that some of the most significant and stirring expressions are left out of the most complete reports of the speeches yet given.

"The officers of the Association for the coming year are, President, Hon. Felix R. Brunot, Pittsburg, with 99 Vice-Presidents, among whom are 4 governors, 5 State superintendents of public instruction, 9 bishops, 15 judges of higher courts, and 41 college presidents and professors, and the others are all eminent men; General Secretary, Rev. D. McAllister, N. Y.; Corresponding Secretary, Rev. T. P. Stevenson, Philadelphia."

In his opening address, the President of the National Association, and chairman of this fifth Convention, Hon. Felix R. Brunot, said that their "cause had made the progress of twenty years in five;" and the general Secretary, D. McAllister, said of the past year that it had "numbered a larger array of accessions to our ranks than any two, or three, or perhaps five, preceding years."

Instead of a large national convention in 1875, four conventions, more local in their nature, were held in different parts of the country, as follows :—

One in Tremont Temple, Boston, Mass., Dec. 16, 1874; one in St. Louis, Mo., Jan. 27 and 28, 1875; one for Kansas and adjacent States, Feb. 10 and 11; and one for Ohio and adjoining States, early in March.

Of the meeting in St. Louis, the *Christian Statesman* of February, 1875, said :—

"The Convention of citizens of Illinois, Iowa, Missouri, and neighboring States, in the city of St. Louis, on the 27th and 28th of last month, was a triumphant success. In a city where there was but a small constituency committed in advance to the support of the proposed amendment, public attention has been earnestly drawn to the movement; a large audience was called out at all the sessions of the Convention, and full reports of the able addresses delivered have been published in the city papers. By special arrangement, the St. Louis *Globe* gave a full report, like that of the Pittsburg *Commercial* or the *Globe* of Boston, but the other papers also contained full and respectful accounts of the proceedings. Fully one thousand people were present at the opening session, and at least three hundred at the day sessions on Thursday. Three hundred and ninety-four names were enrolled as members of the Convention. The address of J. C. Wells, Esq., a lawyer from Chillicothe, Illinois, was marked by the same fervor of argument and fervent Christian spirit which lend so much power and attractiveness to his able little book entitled 'Our National Obligation.' Mr. Wells was also chosen President of the Convention. **The** friends in St. Louis and vicinity are to be congratulated on this result."

"The closing resolution adopted at the Convention reads :—

"'*Resolved*, That, recognizing the importance of this subject, we pledge ourselves to present and advocate it until the nation shall declare its Christian character, as it has, with one consent, already asserted its freedom in the charter of our rights and liberties.'"

Nov. 9, 1875, a special meeting of the National **Association** was held in Philadelphia, Pa., **at which meeting** the Association took steps which have since been carried out, to become incorporated in law, under the name **of the** "National Reform Association." The *Christian Statesman* of Nov. 20, 1875, contained the following notice of this meeting :—

"The evening session was well attended, and was altogether the most encouraging meeting in behalf of the cause held in this city for many years."

The subsequent action of **the** executive committee is reported as follows :—

"The executive committee has since taken **steps to obtain a** charter of incorporation for the Society, **and to secure an office** which shall be a recognized head-quarters for its operations and depository of its publications, especially during the centennial **year.**"

An important meeting was held in Philadelphia at the time of the Centennial Exposition, and meetings have been held each year **since**, in all parts of the country.

The Association has at the present time **the** following board of officers : **A** president, corresponding secretary, financial secretary, recording secretary, treasurer, four district secretaries, and fifty-three vice-presidents. Among these, besides the President, Hon. Felix R. Brunot, Pittsburg, Pa., are seven Reverends, twenty-eight D. **D.'s** (sixteen of these **are** presidents of, or professors **in**, colleges **and** other institutions of learning, and most of the others are bishops and presiding elders), **nine** LL. **D.'s,** four justices of supreme courts, two editors, two generals, etc.

Whatever influence great names can impart to any cause **is** certainly secured in favor of this. **Mr.** F. E. Abbott, then editor of the *Index*, published in Boston, Mass., who was present at the Cincinnati Convention, and presented a protest against **its** aims **and** efforts, thus speaks o**f those who** stand **at the** head of this movement :—

"We found them to be so thoroughly sincere **and earnest in** their purpose, that they did not fear the effect of a decided but temperate protest. This fact speaks volumes in their praise **as** men of character and convictions. We saw no indications of the artful management which characterizes most conventions. The leading men, Rev. D. McAllister, Rev. A. M. Milligan, Prof. Sloane, Prof. Stoddard, Prof. Wright, Rev. T. P. Stevenson, impressed us as able, clear-headed, and thoroughly honest men ; and we could not but conceive a great respect for their motives and their intentions. **It** is such qualities **as** these in the leaders of the **movement** that give it its most formidable character. They have definite and consistent ideas ; they perceive the logical connection of these ideas, **and** advocate them in a very cogent and powerful manner ; and they propose to push them with determination and zeal. Concede their premises, and it is impossible to deny their conclusions; and since these premises are axiomatic truths with the great majority of Protestant Christians, the effect of the vigorous campaign **on** which they are entering cannot be small or despicable. The very respect with which we were compelled to regard them only increases our sense of the evils which lie germinant in their doctrines ; and we came home with the conviction that religious liberty in America must do battle for its very existence hereafter. The movement in which these men are engaged has too many elements of strength to be contemned by any far-seeing liberal.

Blindness or sluggishness to-day means slavery to-morrow. Radicalism must pass now from thought to action, or it will deserve the oppression that lies in wait to overwhelm it."

To show the strong convictions of many minds that the conflict here indicated is inevitable, we present some further extracts from the *Index*.   In its issue of Feb. 12, 1874, it says :—

"Yet in this one point the Christianizers show an unerring instinct.   The great battle between the ideas of the State and the ideas of the Church will indeed be fought out in the organic law of the nation.   The long and bitter conflict of chattel-slavery with free industry began in the world of ideas, passed to the arena of politics, burst into the hell of war, and expired in the peaceful suffrages by which Freedom was enthroned in the Constitution. The old story will be repeated ; for it is the same old conflict in a new guise, though we hope, and would fain believe, that the dreaded possibility of another civil war is in fact an impossibility. But that the agitation now begun can find no end until either Christianity or Freedom shall have molded the Constitution wholly into its own likeness, is one of the fatalities to be read in the very nature of the conflicting principles.   The battle of the amendments is at hand.   A thousand minor issues hide it from sight ; but none the less it approaches year by year, month by month, day by day.   Cowardice to the rear !   Courage to the front !"

The sentiment here expressed, that "the agitation now begun can find no end until either Christianity or Freedom [by which the *Index* means infidelity] shall have molded the Constitution wholly into its own likeness," is becoming the settled conviction of many minds.   It is not difficult to foresee the result. Infidel, the Constitution can never become ; hence it will become wholly the instrument of that type of Christianity which the Amendmentists are now seeking.

Again the *Index* says :—

"The central ideas of the Church and of the Republic are locked in deadly combat—none the less so, because the battle-ground of to-day is the invisible field of thought. To-morrow the struggle will be in the arena of politics, and then no eye will be so blind as not to see it."

At the Pittsburg Convention in 1874,—

"Dr. Kieffer said that this movement was more political than ecclesiastical, appealing to the patriotism of all classes alike, and should be accepted by all. Dr. Hodge said it was in no sense sectarian, and the ends it sought could be accepted by one denomination as well as by another,—by the Catholic as well as by the Protestant. He said it was destined to unite all classes. And their work was all in this direction."

The following, also from the *Index*, we copy from the *Christian Statesman* of Jan. 2, 1875. We do not indorse its statements as applied to real Christianity, but it probably expresses the view which will be taken of this matter by the churches generally, and so may be regarded as an indication of the course that will be pursued by them. While the political religionist can see in present movements the prelude of a mighty revolution, we believe it to be the same that students of prophecy have for years been led by the word of God to expect. The *Index* says :—

"Nothing could be more apparent to one who intelligently followed the argument from its own premises, than that this movement expresses at once the moral and the political necessities of Christianity in this country. It is not a question of words, but rather a question of the vital interests of great institutions. Christianity must either relinquish its present hold on the government, —its Sunday laws, its blasphemy laws, its thanksgivings and fasts, its chaplaincies, its Bible in schools, etc.,—or else it must secure the necessary condition of retaining all these things by inserting some guarantee of their perpetuity in the national Constitution. Looking simply at the small present dimensions of the movement, —at the fewness of its devoted workers, the paucity of attendants at the late Convention, and the indifference of the public at large, —one is justified in dismissing it from consideration as of no im mediate importance. But whoever is qualified to detect great movements in their germs, and to perceive that *instituted* Christianity is in vast peril from the constant inroads of rapidly speading disbelief of *dogmatic* Christianity,—whoever is able to discern the certainty that the claims of Christianity to mold political action in its own interest must sooner or later be submitted for adjudication to the supreme law of the land, by which they are not even verbally recognized,—will not fall into the superficiality of inferring the future fortunes of this movement, either from the mediæval character of its pretensions or the present insignificance of its success. It may possibly be that the Christian churches do not really care for their own existence, and are prepared to surrender it without a struggle, but we do not so read history. So soon as they come to comprehend fully the fact that their legal 'Sabbath,' their Bible in schools, and all their present legal privileges, must one by one slip away inevitably from their grasp, unless they defend them in the only possible way, by grounding them on Constitutional guarantees, it seems to us an irresistible conclusion from history and experience that they will arouse themselves to protect these possessions as infinitely important. If they do not, they have achieved a degree of moral rottenness, cowardice, and hypocrisy which we are very slow to attribute to them. These champions of a Christianized Constitution are to-day the POLITICAL BRAIN of the Christian Church. Conceding their premises, which are simply those of the universal Evangelical communion, it is impossible to deny their conclusions. It is these premises that we dispute, not the logicalness of the conclusions themselves; and although we hold that the same premises, if further carried out, must lead to the Roman Catholic position expressed by the Vatican decrees, we none the less admit the necessity of traveling that road from the starting-point, if it is once fairly entered upon. Hence we are as strongly convinced as ever that the Christian-Amendment movement contains the germ of a demand that must sooner or later be heard asserted with perilous emphasis, by the body of orthodox Christian Churches."

The character of this movement is thus described by one who was an eye-witness at the Pittsburg Convention :—

"They show determination to make the movement popular, and

to reach the feelings of the people by every means. In their speeches, they alternate with the most impassioned earnestness and gravest argument the sharpest wit, and even laughable puns and incidents. Staid 'Reverends' clap their hands in applause as heartily as I ever saw done in any kind of gathering, and Old-School Presbyterian Doctors of Divinity, who have generally been noted for clerical dignity, take the greatest delight in raising the cheers of the crowd by their keen thrusts and witticisms. The *Commercial* was publicly recommended as giving the official report, and of the speech of the President of Washington and Jefferson College it said, 'Dr. Hay's address was received with frequent marks of approbation, and his witty points drew forth shouts of laughter.' Judging from what I have seen, the standard of piety is not to be elevated by this work."—*J. H. W., in Review of Feb. 17, 1874.*

Between the professions of this Association, and the objects which they are openly laboring to obtain, there is an utter inconsistency, as the following considerations will show. In the *Review* of March 24, 1874, the writer last quoted says :—

"We are sometimes perplexed to account for the singular operations of the human mind. When we see men of good natural ability and of superior privileges of mental and moral culture, persistently clinging to the weaker side in argument, and seeming able to discover light only on the darkest side of a proposition, or endeavoring to sustain themselves by taking contradictory positions, our charity is taxed to the utmost to give them credit for the ability they seem to possess and for the integrity of purpose they claim. Seldom have our reflections been more forcibly turned in this direction than in viewing the course pursued by the advocates of the Religious Amendment. A late number of the *Christian Statesman*, speaking of the Seventh-day Adventists, says :—

"'From the beginning of the National Reform Movement, they have regarded it as the first step toward the persecution which they, as keepers of the seventh day, will endure when our Sabbath laws are revived and enforced. One can but smile at their apprehensions of the success of a movement which would not harm a hair of their heads ; but their fears are sincere enough, for all that.'"

Pursuing the line of argument into a consideration of the question whether there is anything in the professions of the Amendment party calculated to change our opinion in this respect, he continues :—

"If a profession of good motives and of a desire to steer clear of a union of Church and State on the part of the Amendment party could give us assurance on this point, then might we cease to notice this subject. On this point they are very explicit. A few quotations will suffice to present their claims. Said Hon. Mr. Patterson, in the Pittsburg Convention :—

"'Be not misled by the assertion that the movement agitated by this Convention tends to religious intolerance, to wedding Church and State. No such tendency exists. On the contrary, this movement claims nothing but to secure in the preamble of our national Constitution an acknowledgment of the supremacy of God and the Christian character of our nation, such as is now generally and authoritatively conceded to be the law of our land.'

"This, surely, is lamb-like enough to throw us all off our guard. The following remarks by President Brunot (pronounced *Brūno*) on taking the chair, are equally innocent to view :—

"'The fourth article of the Constitution declares that "no religious test shall ever be required as a qualification to any office or public trust under the United States," and the first amendment in the Constitution provides that "Congress shall make no law respecting an establishment of religion, or prohibiting the free exercise thereof." We have not proposed to change these. We deem them essential, in connection with the amendment we ask, to the preservation of religious liberty, and with it, an effective guard against a union of Church and State.'

"And again : 'The attempt to destroy the inalienable right of freedom of conscience in religion in this, our favored land, would meet with its very first organized resistance from this Association.'

"And Dr. Kerr said :—

"'We want no union of Church and State. Let that question be raised in this country, and there is no element of the opposition that would rise against it that would be more decided and determined than that represented in this Convention. We wish no restraint of the rightful liberties of any man.'

"These utterances are pleasant to read, and doubtless they, and others like them, have had much to do in enlisting so strong an interest in favor of the amendment. And were these sayings, or those of like nature, all that they had put forth, we should feel constrained to regard the men and their work in a light somewhat different from that in which we now view them.

"We come now to examine another class of expressions, of a positive nature. What we have quoted is negative,—a disclaimer, a relation of what they do not wish to do. Very explicitly have they stated their desires and intentions. True, we cannot reconcile what they have said under these two heads, and it is this which so perplexes us in regard to their professions. It is to be hoped that they will sometime attempt to show that their statements may be harmonized, or else confine their avowals to one side of the question, that all may understand, without study or doubt, just the position they occupy.

"Dr. Stevenson, Corresponding Secretary of the National Association, and editor of the *Statesman*, in the opening address at the Convention, said :—

"'Through the immense largesses it receives from corrupt politicians, the Roman Catholic Church is, practically, the established church of the city of New York. These favors are granted under the guise of a seeming friendliness to religion. We propose to put the substance for the shadow,—to drive out the counterfeit by the completer substitution of the true.'

"These words are somewhat ambiguous, but none the less important, on this subject ; for, taken in any possible way, they are full of meaning. It may be a question whether this 'seeming friendliness to religion' is the shadow, and real friendliness to religion in politics is the substance, or whether the Catholic Church is the counterfeit and Protestantism the true ; but in either case the establishment of the Church, or a Church, or Churches, more completely than at present established, though they are practically existing now, is the object aimed at in this paragraph. The latter form, the establishment of the Churches, appears to be the object ; for in the next sentence he says :—

"'What we propose is nothing of a sectarian character. It will give no branch of American Christians any advantage over any other.'

"A remark made by Prof. Blanchard is a complement to the

above. He has given us a definition of 'union of Church and State' as opposed by them. Thus he said :—

"'But union of Church and State is the selection by the nation of one Church, the endowment of such a Church, the appointment of its officers, and the oversight of its doctrines. For such a union none of us plead. To such a union we are all of us opposed.'

"In reading this, we are reminded of the turn taken by the Spiritualists, when they deny that they are opposed to marriage ; they explain by defining marriage to be a union of two persons not to be regulated nor guarded by civil law, which exists only as long as the parties are agreed thereto, requiring no law to effect a divorce ! To such marriage the most lawless libertine would not object. We are sorry that the respectable advocates of the amendment take a position so nearly parallel to the above-cited position of Spiritualists. They give a definition of union of Church and State such as no one expects nor fears,—such, in fact, as is not possible in the existing state of the Churches,—and then loudly proclaim that they are opposed to union of Church and State ! But to a union of Church and State in the popular sense of the phrase ; a union, not of one Church, but of all the Churches recognized as orthodox, or evangelical ; a union not giving the State power to elect Church officers, nor to take the oversight of Church doctrines, but giving the Churches the privilege of enforcing by civil law the laws, institutions, and usages of religion according to the faith of the Churches, or to the construction put upon those institutions and usages by the churches,—to such a union, we say, they are not opposed. They are essentially and practically, despite their professions, open advocates of union of Church and State.

"President Brunot and others have referred to the first amendment to the Constitution as a safeguard against establishing a national religion. Yet in the face of this reference he says:—

"'We propose "such an amendment to the Constitution of the United States (or its preamble) as will suitably acknowledge Almighty God as the author of the nation's existence and the ultimate source of its authority, Jesus Christ as its ruler, and the Bible as the supreme rule of its conduct," and thus indicate that this is a Christian nation, and place all Christian laws, institutions, and usages on an undeniable legal basis in the fundamental law of the land.'

"Now the question arises, If all this were accomplished, would

the Christian religion be established in and by this government?
If it be answered that it would not, then another question, Would
individuals be at liberty under the law of the land to disregard
those Christian institutions and usages? If not, if both of these
questions be answered in the negative, then what would be the existing state of things? Could it be defined?

"This will never do; such talk is idle. To place Christian
usages on a legal basis is to enforce them by law, and to enforce
them is to 'establish' them. When they are placed on an 'undeniable legal basis in the fundamental law of the land,' they are
fully established, and to deny this is only to trifle with language.
But again, you cannot distinguish between 'all Christian laws, institutions, and usages,' and the Christian religion. By establishing them, you establish it, of necessity. To deny this is to manifest a lack of discrimination or of candor. We speak with due
respect, but we have to deal with facts of the greatest magnitude
and importance, and which affect us in those things which we
hold most sacred and dear. The advocates of this movement are
able men. We hope they will not ignore these points, but so explain them as to reconcile themselves with themselves, if it can be
done."

The New York *Independent*, in January, 1875,
showed up the inconsistency of this movement in a
few paragraphs so pointed and pungent that we quote
them entire, as follows:—

"This being a Christian nation, we have a right to acknowledge
God in the Constitution; because, as things are now, this is not a
Christian nation, and needs such recognition to make it one.

"This having always been a Christian nation, we have a right
to keep it such; and therefore we need this amendment, since
hitherto, without it, we have only been a heathen nation.

"In other words, we need to make this a Christian nation, because we are already such, on the ground that if we do not make
it such, we are not a Christian nation.

"Because the people are substantially all Christians, we have a
right, and have need, to make the Constitution Christian, to check
our powerful element of unbelievers.

"We mean to interfere with no man's rights, but only to get
certain rights, now belonging to all, restricted to Christians.

"This religious amendment is to have no practical effect, its object being to check infidelity.

"It is to interfere with no man's rights, but only to make the unbeliever concede to Christians the right to rule in their interest, and to give up like claims for himself.

"It is meant to have no practical effect, and therefore will be of great use to us.

"We want to recognize God, and Christianity as our national duty to Deity, but intend to give no effect to such recognition, pleasing God by judicially voting ourselves pious, and doing nothing more.

"We shall leave all religions in equality before the law, and make Christianity the adopted religion of the nation.

"Christianity, being justice, requires us to put down infidelity by taking advantage of our numbers to secure rights which we do not allow to others.

"Justice to Christians is one thing, and to infidels another.

"We being a Christian people, the Jewish and unbelieving portion of our people are not, of right, part of the people.

"And so, having no rights which we, as Christians, are bound to respect, we must adopt this amendment in our interest.

"Passing this act will not make any to be Christians who are not Christians; but it is needed to make this a more Christian nation.

"The people are not to be made more Christian by it; but, since the nation cannot be Christian unless the people are, it is meant to make the nation Christian without affecting the people.

"That is, the object of this amendment is to make the nation Christian without making the people Christians.

"By putting God in the Constitution he will be recognized by nobody else than those who already recognize him; and therefore we need this amendment for a fuller recognition of him.

"If we say we believe in God and Christ in the Constitution, it is true of those believing in him and a lie as to the rest; and as the first class already recognize him, we want this amendment as a recognition by the latter class, so that our whole people shall recognize him.

"Whether we have an acknowledgment of God in the Constitution or not, we are a Christian nation; and, therefore, it is this recognition of God that is to make us a Christian nation."

As to the probability of the success of this movement, there is at present some difference of opinion.
While a very few pass it by with a slur as a mere
temporary sensation of little or no consequence, it is
generally regarded, both by its advocates and its op-
posers, as a work of growing strength and importance.
Petitions and remonstrances are both being circulated
with activity; and shrewd observers, who have watched
the movement with a jealous eye, and therefore hoped
it would amount to nothing, now confess that it
"means business." No movement of equal magnitude
of purpose has ever sprung up and become strong,
and secured favor so rapidly as this. Indeed, none
of equal magnitude has ever been sprung upon the
American mind, as this aims to remodel the whole
frame-work of our government, and give to it a strong
religious caste,—a thing which the framers of our
Constitution were careful to exclude from it. They
not only ask that the Bible, and God, and Christ shall
be recognized in the Constitution, but that it shall indicate this as "a Christian nation, and place all Christian laws, institutions, and usages in our government
on an undeniable legal basis in the fundamental law
of the nation."

Of course, appropriate legislation will be required
to carry such amendments into effect, and somebody
will have to decide what are "Christian laws and institutions." And when this question is raised, who
will be appealed to as qualified to determine the matter in question?—The doctors of religion, of course.
Then what shall we have?—The Church sitting in
judgment on men's religious opinions, the Church
defining heresy, and the State waiting at its beck to
carry out whatever sentence shall be affixed to a de-

viation from what the Church shall declare to be
"Christian laws and institutions." But was not this
exactly the situation in the darkest reign of Roman
Catholicism? And would not its production here be
a very "image to the beast"?—Yea, verily. But this
is the inevitable sequence of the success of this effort
to secure a religious amendment of the Constitution.
From what we learn of such movements in the past
in other countries, and of the temper of the churches
of this country, and of human nature when it has
power suddenly conferred upon it, we look for no
good from this movement. From a lengthy article
in the Lansing (Michigan) *State Republican* in reference to the Cincinnati Convention, we take the following extract :—

"Now there are hundreds and thousands of moral and professedly Christian people in this nation to-day who do not recognize
the doctrine of the Trinity,—do not recognize Jesus Christ the
same as God. And there are hundreds and thousands of men and
women who do not recognize the Bible as the revelation of God.
The attempt to make any such amendment to the Constitution
would be regarded by a large minority, perhaps a majority, of our
nation as a palpable violation of liberty of conscience. Thousands
of men, if called upon to vote for such an amendment, would hesitate to vote against God, although they might not believe that the
amendment is necessary or that it is right ; and such men would
either vote affirmatively or not at all., In every case, such an
amendment would be likely to receive an affirmative vote which
would by no means indicate the true sentiment of the people.
And the same rule would hold good in relation to the adoption of
such an amendment by Congress or by the Legislatures of three-
quarters of the States. Men who make politics a trade would hesitate to record their names against the proposed Constitutional
Amendment, advocated by the leaders of the great religious denominations of the land, and indorsed by such men as Bishop Simp-
son, Bishop McIlvaine, Bishop Eastburn, President Finney, Prof.
Lewis, Prof. Seelye, Bishop Huntington, Bishop Kerfoot, Dr. Pat-

terson, Dr. Cuyler, and many other divines who are the represent ative men of their respective denominations."

Not only the representative men of the churches are pledged to this movement, but governors, judges, and many who are among the most eminent men of the land in other directions, are working for it. Who doubts the power of the "representative men of the denominations" to rally the strength of their denominations to sustain this work at their call? We utter no prophecy of the future; it is not needed. Events transpire in these days faster than our minds are prepared to grasp them. Let us heed the admonition to "watch!" and with reliance upon God, prepare for "those things which are coming on the earth."

But it may be asked how the Sunday question is to be affected by the proposed Constitutional Amendment. Answer: The object, or to say the least, *one* object, of this amendment, is to put the Sunday institution on a legal basis, and compel its observance by the arm of the law. At the National Convention held in Philadelphia, Jan. 18 and 19, 1871, the following resolution was among the first offered by the Business Committee :—

"*Resolved*, That, in view of the controlling power of the Constitution in shaping State as well as national policy, it is of immediate importance to public morals and to social order, to secure such an amendment as will indicate that this is a Christian nation, and place all Christian laws, institutions, and usages in our government on an undeniable legal basis in the fundamental law of the nation, specially those which secure a proper oath, and which protect society against blasphemy, Sabbath-breaking, and polygamy."

By Sabbath-breaking is meant nothing else but Sunday-breaking. In a convention of the friends of Sunday, assembled Nov. 29, 1870, in New Concord, Ohio, the Rev. James White is reported to have said :—

14

"The question [of Sunday observance] is closely connected with the National Reform Movement ; for until the government comes to know God and honor his law, we need not expect to restrain Sabbath-breaking corporations."

Here again the idea of the legal enforcement of Sunday observance stands uppermost.

Once more : The Philadelphia *Press*, of Dec. 5, 1870, stated that some Congressmen, including Vice-President Colfax, arrived in Washington by Sunday trains, Dec. 4, on which the *Christian Statesman* commented as follows (we give italics as we find them) :—

"1. *Not one of those men who thus violated the Sabbath is fit to hold any official position in a Christian nation.* * * * *

"He who violates the Sabbath may not steal, because the judgment of society so strongly condemns theft, or because he believes that honesty is the best policy ; but tempt him with the prospect of concealment or the prospect of advantage, and there can be no reason why he who robs God will not rob his neighbor also. For this reason, the Sabbath law lies at the foundation of morality. Its observance is an acknowledgment of the sovereign rights of God over us.

"2. *The sin of these Congressmen is a national sin*, because the nation hath not said to them in the Constitution, the supreme rule for our public servants, 'We charge you to serve us in accordance with the higher law of God.' These Sabbath-breaking railroads, moreover, are corporations created by the State, and amenable to it. The State is responsible to God for the conduct of these creatures which it calls into being. It is bound, therefore, to restrain them from this as from other crimes, and any violation of the Sabbath by any corporation, should work immediate forfeiture of its charter. And the Constitution of the United States, with which all State legislation is required to be in harmony, should be of such a character as to prevent any State from tolerating such infractions of fundamental moral law.

"3. Give us in the national Constitution the simple acknowledgment of the law of God as the supreme law of nations, and *all the results indicated in this note will ultimately be secured.* Let no one say that the movement does not contemplate sufficiently practical ends."

Let the full import of these words be carefully considered. The writer was by some unaccountable impulse betrayed into a revelation of the real policy and aim of this movement. He holds up to the public view those Congressmen who traveled on Sunday, as men who would rob and steal if they saw an opportunity to do so without danger of detection! Not one of them, he says, is fit to hold any office in the government. He would make this religious test a qualification for office, contrary to the Constitution. Every corporation that infringes upon Sunday should be immediately destroyed by a forfeiture of its charter. And what then of the individual, in this respect, who does not observe the Sunday? Of course he could fare no better than the corporations,—he must be at once suspended from business. What does the prophecy say the enactment will be?—"That no man might buy or sell save he that had the mark, or the name, of the beast, or the number of his name." Could there be a more direct fulfillment than this would be if once carried out, as the religious amendmentists are trying to do?

From all this we see the important place the Sabbath question is to hold in this movement,—the important place it even now holds in the minds of those who are urging it forward. Let the amendment called for be granted, "and all the results indicated in this note," says the writer, "will ultimately be secured;" that is, individuals and corporations will be restrained from violating the Sunday observance. The acknowledgment of God in the Constitution may do very well as a banner under which to sail; but the practical bearing of the movement relates to the compulsory observance of the first day of the week.

An article in the *Christian at Work* of April 20, 1882, spoke of a proposed plan to induce railroad corporations and the leading industries of the country to suspend business on Sunday. The writer thought the plan would fail, because it did not have "the force of a penalty," and said :—

"There is need of the power of government behind the plan,—the strength of the national government in support of the rule; for the great business corporations of the country have risen above, and reach beyond, the authority of a Commonwealth. And not till the people have made the Federal Government the escutcheon of the Sabbath [Sunday], may we expect the rival industries to honor that sacred day."

And while this writer thus sturdily called for law, he believed that if the Church "insisted on her rights" as loudly as the "infidel resisted them," they could be easily secured.

Even now the question is agitated why the Jew should be allowed to follow his business on the first day, after having observed the seventh. The same question is equally pertinent to all seventh-day keepers. A writer signing himself "American," in the Boston *Herald* of Dec. 14, 1871, said :—

"The President in his late message, in speaking of the Mormon question, says, 'They shall not be permitted to break the law under the cloak of religion.' This undoubtedly meets the approval of every American citizen, and I wish to cite a parallel case, and ask, Why should the Jews of this country be allowed to keep open their stores on the Sabbath, under the cloak of their religion, while I, or any other true American, will be arrested and suffer punishment for doing the same thing? If there is a provision made allowing a few to conduct business on the Sabbath, what justice and equality can there be in any such provision, and why should it not be stopped at once?"

And this question, we apprehend, will be very summarily decided, adversely to the Jew and every other seventh-day observer, when once the Constitutional Amendment has been secured.

At a Ministerial Association of the Methodist Episcopal Church, held in Healdsburg, Cal., April 26–28, 1870, Rev. Mr. Trefren, of Napa, speaking of S. D. A. ministers, said, "I predict for them a short race. What we want is law in the matter." Then, referring to the present movement to secure such a law, he added : "And we will have it, too ; and when we get the power into our hands, we will show these men what their end will be."

In 1876 the question was raised in Keokuk, Iowa, "whether a Seventh-day Adventist could be compelled to attend court as a witness on Saturday ;" and Judge Blanchard decided that he could be, and that "a refusal would be contempt of court."

The *Signs of the Times*, of Oakland, Cal., in its issue of Dec. 22, 1881, said :—

"After a sermon recently preached by an Oakland D. D., in favor of enforcing the Sunday law, some of the members of the congregation were heard giving utterance to strong commendations of the sermon and of the law. Said one, 'I am glad the Seventh-day Adventists will have to come to time.'"

This feeling is not confined to the Pacific States. A correspondent of the *Review and Herald*, Battle Creek, Mich., writing from Illinois in 1883, said :—

"A short time ago, at the dedication of a certain church, I heard a minister—who is also president of one of the leading colleges in our State, and of enough importance to have D. D. to his name—say that he was glad that the sectarian walls are being thrown down, and that people are becoming more liberal. 'Yes,' says he, 'I thank God for a *Roman Catholic* Church ; for there is no religious body that is any more zealous in trying to establish a law for the protection of the Sabbath [Sunday].' Another minister, where I was holding meetings a few weeks since, in a sermon against us, said: 'You Americans all have great respect for Noah Webster; there is not one of you but what considers him absolutely infallible; and if you will look in his dictionary at the word *Sunday*, you will find that he says that it is the Christian Sabbath. It is true that before Christ, the Jewish people kept the seventh day; but since Christ the lines of longitude and latitude have been such that it is impossible to keep it. And furthermore, the custom of our country makes it obligatory upon us to observe Sunday sacredly. But these *miserable* Adventists come around in the face of all this, and tell us that we must keep the old Jewish Sabbath. They are a set of ABOMINABLE TRAITORS, who are *trying to produce dissension* in our land, and OPPOSE the laws of our country; the place for EVERY ONE of them is in our State prisons, and what we want is a LAW that will put them there; and, thank God, the time is not far distant when we will have it.'"

There are abundant indications that this pious feeling largely prevails in many sections of our country.

From a work recently issued by the Presbyterian Board of Publication, entitled "The Sabbath," by Chas. Elliott, Professor of Biblical Literature and Exegesis in the Presbyterian Theological Seminary of the Northwest, Chicago, Ill., we take the following paragraph:—

"But it may be asked, Would not the Jew be denied equality of rights by legislation protecting the Christian Sabbath and ignoring the Jewish? The answer is, We are not a Jewish, but a Christian nation; therefore our legislation must be conformed to the institutions and spirit of Christianity. This is absolutely necessary from the nature of the case."

There is no mistaking the import of this language. No matter if the Jew does not secure equal rights with others. We are not a Jewish nation, but a Christian; and all must be made to conform to what the majority decide to be Christian institutions. This affects all who observe the seventh day as much as it does the Jews; and we apprehend it will not be a difficult matter to lead the masses, whose prejudices incline them in this direction, to believe that it is "absolutely necessary" that all legislation must take such a form, and cause them to act accordingly.

Several years since, Dr. Durbin, of the *Christian Advocate and Journal*, gave his views on this subject as follows :—

"I infer, therefore, that the civil magistrate may not be called upon to enforce the observance of the Sabbath [Sunday] as required in the spiritual kingdom of Christ; but when Christianity becomes the moral and spiritual life of the State, the State is bound, through her magistrates, to prevent the open violation of the holy Sabbath, as a measure of self-preservation. She cannot, without injuring her own vitality and incurring the Divine displeasure, be recreant to her duty in this matter."

At a meeting held at Saratoga Springs, N. Y., Aug. 12, 1860, ex-President Fillmore said that "while he deemed it needful to legislate cautiously in all matters connected with public morals, and to avoid coercive measures affecting religion, the right of every citizen to a day of rest and worship could not be questioned, and laws securing that right should be enforced."

And the *Christian Statesman* of Dec. 15, 1871, in speaking of the general disregard of the Sabbath [Sunday] in the arrangements for welcoming the Grand Duke Alexis of Russia, said :—

"How long will it be before the Christian masses of this country can be aroused to enact a law compelling their public servants to respect the Sabbath?"

That the Sunday question has entered into the arena of politics to stay till some decision is reached in regard to it, is now too apparent to be questioned;

and this is an immense stride in the direction of the fulfillment of the prophecies referring to this subject, as herein set forth.

In August, 1882, a copy of a paper published in Chicago, and called the *Illinois American*, was placed in our hands. It purported to be the organ of the American party, and it was announced that the party intended to establish similar papers in all the leading States of the Union. That party claims to embody in its platform " all the *great* reforms of the day." One reform which it considers essential is the enforcement of Sunday as the Sabbath, after the manner of the National Reform Association. In proof of this, we have but to quote the first two planks in its platform :—

"We hold, 1. That ours is a Christian and not a heathen nation, and that the God of the Christian Scriptures is the author of civil government ; 2. That God requires and man needs a Sabbath."

This Sabbath is, of course, the first day of the week ; and whatever papers this party shall establish, will be the political organs of the Religious Amendment Movement, as the *Christian Statesman* is the religious organ. They enter the field as a national party, and nominated candidates for the presidential election of 1884, as follows : For President of the United States, Jonathan Blanchard, D. D., President of Wheaton College, Illinois ; for Vice-President, John A. Conant, of Connecticut.

The fanatical temper of the leading candidate, on the Sunday question, is plainly read in a few facts : 1. He is one of the vice-presidents of the National Reform Association, and a prominent worker in that movement ; 2. In October, 1881, a circular was sent out from Wheaton College chapel, of which he was quite evidently the inspiring spirit, addressed to the "Churches of Christ throughout the United States," setting forth that our great national calamity, the assassination of President Garfield, was a judgment of God upon the nation for its sins, chief among which is Sabbath (Sunday) breaking ; and beseeching "that the churches of Christ, individually or collectively, unite in requesting Congress to forbid, by proper enactment, the transaction of public business upon the Sabbath-day by any department of government, and that petitions to this effect be prepared or obtained from the Sabbath Association of Philadelphia, to be presented by that society at the opening of Congress on December next."

We know many will be inclined to look upon the formation of this new American party as an idle move, and upon its efforts and object as vain and impossible. But the significant fact still remains that somebody has thought enough of these things to inaugurate this movement, and everything must have a beginning. Moreover, we all know that sometimes the beginnings of great revolutions are exceedingly small. The acorn which the little child so easily holds in its hand, comes at length to be the sturdy oak, which the mightiest tempest cannot uproot.

In one State already, the Sunday question has been made the main issue, in a State election, between the two great parties, Democratic and Republican. In the fall election of 1882, California made this issue, and gave to our country the first spectacle of a strictly religious question in the arena of politics. In this struggle Sunday was led to the front under the mantle of a "police regulation," a merely "civil institution." The working-man, said the Sunday advocate, must be secured in his right to a day of rest. This claim was too transparent to conceal from view the real object; for the law which it was sought to enforce was not the law of the *civil* code, which makes Sunday a legal holiday and gives every one the privilege of resting on it who chooses to do so, but the Sunday law of the *penal* code, which was enacted for the purpose of making all desecration of the day an offense against *religion*, and punishing it as such. Now if the design was simply to secure rest to the people on that day, the civil code already provided for that, and no one proposed to interfere with the action of that law; but if it was to enforce Sunday as a religious institution, on religious grounds alone, the law of the penal code was the one to enforce; and in that direction the effort was made. The object was therefore sufficiently apparent.

The Democrats having inserted in their platform a plank calling for the repeal of the Sunday law, the Republicans, in their State Convention, which convened in Sacramento, Cal., Sept. 30, 1882, introduced into their platform a plank calling for the maintenance of the law. Thus the issue was fairly joined. The scene in the Sacramento Convention when the Sunday plank was read, baffles description. The four hundred and fifty delegates broke into a vociferous shout; they clapped their hands, stamped with their feet, threw up their hats, and hugged each other in a delirium of joy. It was a wild, insane spirit, on which neither argument nor the testimony of Scripture would make any impression. We imagine it is just such a blind, impetuous spirit which is essential to the success of the Sunday movement.

The Democrats carried the election, and the Sunday law was in due time repealed. And now the friends of the institution turn more vigorously than ever toward the national movement which is working for the religious amendment.

In New York, Ohio, Indiana, and Illinois, the agitation of the Sunday question has been remarkable. In February, 1883, a correspondent wrote from Indiana : "Almost every paper in the State is crying out for Sunday law and Sunday reform."

No less significant is the fact that the Sunday agitation is appearing in foreign countries simultaneously with the Sunday movement in this country. The N. Y. *Independent* of Oct. 1, 1885, published the following significant article touching the question of Sunday-keeping in Europe :-

"No *desideratum* of the social an   religious world is now being more actively agitated in Central Europe than the project of a better observance of the Lord's day. It seems that the so-called 'Continental Sunday' is doomed 'to go ;' and no friend of public and private morals will do otherwise than rejoice that its day of doom appears to have come. For years an international association, organized for the purpose of educating public sentiment on this point, has been busily at work, with head-quarters at Geneva, and by means of branch associations, publications, annual delegate meetings, petitions, and the like, has managed to keep the subject constantly before the public. The movement is just now assuming a new character, and is entering upon a new stage that promises some healthy results. The political authorities are beginning to recognize the agitation, and are taking active steps in the right direction. In various cantons of Switzerland—such as St. Gall, Berne, Aargau, and others—more stringent laws have been enacted. In Austria such laws went into force a few months ago, and already good results are reported. Now the German governments have taken hold of the matter, and are trying to find out what to do in the premises. Prussia is leading in the movement. The Minister of Cultus has issued a circular letter to the presidents of the various provinces, directing a stricter obedience to the Sunday

laws already in existence ; namely, that, during the principal services Sunday morning and afternoon, and also on the great Church
festivals, all work that can interrupt the devotions must cease, and
promising that, in the near future, further laws will be passed by
the government. The Imperial government is taking similar steps
for the whole German empire. During the past winter lively de-
bates were held on the subject in the Reichstag, or Imperial Parliament, which gave occasion to many classes of the people to express their sentiments on this burning question. These facts have
influenced the government to issue a circular letter to representative manufacturers and other 'work-givers,' and also to workmen,
asking answers to the following questions : 1. Is Sunday work
common in all branches of industry ?   2. Is Sunday work the rule
or the exception ?   3. Is this work done (*a.*) in the whole business,
(*b.*) for all the workmen, (*c.*) for the whole Sunday or for a part ?
4. What causes this work, (*a.*) technical reasons or (*b.*) economic
reasons ?   5. What results would the forbidding of such work
have (*a.*) for the capitalist, (*b.*) for the workingman, in regard to
his income ?   Would this loss find a compensation in any gain ?
6. Is it possible to carry laws forbidding work on Sunday, (*a.*) without any exceptions, (*b.*) with what exceptions, and for what reasons?
The answers received to these questions by the government officials
will have a great deal to do in shaping the proposed legal measures in regard to Sunday observance to be introduced into the next
German parliament."

Who can explain the fact that Sunday seems everywhere coming to the front, except on the ground
that we have reached the time pointed out in prophecy when such a movement should be seen ? The
Chester (Eng.) *Chronicle* of July 9, 1881, reported a
meeting of 3,000 persons in Liverpool in favor of closing all public houses on Sunday. The *Christian
Statesman* of July 22, 1880, gave information from
England to the effect that a "Working-man's Lord's-
Day Rest Association" had been formed there, and
that two of England's prime ministers, Beaconsfield
and Gladstone, had given their voice against the
opening of museums, etc., on Sunday. The same

policy is enforced by some, at least, of the English in their dependencies. One of the first acts of the Marquis of Ripon, who was made Viceroy of India in 1880, was, according to the *Christian Weekly*, to issue an order forbidding official work of any kind on Sunday.

In France the question is also agitated. The Senate having occasion to consider some proposed changes in the Sunday laws, an eminent senator, M. Barthélemy Saint Hilaire, according to the French journal, *Le Christianism au 19e Siécle*, of June 11, 1880, opened the eyes of his hearers by a clear argument showing that the seventh day, and not the first day, is the Sabbath of the Bible.

In Switzerland and Germany, also, this question is before the people. In the latter country, according to the New York *Independent*, a meeting was held a few years ago, numbering some 5,000 persons, to encourage a more strict observance of Sunday. Many of these were socialists.

Austria also shares in the general movement. A New York paper in January, 1883, published the following item :—

"A telegram from Vienna, Austria, says : 'A meeting of 3,000 workmen was held to-day, at which a resolution was passed protesting against Sunday work. A resolution was also passed in favor of legal prohibition of newspaper and other work on that day.'"

To come back again to our own country, we have the following singular circumstance to record : The *Illustrated Christian Weekly* of March 3, 1883, spoke of the novel spectacle of a strike for religious purposes, as follows :—

"A hundred men employed by the Chesapeake and Ohio Railway have struck, not for higher wages, but for their Sunday."

There is a local Sabbath (Sunday) Committee in many of the great cities, and an International Sabbath Association to secure the co-operation of other nations. This Association has its offices in Philadelphia, Pa.

The Churches can carry their point whenever they can become sufficiently aroused to take general and concerted action in the matter. David Swing, at a ministers' meeting in Chicago in 1879, held for the purpose of deliberating in regard to a better observance of Sunday, according to a report in the *Inter Ocean*, said :—

"Group together these Churches, — Presbyterian, Methodist, Baptist, Congregational, Episcopal, and Catholic,—and they make up a powerful group of generals and soldiers. They can throw great armies into the field. Whoever should hope to lift up suffering humanity without asking the aid of all these heroes of old battle-fields, would simply show how feeble he is in the search of great means to a great end."

Thus Protestants propose to act in concert with Catholics in this matter, and profess no lack of assurance in regard to accomplishing what they undertake. And so impatient are some to reach the desired result, that they are even considering whether they cannot regard the Constitution already Christian, and proceed to act accordingly, without waiting for the religious amendment. Thus, Bishop A. Cleveland Coxe, D. D., writing on "National Christianity," in the N. Y. *Independent* of July 8, 1880, expresses respect for the "integrity, piety, efforts, and objects of the National Reform Association," but thinks it would be conceding too much to the infidel element to acknowledge that the Constitution is not Christian as it now stands. He thinks the better way would be to consider that it is already Christian, and then unitedly move against all opposing influences. And he suggests that by the time the centennial anniversary of the adoption of the Constitution shall be reached, Sept. 17, 1887, a league shall have been formed, embracing all Christians in an organization which politicians shall respect and evil-doers fear, and then such a celebration of the adoption of " Our Christian Constitution" shall be held as will cause the material splendor of 1876 to pale before its moral grandeur, and make "AMERICAN CHRISTIANITY as evident to the world as our other characteristics are already."

Something important may grow out of this suggestion. It will at any rate be safe to say that we shall see what we shall see.

This notice of current movements would hardly be complete without a glance at the seductive apparent change of issue which is now coming to be quite prominently brought to the front ; and that is, that the Sunday is not to be enforced as a *religious* institution, but only as a *civil* institution ; that to enforce the keeping of the day as an act of religion, would be to violate the spirit of the Constitution and strike a blow at religious liberty, but that the State has a right to enforce it as a " sanitary measure," a "police regulation," a merely "civil enactment," and with this seventh-day keepers must comply, or move elsewhere.

The *International Sabbath Association Recorder*, published at 19 So. Twelfth St., Philadelphia, Pa., has for one of its mottoes these words of Adam Smith :—

"The Sabbath as a *political* institution is of inestimable value, independently of its claim to divine authority."

Richard W. Thompson, when Secretary of the Navy, in 1880, at a meeting of the New York Sabbath Committee, as reported in the N. Y. *Herald* of March 8, 1880, said :—

"I take it there is no principle better fixed in the American mind than the determination to insist upon the conformity by foreigners to our Sunday legislation. We are a Sabbath-keeping people. [Applause.] Men say that we have no power to interfere with the natural right of individuals ; that a man may spend Sunday as he pleases. But society has a right to make laws for its own protection. They are not religious laws. The men engaged in this grand work of securing the enforcement of the Sabbath laws, do not want to force you into any church ; for these gentlemen represent all denominations. They want to make you observe the Sabbath-day as a day of rest merely,—*peaceably if they can, forcibly if they must,*—only so far as it is necessary to protect society. Destroy the Sabbath, and you go out of light into darkness. A government without the Sabbath as a civil institution, could not stand long enough to fall. [Applause.]"

And yet with all these professions they find it impossible to conceal the fact that it is, after all, a *religious* observance which they wish to secure. Thus Mr. Thompson continues :—

"Why are we so specially interested in Sabbath laws ?—Because there is no other government that depends so much on the *morality* of its citizens as ours. Here, where we have a republic with its existence depending on the mass of the people, it is necessary to have a general *observance of the Sabbath.*"

The italics in the foregoing quotation are ours ; and we thus emphasize these words because we must insist that the devoting of a day to cessation from labor in obedience to a law of the State is in no sense the "observance of the Sabbath," even though the right day were selected for that purpose. For the very idea of the Sabbath is a religious idea. It is derived from the word of God. There is no Sabbath in any Scriptural sense, except the day that God made such by resting upon it. And when the day is observed as a religious act, on the authority of God's word and as his word directs, the Sabbath is observed, but not otherwise. Neither is compliance with a State law to stop work on a certain day, in any just sense the practice of "morality," unless the State is the source of that grace, and civil laws are moral laws. Yet Mr. T.'s language betrays the fact that it is the "morality," and the "observance of the Sabbath," that it is intended to enforce.

The people of Louisville, Ky., in the call for a mass-meeting, Feb. 10, 1879, "for the purpose of securing a better observance of our weekly rest-day," endeavored to draw this distinction sharp, as follows :—

"With regard to the Sabbath as a religious institution, we propose to do nothing whatever in this meeting. We withdraw from the discussion every religious question. Your attention will be called exclusively to the Sabbath as a civil institution, a day of rest from labor and public amusements, set apart for that purpose by the immemorial usage of the American people and the laws of the land."

Mr. Joseph Cook, in a Boston lecture in May, 1879, claimed the same distinction. He said :—

"Sabbath laws are justified in a republic by the right of self-preservation. . . . An important distinction exists between Sunday observance as a religious ordinance and as a civil institution. American courts, while enforcing the Sunday laws, disclaim interference with religion," etc.

Such a presentation of the subject will captivate many minds, and lead thousands to act from a standpoint of secular policy as they would not dare to act from that of religious toleration.

Even the N. Y. *Independent*, after its scathing exposure of the inconsistency of the Religious Amendment Movement, as given on p. 205, is, in its issue of Jan. 4, 1883, carried away with this kind of logic.

15

The case calling out its remarks was this: Certain Jews in New York City made application for an injunction restraining the police from arresting them for pursuing their ordinary business on the first day of the week, on the ground that they were observers of the seventh day. The injunction was temporarily granted by Judge Arnoux, but was soon after dissolved, on the plea that the business of the applicants would not come under the head of "works of mercy or necessity." The New York penal code makes only this provision for observers of the seventh day :—

"It is a sufficient defense to a prosecution for servile labor on the first day of the week, that the defendant uniformly keeps another day of the week as holy time, and does not labor on that day ; and that the labor complained of was done in such a manner as not to interrupt or disturb other persons in observing the first day of the week as holy time."

It is now argued that this is no ground for exemption from arrest for Sunday labor ; for such labor is a violation of the letter of the law, and the law does not presume that a man has a defense till he makes one. Therefore, although a man is well known to be a conscientious observer of the seventh day, he may be arrested whenever found working on the first day, and put to all the annoyance and trouble of making a defense. And such a course of action is defended as right.

To the question, Would not this be a hardship to the Jews and Seventh-day Baptists? the *Independent* makes answer that this is incidental to their living in a community which makes Sunday the day of rest, and cannot be avoided without destroying the day of rest altogether.

Again it says that if the Sunday law—

" Is not equally well fitted to the Jews, as it is not, who form but a mere fragment of the people, this is an inconvenience to them which they must bear, and which the law cannot remove without imposing a much greater inconvenience upon a far larger number of persons."

Now comes the distinction on the strength of which these sentiments are uttered. Again we quote :—

"If it [the Sunday law] enforced any kind of religious observance upon them, this would be unjust ; but there is no injustice in requiring them to observe Sunday as a day of rest in a community in which, for good and sufficient general reasons, the day is so observed. If they do not like it, we see no remedy for them except in a withdrawal from such a community."

Notwithstanding such declarations, the general reader will, we think, be able to look beneath this woolly exterior, and discern the true nature of the Sunday-law movement, and why it has seen fit to array itself in sheep's clothing. It will, without doubt, be conceded by all that the present clamor for Sunday legislation is owing entirely to the fact that the great majority of religionists regard the day as a divine institution, and its observance as a religious duty. But some do not so regard it, because they understand that God has set apart another day for the Sabbath, and does not require the observance of this one ; and when such are compelled to observe the first day, in what position are they at once placed ?—They are made to keep the day because others regard it as a divine institution, while they do not so regard it, and to pay homage to a religious custom which they know to be false. They are deprived of one-sixth of the time which God has given them for labor, and are thus robbed of one-sixth of their means of support, if they live by the labor of their hands, as most of them do, because a stronger religion demands it, and the

State confirms that demand. Is there not here religious discrimination? Are not the consciences of one class oppressed in the interest of another class? Is not this an interference on the part of the State with the spiritual freedom of its subjects? Is not this religious intolerance and persecution for conscience' sake? Such, in reality, it is, however much people may try to disguise it by other names.

In a later issue, dated March 1, 1883, in reply to the question from a correspondent, "Will you please tell me how this has nothing to do with religion?" the *Independent* says :—

"We can only repeat that it is a great disadvantage to be in the minority. People there may be right; but they must suffer and submit."

Every one, from the days of the apostles down, who has suffered from religious oppression, could testify in regard to the disadvantage of being in the minority. But is this government, which professes to guarantee to the weakest and humblest citizen his just rights, now to take the position that such rights cannot be secured unless he is with the majority?

Again the *Independent* says :—

"All the State wants is that the citizen shall have one day in seven for rest, not for religion."

But can any one tell why the large majority cannot "rest" just as well on the first day, even if the small minority who keep the seventh day go about their legitimate and honorable occupation? If it is "rest" merely that is wanted, does my work hinder my neighbor from resting? But no! if you are seen at work, you shall be arrested. Therefore, it is not simply the privilege of rest for those who desire it, but a compulsory rest, whether you wish it or not, because others desire that you shall rest as well as themselves. Again we quote :—

"If they insist on so working as to interfere with the rest-day of the majority, they must either move, or be moved away. We are sorry, but there is no help for it."

We know of no observers of the seventh day who have the least intention of interfering, or desire to interfere, with others in their observance of the first day. They ask for no right to do anything of this kind. They would religiously refrain from disturbing either the private rest or the public devotion of any on that day. But we apprehend that the very fact that they do not keep the day, nor acknowledge its claims, will be construed to amount to a sufficient "interference" and "disturbance" to call for repressive measures. Let them "move or be moved."

The opposition to the religious amendment manifested in many parts of the country, especially by the liberal or infidel element, is thought by many to be an insuperable barrier in the way of its success. But if we mistake not, this is the very stimulus which will excite its friends to such exertions that it will ultimately be secured ; for the opposition assumes such an aggressive attitude that no neutral ground is left ; an irrepressible conflict is precipitated ; it must be victory or defeat of the most decisive kind with either party ; the government must become nominally wholly Christian or in reality wholly secular.

Thus the National Reform Association set forth the object they have in view by the second article of their Constitution, which reads as follows :—.

"The object of this Society shall be to maintain existing Christian features in the American government, and to secure such an

amendment to **the** Constitution **of the** United States **as will indicate** that this **is a** Christian nation, and place all the Christian
laws, institutions, and usages of our government on an undeniable
legal basis in **the fundamental** law of the land."

On the other hand, in opposition to this National
Reform Movement, Liberalism sets forth its sweeping
antagonistic demands in the following platform :—

"1. **We demand that churches and other** ecclesiastical property
shall no longer **be** exempt from just taxation.

"2. We **demand that the** employment of chaplains **in Congress,**
in State **Legislatures, in the navy and** militia, **and in prisons,**
asylums, and all **other institutions supported by public money,**
shall be discontinued.

"3. We demand that **all public** appropriations for educational
and charitable **institutions of a sectarian** character shall cease.

"4. We demand that all religious services now sustained by the
government shall be abolished ; and especially that the use of the
Bible in the public schools, whether ostensibly as a text-book or
avowedly as a book of religious worship, shall be prohibited.

"5. We demand that the appointment, by the President of the
United States or by the Governors of the various States, of all religious festivals and fasts, shall wholly cease.

"6. We demand that the judicial oath, in the courts and in all
other departments of the government, **shall** be abolished, and that
simple affirmation **under the pains and** penalties of **perjury** shall
be established in **its stead.**

"7. We demand that all laws directly or indirectly enforcing
the observance of Sunday as the Sabbath shall be repealed.

"8. We demand that all laws looking to the enforcement of
'Christian' morality shall be abrogated, and that all laws shall be
conformed to the requirements of natural morality, equal rights,
and impartial liberty.

"9. We demand that not only in the Constitutions of the United
States and of the several States, but also in the practical administration of the same, no privilege or advantage shall be conceded
to **Christianity** or any other special **religion ;** that our entire political system **shall be founded and administered on** a purely secular
basis ; and **that whatever** changes shall prove necessary to this
end, shall **be consistently,** unflinchingly, **and** promptly made."

The *Inter Ocean* of Nov. 16, 1880, reported the proceedings of a convention held in Chicago the day previous, for the promotion of the "secularization" of the State. "By that," said the report, "they signify the exclusion of the Bible and all religious training from the public schools, and the taxation of church property. A permanent organization was effected."

Thus while frequent conventions are held by the National Reform party, counter conventions are held by the Liberalists; and the forces are marshaling on either side.

The Tulare (Cal.) *Times* of Oct. 20, 1882, said:—

"The Associate Reformed Presbyterian Covenanter organ proclaims 'an irrepressible conflict between the religious and secular theories of government.' The sectarian press reiterates the sentiment, and such politicians as John Sherman, Governor Foster, Jeremiah Black, Judge Sawyer, Senator Harvey, Judge Brooks of North Carolina, Judge Saffold of Alabama, Judge Phelps of Connecticut, Judge Cole of Iowa, Governor Turnes of Nebraska, Judge Rockwell of Massachusetts, and Judge Morrison of California echo the demand for a religious amendment to the Constitution of the United States. General Grant warned the country years ago, that there was impending such a struggle between the 'God in the Constitution party' on the one side, and the friends of the present guarantees for religious freedom on the other side, as would shake the very foundations of our government. And yet such men as ex-Governor Woods have the effrontery to deny that there is any danger of a religious contest. These fomenters of religious tyranny are endeavoring to lull the people and put them to sleep, that their designs may be the more easily accomplished."

The Chicago *Express* of Feb. 16, 1884, contains an article written by Bishop Foster, of the Methodist Church. While traveling in Europe, he takes occasion to speak of those forms of worship there which are supported by law, and the acts that led to such a state of things. He says:—

"That there is but little real, vital, personal, religion in these lands, is among the most patent facts. . . . I know of nothing more sad than the religious condition of Europe, and *the saddest part of it is that it is chargeable to the Church itself, and therefore the more hopeless. If something is not speedily done, the so-called Christian Church will drive Christianity from these ancient lands, if not from the whole world.*"

In speaking of the primary causes which led to this spiritual condition, he says :—

"Did Constantine make the Roman mind Christian by abolishing paganism, and proclaiming the religion of the cross in its stead, and, creating the constituted Roman nation into a Church, make the nation a Christian Church ? or did he not rather paganize Christianity ? "

Speaking still further of the present state of things, he says :—

"By a false theory, the Church has been taken from the people, and *converted into a priestly and political machine, and has ceased to be a Church of Christ,* as much as the papal machine at Rome. . . . This condition of things is the sad inheritance of the union of Church and State."

The editor of the *Express*, in calling attention to these statements of the Bishop, says :—

"The Church in America has also very largely become a political machine, and has been used as a means of raising a campaign fund to retain and maintain the party in power, and return men to office who have betrayed the people, and sold them to the giant corporations of the land. . . . How long, we would ask of Bishop Foster, does he imagine it will be before the Church in America, like the Church in Europe, will be forced to seek an alliance with the State in order to sustain itself, because of the indifference of the people, who perceive its iniquitous practices, and scoff at its pretended Christianity ? Already a union of the two is a thing openly spoken of as desirable.

" We have before us at this moment a religious journal, the *Sabbath Sentinel*, which in its leading editorial warns the Church against the tendency. The rich men within the Church, who have taken shelter there against public condemnation of their crimes of extortion, are ready at any time for the union—more than ready. They would do with their taxes to the Church as they have done with their taxes to the State,—frame the laws in such a way that the poor shall be forced to pay for them. Every one of the causes which produced the union of Church and State in Europe, exists either in full bloom or in embryo in this country; and here, as there, 'if something is not speedily done, the so-called Christian Church will drive Christianity from the land.'

"Again we say, with the Bishop, 'Let the Church of God come out from the world; let it be made of followers and disciples of Christ; let it represent righteousness and truth; let it cut loose from false and entangling alliances; let its priests be clothed with salvation, and its citizens be a holy communion; let it demonstrate its divine lineage,—let this be the watch-cry of Zion, and then it will be a power in the earth, and will silence the taunt of its enemies.'"

In the Richland *Star* of Dec. 4, 1879, published in Bellville, Ohio, an infidel wrote against the National Reform party, which had then recently held a convention in Mansfield, Ohio, concluding his remarks as follows:—

"The lash and the sword have always proved poor ambassadors of Christ. If we live up to our Constitution as it now is, we shall be good citizens, and have all the room we care to occupy as Christians."

To this writer a Mr. W. W. Anderson replied in the next issue of the same paper, in defense of the Association, giving expression, in his remarks, to this sentiment:—

"Either we are a Christian nation, or we are not. Either our Sabbath laws, so essential to good order and the welfare of all classes, are to be maintained, or they are to be abrogated. In the latter case, we shall wade through blood, as Paris did when under infidel rule."

These passages show that the contestants are fully

aware of the nature and magnitude of the struggle upon which the Christian world is now entering.

A minister in Kansas, an agent of the National Reform Association, uses the term, "A Second Irrepressible Conflict," to describe the antagonism now arising between theology and secularism, as embodied in the present movement for a religious amendment of the Constitution of the United States. The opposition to this he likens to the great Rebellion, and asks if we are to have another such rebellion. A few words from his pen will set forth his views in this respect, and indicate the length to which he would be willing to go in its suppression. He says:—

"The great Rebellion, which was put down at such frightful cost, was a rebellion which aimed to *strike down liberty* from its place in the American government. The rising rebellion we have yet to deal with, aims to *strike down Christianity* from the place it has held in our government from its origin to the present hour."

This, he thinks, can be met only by the amendment movement of the National Reform party. And he leaves it to be inferred, as did also the speakers at the National Reform Convention in Cleveland, in December, 1883, that if the success of this movement cost even as great a sacrifice as the suppression of our late political Rebellion cost, the sacrifice should be made rather than that the religious amendment movement should fail. For he says:—

"The success of the present endeavor to conform our government in every respect to its acknowledged secular Constitution, would be followed by consequences *more revolutionary* and *more frightful* [italics his] than would have followed the success of the endeavor of the pro-slavery party of the North and of the South, to conform our government in every respect to our then pro-slavery Constitution."

If this is so, the rising rebellion, before which he

stands appalled, should be put down even at a greater sacrifice than the former.

But it might be well to inquire what has given Liberalism its recent impulse toward the secularization of the State. Is it not the National Reform movement itself? We heard nothing about the "demands" of Liberalism, nor their specially aggressive work, till the amendmentists began to seek the aid of the civil power in behalf of religious customs and dogmas. This naturally threw the Liberalists into an active defensive movement under the menace of the loss of their civil rights. Thus the amendmentists find that they have conjured up a demon which they would now fain exorcise. Neither party can recede from the positions it has taken. The crisis must now come ; and the amendmentists see no way to meet it on their part, but to carry through to the desperate end, the movement by which it has been precipitated.

A very marked and rapid change is taking place in public opinion relative to the proposed religious amendment of the Constitution. Some who were at first openly hostile to the movement, we learn are now giving their influence for its advancement, and clamoring loudly for a Sunday law. And some who at first regarded it with indifference, are now becoming its warm partisans. As a sample of this change of feeling, the following paragraph from the *Christian Press* of January, 1872, may be presented. The *Christian Press* is the organ of the Western Book and Tract Society, Cincinnati, Ohio, and its editor, speaking of the National Association above referred to, says :—

"When this Association was formed, while we were prepared to bid it God speed, we did not then feel that there was any pressing need for the object sought; and as our mission was specially directed to the Christianizing, enlightening, and elevating of the masses of the people, we have said little in our columns on the subject, being assured that if the people are right, it is easy to set the government right. The late combined efforts, however, of various classes of our citizens to exclude the Bible from our schools, repeal our Sabbath laws, and divorce our government entirely from religion, and thus make it an atheistic government,— for every government must be for God or against him, and must be administered in the interests of religion and good morals, or in the interests of irreligion and immorality,—have changed our mind, and we are now prepared to urge the necessity for an explicit acknowledgment in the national Constitution of the authority of God, and the supremacy of his law as revealed in the Scriptures of the Old and New Testaments."

The course of the *Examiner and Chronicle*, the leading Baptist journal of our country, is another case in point. When the movement for the religious amendment of the Constitution was inaugurated, this paper, alluding thereto, said :—

"We have wondered at the magical effects ascribed to the sacraments according to high-church theology. But turning a nation of atheists to Christians by a few strokes of the pen, by a vote in Congress, and ratifying votes in three-fourths of the State Legislatures, is equally miraculous and incomprehensible. This agitation for a national religion, officially professed, has for its logical outcome, persecution—that, and nothing more or less. It is a movement backward to the era of Constantine; as far below the spirituality of the New Testament as it is below the freedom of republican America."

But in 1879 the same paper, in an article on "The Day of Rest," changed its tone in reference to national action on this question, as follows :—

"By these and other considerations, therefore, we are justified in holding that the spirit of the fourth commandment, with all its divine sanctions and sacred privileges, applies in full force to the Christian day of rest. To preserve it from profanation, to maintain its inestimable privileges, to secure to all the sanitary, moral, family, and civic benefits of which M. Proudhon wrote, as well as the undisturbed enjoyment of religious service on that day, is a duty which Christians owe at once to their country and their God. And in this work *governments should aid*, within their sphere, in the interest of public morals, and the general well-being of society."

Again, the *Universalist* of Oct. 6, 1877, published in Boston, Mass., contained a report of the Massachusetts Convention of Universalists, held in Worcester, Mass., Sept. 25, 1877. In that Convention a resolution "heartily sympathizing with the aims of the National Reform Association in seeking a legal recognition of God and his government," was introduced. The committee to whom it was referred recommended its adoption. In the discussion which followed, Mr. H. Kimball said, "We may initiate a religious war, of all wars the most bitter." Dr. Flanders said, "There is danger in the resolution." Rev. Mr. Chambré said, "It is a reactionary movement, hostile to the religious liberty whereof Universalists have been the special champions." Rev. G. W. Haskell said that "the Association which seeks the change in the Constitution only keeps its Calvinism in abeyance. That will come in due time if it gets encouragement."

After all these plain utterances, a motion for indefinite postponement was lost. A motion to strike it out was lost. The motion to adopt was then carried by a vote of 61 to 47.

This strange action on the part of the Universalists may be attributed largely to the course of the Liberal League in calling for the abolition of all recognition of God and religion in State instruments and operations, and making the government wholly secular; for this is arousing the fears of all classes of professed Christians, and inciting them to repel what they consider the danger. Nothing can tend more strongly to precipitate the conflict on the Amendment question.

The tendency of religious opinion is still further shown in the position taken by the *Christian Instructor* in the year 1884. Judge Black of Pennsylvania, having argued before the House Judiciary Committee at Washington, Jan. 30, 1883, against the bill "To Suppress Polygamy in the Territories, the *Instructor* said :—

"When distinguished jurists are taking such positions relating to questions of Christian morals, is it not time, is it not imperative, that the Christian people of this nation should demand the religious amendment of the Constitution ? Many say, as they have been saying, 'It is best to let well enough alone.' It is becoming manifest, however, that well enough cannot be left alone. The silence of the Constitution is being interpreted and used against the Christian institutions of the nation. The Constitution must cease to be silent, and, by the amendment, must unmistakably declare that this is a Christian nation, and that its morality is the morality of the revealed will of God. Only thus is it possible to have our Christian institutions and usages permanently preserved."

The following resolutions may also be taken as sample expressions of the sentiment that prevails to a large extent among church members of different denominations, in reference to the proposed religious amendment of the Constitution of the United States.

The St. Joseph District Conference of the M. E. Church, Marysville, Mo., passed a resolution Oct. 4, 1882, of which the following is the substance :—

"*Resolved,* That we do most heartily commend and indorse the object of the National Reform Association, and we pledge to them our prayers for success in securing their commendable and much needed amendment to our National Constitution."

The General Conference of the M. E. Church, at

Philadelphia, May 27, 1884, unanimously passed the following :—

> "*Resolved*, That we will use our efforts to secure such a change in the Constitution of our country as shall recognize the being of God, our dependence upon him for prosperity, and also his word as the foundation of civil law."

The Iowa State Western Baptist Association, at Shenandoah, Oct. 5, 1882, unanimously embodied the same sentiment in the following resolution :—

> "*Resolved*, That we earnestly approve of that part of the plan adopted by the National Association which aims at the enactment of such laws as will lead to the better observance of the Sabbath, and the use of the Bible in our public schools."

The Kansas Annual Conference of the Protestant Methodist Church, at Whitewater Center, Sept. 16, 1882, also unanimously passed the following :—

> "*Resolved*, That, as a Christian nation, it is the sense of this Conference that we should demand ingrafted in the United States Constitution an amendment acknowledging our faith in, and dependence upon, Almighty God."

Almost as fast as the matter is brought to the attention of the Churches and Conferences, similar sentiments are called out. The danger is that many will be drawn into the movement without perceiving its true import, and the evils to which it will lead ; that they will favor an amendment of the Constitution, thinking it will be made better, not understanding that the final result will be to transform it from the grand ægis of our liberties into an instrument of unrighteousness and oppression.

Yet notwithstanding all these indications of the sentiment fast growing up in the religious circles of this country to establish religion by law, some are still skeptical in regard to the possibility of any such

revolution; and when we express the opinion that
the majority of the professors of religion, and others,
are to combine so far as to enact a general law for the
observance of the so-called "Christian" or "American" Sabbath, we are met with expressions of the utmost incredulity in regard to such a movement. A
law of that kind, they say, can never be carried, as it
would interfere with too many kinds of business, and
there are too many liberals and irreligious persons to
oppose it. And yet when pressed right down to an
expression of their own views in the matter, these
very persons will take the position that there ought
to be such a law. Now do they not see that all that
is necessary is to have such persons take their position and act, and the requisite majority is secured;
for they but represent a feeling that generally prevails.

An illustration in point comes from a correspondent, who writes:—

"In conversation with a number of persons a few days ago, I
stated our views in regard to the Sunday movement, whereupon
all ridiculed the idea of such a thing in a country of liberty, making mention of railroads, amusements, etc. But scarcely five minutes had elapsed when all said that they thought such a law ought
to be passed, and signified their willingness to vote for it!"

Many have been waiting with no little interest to
hear Catholics speak on this question, querying what
position they would assume. An incident which occurred in the summer of 1880, plainly foreshadowed
their policy in this matter. At the time referred to,
S. V. Ryan, the Catholic Bishop of Buffalo, N. Y., issued a circular denouncing the profanation of the first
day of the week, and declaring that none would be
recognized as Catholics who would not strictly ob-

serve the Lord's day. He urged his plea solely on the authority of the Church, claiming, truly, that the day was wholly an institution of the Church. Notwithstanding this, the *Christian World* hastened to welcome this new ally in the Sunday cause. Publishing the remarkable document, which appeals to the "Blessed Mother" as witness to its truth, the *World* urges the consideration and preservation of the circular, and says :—

"It would certainly furnish great ground of gratitude to every truly pious heart, if we might count upon the Roman Catholic ministers of religion as faithful allies in the struggle."

In reference to the Catholic claim that the Sunday institution rests wholly upon the authority of the Church, the *World* says :—

"The historical statement with regard to the position of the Roman Catholic Church on the question of the Lord's day is, unfortunately, far from correct. . . . And yet we prefer to waive an inquiry into the truth or falsity of Bishop Ryan's claims, and to congratulate our Roman Catholic citizens and ourselves on the position which some, at least, of the prelates of this Church in this country are disposed to assume."

Is it not marvelous that a religious journal, professing to be a defender of the truth, should take such a position as this? Here is an assertion put forth by the great Roman Catholic hierarchy that Sunday is an institution of their Church,—and Protestants are challenged to meet it,—an assertion which, if true, nullifies every claim of the first-day Sabbath to divine support, takes out from under it every prop which a true Protestant would depend upon to sustain it, and makes it simply a human institution, not binding in any degree upon the consciences of men. In the face of such an assertion the first question to be settled is, whether this claim is true or not.   But this Protestant writer proposes to waive all inquiry into the matter, virtually saying, We care not whether the claim is true or false, nor what the origin of the institution is, nor upon what authority it rests, if only we can have your assistance in trying to carry our point, and enforce it upon the people.   Can any one suppose that the fear of God and the love of the truth for the truth's sake, constitute the motive for such a course of action ?

In this connection a reference to the change of attitude on the part of Protestantism toward Catholicism, will not be considered wholly a digression from the main argument ; for this movement has a significant bearing on the question before us.   The "image," as elsewhere emphasized in this work, is to be made *to* the beast, Romanism.   This would indicate cordial friendliness toward, and a certain degree of deference to, Catholicism, on the part of the image-making power, which we have shown to be Protestantism. And this friendliness of feeling on the part of Protestants, is even now prominently manifested in some quarters.   The time was, and has been all along until within a few years, when Protestants were Protestants indeed, protesting against the errors and abuses of the Roman Catholic Church.   But there seems to be now a widespread inclination to stretch their hands across the chasm which has divided them, and welcome the Catholic Church to union and fellowship, not because the Catholics have reformed in any of the objectionable features of their system, but because Protestants are seemingly becoming very indifferent to them.   How else can we account for a remarkable scene which took place in Westminster Abbey, Oct. 19, 1884, when in that professedly Protestant sanctuary, a procession of five hundred Catholics were admitted to kneel at the shrine of Edward the Confessor, and pray—for what? For the success and good of Protestantism?—No ; but for the conversion of England to the Roman Catholic faith! This is not mere toleration ; it is surrender.

Certain Protestants in this country seem inclined to include all in one Church, calling themselves "the Protestant branch of the great Catholic Church." But do Catholics propose to make any concessions, and meet Protestants half way in these fraternal gestures?—Not at all. Protestants may go the whole way in the disgraceful surrender of principles which have cost the struggles of three hundred years ; and then perhaps the Catholic Church will receive them back into her bosom as erring, repentant children. But the Catholic Church is the same to-day in its intolerant and blood-thirsty instincts that it always has been. It makes its boast that it never changes. Once let it gain supreme control in this country, and how soon would every Protestant place of worship in the land be sealed up as silent as the tomb, and every Bible be banished, not from the schools alone, but from the homes and hands of the people, and rigid conformity to the Catholic ritual alone be enforced by flood and flame, dagger and dungeon. To flatter ourselves that the bloody scenes of the Dark Ages were owing to the spirit of the age, and not the spirit of the Church, and could not now be repeated under Romish rule, is to be not only willfully but criminally blind. And to see Protestants shutting their eyes to these facts, and virtually accepting the preposterous pretensions of Catholicism, is astonishing indeed.

These movements on the part of Protestants toward

fraternity with Catholics, become very significant in view of the agitation of the Sunday question, which is becoming so prominent in the land. The Sunday rest-day, being a Papal institution, will naturally claim the support of the Catholics. And in this thing, Protestants who are seeking a Sunday law will gladly welcome them as allies ; and who then can for a moment doubt the ability of these two Churches, the Protestant and Catholic, to carry any measures upon which they might unite ?

According to the Dakota *State Record*, the Bishop of the Episcopal Church of Ohio speaks of "the Protestant portion of the Catholic Church of Rome." He proposes a union between all Protestant sects and the Romish Church on marriage and divorce and the Sabbath (Sunday). He calls these (Protestant sects and the Romish Church) "every portion of the *Christian* Church," and thinks that "it is within reasonable expectation " that this "Christian Church throughout the world will speak the same language on all these moral issues," and that "legislation will not fail to follow the lead of such a public opinion."

Yes, if Protestantism is only a "portion of the Catholic Church of Rome," why should it maintain the position of a schismatic, and keep up the division ? Why not go back at once to the mother Church ? But if that Catholic Church which is represented in the Scriptures as a harlot woman, drunken with the blood of the saints,—a Church which has harried a hundred millions of innocent victims to their graves, which has invented and inflicted upon the humble followers of Christ horrible barbarities, more in number and more fiendish in character than those of all heathendom combined, from the earliest ages,—if such a Church is *Christian*, God pity Christianity! but rather God pity the man whose moral sensibilities have become so benumbed and paralyzed that he can assume such an attitude toward this tragical burlesque of Christianity!

That such words can be spoken by Protestants, and such propositions be urged by them, is one of the most alarming indications of the tendency of the times.

With the anti-Sunday movements of the present day, considering their associations, and the manner and object in and for which they are carried forward, we have no sympathy. They aim at utter no-Sabbathism, freedom from all moral restraint, and all the evils of unbridled intemperance,—ends which we abhor with all the strength of a moral nature quickened by the most intense religious convictions. And while the indignation of the better portion of the community will be aroused at the want of religious principle and the immorality attending the popular anti-Sunday movements, a little lack of discrimination, by no means uncommon, will, on account of our opposition to the Sunday institution, though we oppose it on entirely different ground, easily associate us with the classes above mentioned, and subject us to the same odium.

We therefore here take occasion to put on record a few words defining more fully our position. We wish it to be understood that we are in the most complete accord and the fullest sympathy with all reforms which tend to restrain immorality and conduce to the well-being of society. We bid all temperance reformers Godspeed in their noble efforts. We wish all success to the great work of rescuing men from the evils of intemperance. We wish all crippling, blighting, and paralyzing influences to fall upon the vile traffic in intoxicating liquors, above and below, east, west, north, and south, always and everywhere. We would restrain it, not only on Sunday, but on every day of the week.

So, too, we are in favor of a divorce reform, prison reforms, all sanitary reforms, labor reform as against the encroachments of monopolies, reforms to restrain cruelty to children and to animals, and to prevent the circulation of vile, blasphemous, or obscene matter through the mails. We wish the latter reform might be extended also to the publication and circulation, in any manner, of the dime novel curse and abomination. Let the law which is designed to be a safeguard to society, take hold of all these things, we care not how rigidly.

But with these things, our friends are unfortunately connecting another enterprise as a reform, which lacks the true basis of all reforms ; namely, the divine sanction. They labor to secure the enforcement by law of a day as the Sabbath which the Scriptures nowhere declare to be the Sabbath, in opposition to the day which they do explicitly declare to be the Sabbath. Now we believe in Sabbath reform ; but we say, Let us take the day which the Scriptures everywhere set forth as the divinely-appointed day of rest, and secure its observance by moral suasion under the sanctions of the divine law.

Let it be understood further that we take no exception to laws in behalf of those who conscientiously deem it their duty to observe any day as a day of rest, so far as to secure them from any real disturbance on such days.

If people wish to observe Sunday, let them then be protected from anything which would really interfere with such observance. But we say that those who have conscientiously observed another day as the Sabbath, should not be compelled to keep Sunday also (all disturbance of course excepted), because some one else thinks that day is the Sabbath, any more than the Sunday-keeper should be compelled to keep the seventh day, because we believe that day is the Sabbath. An exemption should be made to cover such cases. To refuse this is to strike a blow at religious liberty in this country. Here is the danger; and this is the ground of our protest.

Meanwhile, some see the evils involved in this movement, and raise the note of alarm. The *Christian Union*, January, 1871, said:—

"If the proposed amendment is anything more than a bit of sentimental cant, it is to have a *legal* effect. It is to alter the status of the non-Christian citizen before the law. It is to affect the legal oaths and instruments, the matrimonial contracts, the sumptuary laws, etc., etc., of the country. This would be an outrage on natural right."

The Janesville (Wis.) *Gazette*, at the close of an article on the proposed amendment, speaks thus of the effect of the movement, should it succeed:—

"But, independent of the question as to what extent we are a Christian nation, it may well be doubted whether, if the gentlemen who are agitating this question should succeed, they would not do society a very great injury. Such measures are but the initiatory steps which ultimately lead to *restrictions of religious freedom*, and to commit the government to measures which are as foreign to its powers and purposes as would be its action if it should undertake to determine a disputed question of theology."

The *Weekly Alta Californian* of San Francisco, March 12, 1870, said:—

"The parties who have been recently holding a Convention for the somewhat novel purpose of procuring an amendment to the Constitution of the United States recognizing the Deity, do not fairly state the case when they assert that it is the right of a Christian people to govern themselves in a Christian manner. If we are not governing ourselves in a Christian manner, how shall the doings of our government be designated? The fact is, that the movement is one to bring about in this country that union of Church and State which all other nations are trying to dissolve."

The New York *Independent*, February, 1870, spoke of the movement as having the same chance of success that a union of Church and State would have.

The Champlain *Journal*, speaking of incorporating the religious principle into the Constitution, and its effect upon the Jews, said:—

"However slight, it is the entering wedge of Church and State. If we may cut off ever so few persons from the right of citizenship on account of difference of religious belief, then with equal justice and propriety may a majority at any time dictate the adoption of still further articles of belief, until our Constitution is but the text-book of a sect beneath whose tyrannical sway *all liberty of religious opinion will be crushed.*"

Meanwhile the movement assumes a very harmless and innocent mien. What hurt can it do, it is asked, just to recognize God in the Constitution? Who could object just to the mention of the Supreme Being and of Christ in our great national charter? We have such recognition now, they plead, in most of our State Constitutions, and it does not seem to work any mischief; why not then put it into the national Constitution?

Thus the advocates of the religious amendment are wont to reason, or at least thus they seem pleased to have other people reason, with the hope, very apparently, that they will act from that standpoint, and thus the more readily give support to their movement. This feature comes out very distinctly in the report of one of the secretaries of the National Reform Association, who has lately [1884] been laboring in Lincoln, Nebraska.

The object sought is thus put in a light which seems, at first view, very innocent and unobjectionable. But let us look at it a little more closely, and see if the most virulent kind of sophistry is not involved therein. If the simple insertion of the names of God and Christ somewhere in the Constitution is all that is designed, we inquire how that can be a matter of such importance as to warrant such a movement as is now on foot in its behalf—the organization of an association, the issuing of books and tracts, the publication of a weekly paper, the calling of conventions, the employing of men to devote the whole or a part of their time to its promulgation, and the pouring out of liberal contributions of money in its support. All this shows upon the very face of it that there is something more in view than the mere mention of God in the Constitution.

But further, if God is already recognized in most of the State constitutions, as they acknowledge is the case, why is not that sufficient? Is he not acknowledged by all the States, and thus, so far as constitutional action can go, by all the people of those States? What is to be gained, then, by putting his name into the Constitution of the nation?

This brings us to the real issue. They desire not simply the name of God in the Constitution, but "such an amendment as shall place all the Christian laws, institutions, and usages of the government, on an undeniable legal basis in the fundamental law of the land." They want this because, as the case now stands, if attempt is made through any State laws to enforce religious enactments, appeal can be taken to the higher court, and such efforts can be shown to be unconstitutional. It is just because the recognition of God in the State constitutions is thus liable to be rendered inoperative, because religious enactments under State laws are virtually null and void, that they want to get a sure foot-hold in the national Constitution, the highest source of authority in the land. And then our whole relation to religious matters would very speedily assume a different complexion; for they desire such an arrangement that men can be coerced into compliance with what the majority shall decide to be religious customs. For instance, they declare— and for this we have their own explicit language— that, this amendment once secured, no one who does not strictly observe the first day of the week as the Sabbath, shall hold any public office under this government; and that any corporation which will not thus regard it, shall immediately forfeit its charter!

Now look at the method of reasoning they condescend to adopt in this matter: God is recognized in State constitutions, and no mischief comes of it; therefore no man should be afraid to have him recognized in the national Constitution. But why does no mischief come of his recognition by State constitutions?—Because such recognition not existing in the national Constitution, the recognition by the State cannot be used to enforce religious tests in national affairs. And what do they intend to gain by such a recognition in the national Constitution? *Answer*: To put matters in such a shape that religious tests *can* be enforced. But this would at once reverse the situation, and transform all their reasoning into a falsehood and a snare. If such enforcement as they are laboring for could now be had by the recognition of religious customs by the State constitutions, no one could say that no mischief came of it ; and if these men could do under State constitutions what they desire to do, they would seek for no amendment of the general Constitution. But now they appeal to the harmless nature of State constitutions on points where they are inoperative, to quiet men's fears and lead them to amend the national Constitution in such a manner as will make these State enactments operative, where they are not now, and thus change the whole complexion of their action. In other words, their reasoning is virtually this : Because a tiger caged can do no harm, therefore we need not fear to take such action as will uncage him, and let him loose upon the community, and it is our duty so to do.

Is such reasoning fair and honest ? Is it not rather the wickedest kind of sophistry ? Their only chance of success in such reasoning is that people preoccupied with other things will not stop to consider the movement sufficiently to see its true intent, as was doubtless the case with some prominent citizens of Lincoln, whom the secretary reported himself as interviewing, and who he claimed gave the movement their sanction. Well did the editor of the Nebraska *State Journal* think there was recognition enough in the Constitution already, and Rev. Mr. Gregory question the propriety of advancing moral reforms by legal enactments, and Rev. Mr. Ingram express alarm lest the movement meant a union of Church and State.

Another argument used by the advocates of the amendment against our government as now constituted, must be abhorrent to every unvitiated Amer-

ican patriot.   It is that the doctrine that governments
derive their just powers from the consent of the governed, is a false principle.   At the Cleveland (O.)
Convention of the National Reform Association, held
in December, 1883, one of the speakers attacked the
statement as found in our Declaration of Independence, and which lies at the very foundation of our national polity, that governments "derive their just
powers from the consent of the governed," and with
a bitterness which was truly surprising, denounced it
as "the old Philadelphia lie."   In defense of his position, he rung the changes on such questions as these :
How could a past generation "consent" for the present?   And how many of those now living under this
government have actually "consented" to it?   How
do minors "consent" to it?   And what criminal would
"consent" to the government?

Such sophistry is well answered by Jos. P. Thompson, D. D., LL. D., in a lecture on the "Doctrine of
the Declaration of Independence," in which he says :—

"'Where,' asks Mr. Jefferson, 'shall we find the origin of *just*
powers, if not in the majority of society ? Will it be in the minority ? or in an individual of that minority ?' This is the key to
the statement of the Declaration, that governments 'derive their
just powers from the consent of the governed.' He was not thinking of a poll of equal rights, that each individual as an 'inalienable' voter might 'consent' to be governed thus or so, but of the
community, the political society, in some method of its own, fram-
ing, commissioning, or consenting to, the government under which
it should live ; and in this view of its meaning, this statement of
the Declaration, like those that precede it, is also true, and of deep
and far-reaching significance for governments and for mankind."

He then draws from the history of both England
and France, facts in confirmation of this view, and
adds :—

Signing the Declaration of Independence, 1776.

Correct portraits of the signers may be seen on pages 272, 273.

"The attachment of a people to their government may be variable ; their sentiment **toward** officers and policy may change with men and measures ; **their loyalty may be that of** enthusiastic devotion, of calm acquiescence, or of patient endurance ; but there inheres in every body politic a latent right of revolution ; and, so long as the people do not revive this right, the government *de facto* is presumed to hold its powers with 'the consent of the governed.'"—*The United States as a Nation*, pp. 82–84.

The idea expressed by the Cleveland speaker was that all government being derived from God, its requirements were to be made known by properly constituted agents, and all that the governed had to do was to quietly submit ; their "consent" was not to be taken into the account at all. Had this man been arguing, under some benighted tyranny, for the "divine right of kings," instead of standing amid the manifold blessings and privileges secured by this Republic, and denouncing the principles of its constitution, after more than one hundred years of such uniform and unbounded prosperity, as no other nation of the earth had ever enjoyed, his statements would not have seemed quite so astounding.

It may still be asked, Has not the State the right to make a law that one day in the week shall be kept as a day of rest ? and would it not be the duty of all citizens to obey such a law, when made ? *Answer:* The State has a right to legislate in reference to all the relations that exist between man and man, to protect and secure the just rights of each. It has a right, therefore, to legislate in regard to such crimes against **society** as Mormon polygamy, though practiced under **the** name of religion, against intemperance, and against some forms of worship which pagans under the sanction of their religion, might introduce upon our shores. But in matters purely religious, matters of conscience between man and his Maker, which in no wise encroach upon the rights of others, the State has no right to interfere. It is going beyond its legitimate province when it does so. The Constitution of the United States recognizes this truth, when, in the first amendment; it provides that " Congress shall make no law respecting an establishment of religion, or prohibiting the free exercise thereof."

But in the matter of the Sabbath, God himself has already promulgated a law ; and certainly the State has no right to interfere with that. It is replied that the State does not propose to interfere with that, but only to establish a day of rest as a " *civil* institution" for the good of society. This will do as a film behind which to try to hide ; but it is not sufficient to conceal the true motive. Speakers and writers alike cry out for a better observance of *the Sabbath* as they call the first day of the week. But resting upon any day merely as a requirement of the State, as a "sanitary measure," a "police regulation," is in no sense the keeping of a Sabbath as an act of worship offered to Heaven. Again, they urge it as a measure to secure a better state of *morality*. Here again the *religious* idea, which is the underlying principle in this movement, crops out.

There is one remarkable fact to be noticed in all this agitation ; namely, however much a day of rest may be urged as a "civil institution," a "police regulation," etc., as if it was not a religious matter, the day selected for the rest-day is always *Sunday*. Why is this ? Will any one be willing to confess himself so obtuse as not to know that it is because the majority regard Sunday, in a religious sense, as *the Sabbath ?*

And this at once discriminates against those who observe the seventh day, inasmuch as, being obliged to keep another day also, they are deprived of one-sixth of their time, and, if laboring men, of one-sixth of their means of support, on account solely of the *religious* prejudices of other people. This strikes at the very root of religious liberty.

If any deny this, and insist that the object is to be absolutely impartial and fair, the matter can be tested by the following proposition : Let some day be selected as the State rest-day, which neither party regards as the Sabbath by divine appointment. Take for instance Tuesday. Now we, having kept the seventh day, could keep Tuesday on the same ground that the Sunday-keeper, having observed the first day, could keep Tuesday also. Here would be equality, one class not being discriminated against more than another. But how many Sunday-keepers would agree to this? No; they would say, having kept Sunday, what is the use of our keeping Tuesday? Exactly. And so we say, After having kept the seventh day, what is the use of our keeping the first day?

If any are still disposed to query why we should object to a general Sunday law, we reply further that to such a law, in itself considered, we do not object. People may make as many Sunday laws as' they please for themselves, and of just such kinds as they please. We do not ask the repeal of any now existing Sunday law. We only ask that those who have conscientiously observed the seventh day, in compliance with the law of God, which says that "the seventh day is the Sabbath of the Lord thy God, in it thou shalt not do any work," and with the physiological law of rest, which demands one day of rest in seven,—we ask that such shall be exempted from the requirements of the Sunday law, and be allowed to go quietly and peaceably about their labor in obedience to the same law of God which says, "Six days shalt thou labor."

And we imagine we hear many responding, "Oh, yes! that is fair; that is just; and of course you will be guaranteed that privilege." But this is just what those who are now so loudly clamoring for a Sunday law do not intend to grant; and this is what we want the people to understand. On this point we have tangible evidence.

Most of the States have exemption clauses in their Sunday laws in favor of observers of the seventh day. Pennsylvania has no such exemption; but she has an old, unrepealed Sunday law of 1794 upon her statute books. Taking advantage of this state of things, some evil disposed persons have caused the repeated oppression, by fine and imprisonment, of a certain Seventh-day Baptist* in that State, for quietly working upon the first day of the week after having conscientiously and scripturally observed the seventh day.

---

* The person referred to is D. C. Waldo, of Venango, Pa. Being a member of the Seventh-day Baptist Church, he conscientiously and religiously observes the seventh day of the week as the Sabbath. Having done this, he deems it his duty to go quietly about his legitimate business upon the first day, in obedience to the same high law which says, "Six days shalt thou labor." He owns a planing-mill in an isolated country position, more than two miles from any first-day meeting-house. Yet under the old 1794 law of Pennsylvania he has been twice prosecuted for thus laboring on Sunday. The last time he appealed to the higher court, at a cost to himself in money, besides his time and trouble, of one hundred and fifty dollars. But the decision of the lower court was sustained. And thus this man suffers for his religious opinions, under a government which guarantees to every man the right to worship God according to the dictates of his own conscience. One other person besides Mr. Waldo has also been prosecuted in that place. 17

Seeing the injustice of such proceedings, a few noble souls have labored to secure an act, not repealing the law, but simply exempting observers of the seventh day from its operation. In 1881-82 this lacked only one vote of becoming a law. But in 1882-83 the same bill was defeated by the surprising majority of 130 against 37. Thus Pennsylvania hugs her disgrace. But what had wrought this change between the winter of 1881-82 and that of 1882-83? One important influence at least, we think, may be seen in the following fact :—

While the bill (No. 122) was pending at the last-named session of the Legislature, some zealous Sunday man placed a copy of it in the hands of Hon. Felix R. Brunot, President of the National Reform Association, and Elliott E. Swift, of Pittsburg, Pa. They immediately sent a copy of the bill to the *Commercial Gazette* of that city, with the accompanying note :—

"The following bill, No. 122, has just been handed us with the statement that it has already passed the second reading in the Legislature of Pennsylvania. Its enactment will lead toward the destruction of the Christian Sabbath in this Commonwealth. It is very desirable that the bill should be understood by our people, and that numerous and emphatic protests be adopted and forwarded immediately We therefore request you to publish it."

The animus of this note is not to be mistaken. No effort is made to repeal the Sunday law, but simply (mark it !) to provide exemption for those who conscientiously keep the seventh day ; and this man, who stands at the head of the National Reform Association, utters a vigorous and emphatic protest—the exemption must not be granted ! and he calls upon "our [his] people," to protest likewise. Ring it out through all the land, that a conscientious Christian man in the State of Pennsylvania, who believes that the seventh day is the Sabbath, as the Bible declares, and keeps it as such, wishes the privilege of quietly following his labor on the first day of the week unmolested by the law which those who believe in keeping Sunday, which he does not believe in, have made for themselves; and the man who stands as the representative of that Association which is calling for a national Sunday law, thunders out, to the extent of his ability, a relentless No! the privilege must not be granted; it will work "the destruction of the Christian Sabbath."

Does the thoughtful reader suppose that when such men gain the power, seventh-day keepers anywhere will be exempted?—Not at all.

In reference to the probable future of the religious amendment movement, Eld. W. H. Littlejohn, in the *Sabbath Sentinel* of May, 1884, spoke as follows:—

"The National Reform party is confident of ultimate success. The men who are behind it are not enthusiasts to that extent that they anticipate an easy victory, or one which is to be realized immediately. Composed as the leaders are of men of learning and experience, their practiced eyes, while seeing with distinctness the goal of their ambition, are able to measure the distance between it and themselves with tolerable accuracy. Surveying the field of contest with a coolness and penetration characteristic of experienced politicians, they have cautiously estimated the strength of the positions of their enemies and the measure of their own resources. Having been active participants in what is termed the great moral contest of the recent past, they have studied the elements which rendered them successful; and they feel assured that the struggle in which they are engaged is equally moral in its character, and therefore certain to triumph sooner or later. Perceiving that the success of the great anti-slavery contest was assured the moment it secured for itself the support, generally speaking, of the pulpits of the land, they very naturally infer that, whenever they shall be able to enlist the same pulpits in the interests of a movement which to their minds is as certainly favored of Heaven as was the one in question, the realization of their expectation will not be far removed.

"With them, therefore, the whole matter turns upon the capture of the ministry of the nation. To that end all their efforts are directed at the present time. If they succeed, there is no power that can stand before them. It must be admitted also that the probability that they will ultimately secure the active support and co-operation of the clergy and the Churches, judging from present appearances, is very strong. They are active and untiring in their efforts, while those in the Churches and outside of the Churches who ought to be alive to the dangers of the situation have but little or nothing to say in the direction of sounding the alarm. One by one the representative bodies of the different denominations are roped into the National Reform movement, and induced by resolutions or otherwise to commit themselves and those for whom they speak to an indorsement of it. In a single year ten Methodist Conferences were induced to give hearty approval to the movement, and five thousand copies of the *Christian Statesman*—the organ of the party—were sent to as many clergymen. Besides the papers spoken of and a flood of other publications, with which the country is being inundated, and all bearing upon the same general subject, ministers and lecturers have been traversing the continent from Maine to California, speaking in the interest of the so-called Reform.

"When it is remembered that there is to the average Christian mind a wonderful fascination in the thought of becoming a champion in the conflict for the recognition of the names of God and Christ in the Constitution of the nation; and when it is borne in mind that it is a comparatively easy task for a polished orator to make his uninformed hearers believe that God will hold them responsible for the desecration of a day that from childhood they have been taught to believe was holy time,—it will be perceived that if not opposed with vigor in this work, it will be comparatively easy for a few energetic and determined spirits to arouse in favor of their enterprise an enthusiasm which will sweep everything before it.

"Never did a party have a more thrilling war-cry than in the words, ''The names of God and Christ in the Constitution, the reading of the Bible in the common schools, and the enforcement of the Sunday laws." All three of these projects are of such a nature as to commend themselves to Christians generally, unless they can be shown that these same projects cannot be realized without imperiling the government and doing great injustice to certain classes of our citizens.

"Nor are professed Christians alone in this. Outside the pale of the Churches are multitudes of men and women who, though not professedly Christians, are nevertheless very friendly to what they believe to be Christian institutions, and who are ready at all times to support them by voice and vote, whenever they can do so without making a public profession of religion. These persons, unless thoroughly aroused to the tendency of the proposed legislation, are certain to enlist under the banners of the new party.

"There is also another feature of this subject that is worthy of attention. Aside from Seventh-day Adventists and Seventh-day Baptists, the apathy of those Christians even who are at heart opposed to the purposes of the National Reform party, is so complete that the public are not apprised of their real feelings. On the other hand, infidels and atheists are so out-spoken in their hostility to that party that the casual observer, unaware of the efforts of the two denominations spoken of above, naturally concludes that the contest is wholly between believers and unbelievers. This fact acts very much to the prejudice of those who are standing manfully for the right. Indeed, this is so true that it will be apparent to any intelligent observer that the supporters of the amendment movement are already gaining no inconsiderable advantage by trying to make it appear that the opponents of their work are found almost wholly among the enemies of God. In a short time they will add to the benefits of a fascinating war-cry the advantage that is derived from hopelessly fastening upon an antagonist an opprobrious epithet. While as a matter of fact Seventh-day Adventists and Seventh-day Baptists are what they are because of their strict adherence to the word of God, and while they are noted for their devotion to the cause of temperance, they will nevertheless be classed with the frequenters of beer gardens, and with such men as Abbott and Ingersoll, whose principles they detest.

"Unless men of every denomination shall speedily cross over the line of indifference, and unite in an effort to enlighten the public mind in reference to the true nature of the proposed legislation by the general government in matters of religion, it will be for ever too late. The drift is altogether in the wrong direction. The Churches once practically captured, the end will not be far off. Sabbatarians, though right in regard to the true Sabbath, and deeply in earnest in their endeavors to stem the tide which is sweeping in the direction of uniting Church and State, are too few in numbers to avert that calamity. In the tempest of passion which is soon to be raised over this subject, their voices will be lost unless they receive immediate help from their fellow-Christians, and the battle for religious liberty will be lost. So far as atheists and infidels are concerned, they are incapable of holding the field against the systematic attacks of the thoroughly drilled and perfectly organized armies of the orthodox Churches. The decision of the question will be simply one of time. The hosts of the Reform party will enter the halls of the capitol, and take into their hands the reins of government. History will repeat itself. Intoxicated with success, and ambitious for the complete realization of their long cherished plan of placing all Christian laws and usages of the government upon an "undeniable legal basis," they will commence to enact laws to secure that end. When this is done, resistance to their plans will no longer be tolerated. Interpreting their success as a token of Divine favor, they will never pause in their career until they have added another to the long list of governments in which religious liberty has been sacrificed on the altar of blind fanaticism.

"Reader, would you avert such a misfortune as long as possible? Then strike hands with those who are struggling hard for the same purpose. Have you looked with innocent pride at the grand old ship of State which for a hundred years has been the object of universal admiration, and the hope of the regions where religious intolerance and political oppression have acted like a blight and a mildew on the national life? Then remember that the hands which have held the helm of that noble craft thus far have all been lifted to Heaven in attestation of a solemn vow to preserve and carry out a Constitution which provides that "Congress shall make no law respecting an establishment of religion or prohibiting the free exercise thereof." Do you think it would be unsafe to allow the majestic old ship to pass under the control of those who would turn her prow away from the course she has hitherto pursued, directing her into unexplored seas, filled with dangerous rocks and tossed by fierce tempests? If so, throw your personal influence against a political organization that seeks to do the very thing which you so much dread."

For a union of Church and State, in the strict mediæval form and sense, we do not look. In place of this, we apprehend that what is called "the image," a creation as strange as it is unique, comes in, not as a State Church, supported by the government, and the Church in turn controlling the State, but as an ecclesiastical establishment empowered by the State to enforce its own decrees by civil penalties; which, in all its practical bearings, will amount to exactly the same thing.

Some one may now say, As you expect this movement to carry, you must look for a period of religious persecution in this country; nay, more, you must take the position that all the saints of God are to be put to death; for the image is to cause that all who will not worship it shall be killed.

There would, perhaps, be some ground for such a conclusion, were we not elsewhere informed that in the dire conflict God does not abandon his people to defeat, but grants them a complete victory over the beast, his image, his mark, and the number of his name. Rev. 15:2. We further read respecting this earthly power, that he causeth all to receive a mark in their right hand or in their foreheads; yet chapter 20:4 speaks of the people of God as those who do not receive the mark, nor worship the image. If, then, he could "cause" all to receive the mark, and yet all not actually receive it, in like manner his causing all to be put to death who will not worship the image does not necessarily signify that their lives are actually to be taken.

But how can this be? *Answer:* It evidently comes under that rule of interpretation in accordance with which verbs of action sometimes signify merely the will and endeavor to do the action in question, and not the actual performance of the thing specified. The late George Bush, Professor of Hebrew and Oriental Literature in New York City University, makes this matter plain. In his notes on Ex. 7 : 11 he says :—

"It is a canon of interpretation of frequent use in the exposition of the sacred writings that verbs of action sometimes signify merely the *will* and *endeavor* to do the action in question. Thus in Eze. 24 : 13 : 'I have *purified* thee, and thou wast not purged ;' *i. e.,* I have endeavored, used means, been at pains, to purify thee. John 5 : 44 : 'How can ye believe which *receive* honor one of another ;' *i. e.,* endeavor to receive. Rom. 2 : 4 : 'The goodness of God *leadeth* thee to repentance ;' *i. e.,* endeavors, or tends, to lead thee. Amos 9 : 3 : 'Though they be *hid* from my sight in the bottom of the sea ;' *i. e.,* though they aim to be hid. 1 Cor. 10 : 33 : 'I *please* all men ;' *i. e.,* endeavor to please. Gal. 5 : 4 : 'Whosoever of you are *justified* by the law ;' *i. e.,* seek and endeavor to be justified. Ps. 69 : 4 : 'They that *destroy* me are mighty ;' *i. e.,* that endeavor to destroy me. Eng., 'That *would* destroy me.' Acts 7 : 26 : 'And *set them at one* again ;' *i. e.,* wished and endeavored. Eng., ' *Would* have set them.'"

So in the passage before us. He causes all to receive a mark, and all who will not worship the image to be killed ; that is, he wills, purposes, and endeavors to do this. He makes such an enactment, passes such a law, but is not able to execute it ; for God interposes in behalf of his people ; and then those who have kept the word of Christ's patience are kept from falling in this hour of temptation, according to Rev. 3 : 10 ; then those who have made God their refuge are kept from all evil, and no plague comes nigh their dwelling, according to Ps. 91 : 9, 10 ; then all who are found written in the book are delivered, according to Dan. 12:1; and, being victors over the beast and his image, they are redeemed from among men, and raise a song of triumph before the throne of God, according to Rev. 14:4; 15:2.

The objector may further say, You are altogether too credulous in supposing that all the skeptics of our land, the Spiritualists, the German infidels, and the irreligious masses generally, can be so far brought to favor the religious observance of Sunday that a general law can be promulgated in its behalf.

The answer is, The prophecy must be fulfilled, and if the prophecy requires such a revolution, it will be accomplished. But we do not know that it is necessary. Permit the suggestion of an idea which, though it is only conjecture, may show how enough can be accomplished to fulfill the prophecy without involving the classes mentioned. This movement, as has been shown, must originate with the Churches of our land, and be carried forward by them. They wish to enforce certain practices upon all the people; and it would be very natural that in reference to those points respecting which they wish to influence the outside masses, they should see the necessity of first having absolute conformity among all the evangelical denominations. They could not expect to influence non-religionists to any great degree on questions respecting which they were divided among themselves. So, then, let union be had on those views and practices which the great majority already entertain. To this end, coercion may first be attempted. But here are a few who cannot possibly attach to the observance of the first day, which the majority wish to secure, any religious obligation; and would it be anything strange for the sentence to be given, Let these few factionists be made to conform, by persuasion if possible, by force if necessary? Thus the blow may fall on conscientious commandment-keepers before the outside masses are involved in the issue at all. And should events take this not improbable turn, it would be sufficient to meet the prophecy, and leave no ground for the objection proposed.

To receive the mark of the beast in the forehead, is, we understand, to give the assent of the mind and judgment to his authority in the adoption of that institution which constitutes the mark. By parity of reasoning, to receive it in the hand would be to signify allegiance by some outward act, perhaps by signifying a willingness to abstain from labor—the work of their hands—on that day, though not indorsing its religious character.

The number, over which the saints are also to get the victory, is the number of the papal beast, called also the number of his name, and the number of a man, and said to be six hundred threescore and six. Rev. 13:18. Where is that number to be found? The pope wears upon his pontifical crown in jeweled letters, this title: " *Vicarius Filii Dei*," " Vicegerent of the Son of God," the numerical value of which title is just six hundred and sixty-six. Thus V stands for 5; I, 1; C, 100; a and r, not used as numerals; I, 1; U, anciently written as V and standing for 5; s and f, not used as numerals; I, 1; L, 50; I, 1; I, 1; D, 500; e, not used as a numeral; I, 1. Tabulating this, we have the following :—

V	=	5
I	=	1
C	=	100
I	=	1
U(V)	=	5
I	=	1
L	=	50
I	=	1
I	=	1
D	=	500
I	=	1

666

The most plausible supposition we have seen on this question is that in this name we find the number sought for. It is the number of the beast, the papacy; it is the number of his name, for he adopts it as his distinctive title; it is the number of a man, for he who bears it is the "man of sin." We get the victory over it by refusing those institutions and practices which he sets forth as evidence of his power to sit supreme in the temple of God, and by adopting which we should acknowledge the validity of his title, by conceding his right to act for the Church in behalf of the Son of God.

And now, reader, we leave this subject with you. We confidently submit the argument as one which is invulnerable in all its points. We ask you to review it carefully. Take in, if thought can comprehend it; the wonderful phenomenon of our own nation. Consider its location, the time of its rise, the manner of its rise, its character, Satan's masterpiece of lying wonders which he has here sprung upon the world, and the elements which are everywhere working to fulfill in just as accurate a manner all the remainder of the prophecy in regard to the dragon voice, the erection of the image, and the enforcing of the mark. Can you doubt the application? We know not how. Then the last agents to appear in this world's history are on the stage of action, the close of this dispensation is at hand, and the Lord cometh speedily to judge the world. But between us and that day stands an issue of appalling magnitude. It is no less than this: To yield, on the one hand, to unrighteous human enactments, soon to be made, and thus expose ourselves to the unmingled wrath of an insulted Creator; or, on the other, to remain loyal to God, and brave the utmost wrath of the dragon and his infuriated hosts. In reference to this issue, the third message of Rev. 14 : 9–12 is now going forth as a solemn and vehement warning. If you have read the foregoing pages, this warning has come to you. In tender solicitude we ask you what you intend to do with it. To aid in sounding over the land this timely note of alarm, to impress upon hearts the importance of a right position in the coming issue, and the necessity of pursuing such a course as will secure the favor of God in the season of earth's direst extremity, and a share at last in his glorious salvation, is the object of this effort. And if with any it shall have this effect, the prayer of the writer will not be utterly unanswered, nor his labor be wholly lost.

———————

The portraits of fifty of the fifty-six signers of the Declaration of Independence (a document so often referred to in this work) have been preserved. Presuming that the reader would be interested to see them, we herewith present them in the order in which their names were attached to that venerable instrument.

JOHN HANCOCK.

BUTTON GWINNETT.

LYMAN HALL.

GEO. WALTON.

WM. HOOPER.

JOSEPH HEWES.

EDWARD RUTLEDGE.

THOS. HEYWARD, JUNR.

THOS. LYNCH, JUNR.

ARTHUR MIDDLETON.

269

SAMUEL CHASE.

WM. PACA.

THOS. STONE.

CHARLES CARROLL OF CARROLLTON.

GEORGE WYTHE.

RICHARD HENRY LEE.

THOS. JEFFERSON.

BENJ. HARRISON.

THOS. NELSON, JR.

FRANCIS LIGHTFOOT LEE.

ROBT. MORRIS.　　　　　BENJAMIN RUSH.

BENJA. FRANKLIN.　　　GEO. CLYMER.　　　JAS. SMITH.

GEO. TAYLOR.　　　JAMES WILSON.　　　GEO. ROSS.

GEO. READ.　　　THOS. M. KEAP.

271

WM. FLOYD.

PHIL. LIVINGSTON.

FRANS. LEWIS.

LEWIS MORRIS.

RICHD. STOCKTON.

JNO. WITHERSPOON.

FRANS. HOPKINSON.

ABRA. CLARK.

JOSIAH BARTLETT,

WM. WHIPPLE.

SAML. ADAMS.

JOHN ADAMS.

ROBT. TREAT PAINE.

ELBRIDGE GERRY.

STEP. HOPKINS.

WILLIAM ELLERY.

ROGER SHERMAN.

SAML. HUNTINGTON.

WM. WILLIAMS.

OLIVER WOLCOTT.

APPENDIX.

SINCE the foregoing pages went to press, events have transpired in Arkansas and Tennessee, going to show very clearly what the practical workings of the Sunday law will be whenever and wherever it may be secured.

It is but a short time since the attention of the people in some places in Arkansas, began to be called to the importance of observing the seventh day of the week as the Sabbath according to the fourth commandment of the decalogue, by the advocates of that faith. As converts to that view and practice began to appear, it excited strong opposition on the part of some, as it has in other places, and as truth has always done ever since error has endeavored to usurp control over the minds of men. How far the action which has since followed has been owing to this opposition, we do not say. We only state the facts, and leave the reader to draw his own conclusions.

In the winter of 1884–5, a bill was introduced into the Legislature of that State to abolish the clause in the existing Sunday law which exempted from its operation those who conscientiously observed the seventh day. Up to this time the laws of that State had been very just and liberal in this respect. But now a petition was presented that the exemption clause be stricken out, bringing all alike, without regard to their religious faith or practice, under subjection to the enactment to keep the first day of the week as the Sabbath. The petition claimed to have been called out by the fact that certain Jews in Little Rock, regarding the seventh day as the Sabbath, kept open stores and transacted their usual business on the first day of the week. Considering the fact that their places of business were open also on the seventh day, this brought them into unfair competition with the other merchants of the place. There was certainly no necessity for a change of the law to meet this difficulty; for the law exempted those only who conscientiously observed the seventh day; and these Jews, by keeping open places of business on the seventh day, showed that there was no such conscientious observance on their part, and consequently that they could not justly claim the exemption of the law. But ostensibly on this ground the petition was urged, and the repeal of the exempting clause secured.

What has been the result? We have not learned that the aforesaid Jews in Little Rock, or any other part of the State, have been molested; that railroads, hotel-keepers, livery men, or those engaged in any like vocations, have been in anywise restrained. But those persons above referred to, who, from a Christian point of view, had commenced to observe the seventh day in preference to the first; who were not engaged in such business as brought them into competition with others; who, having conscientiously observed the seventh day, proposed to go quietly and industriously about their lawful business on the first day of the week,—these soon found that they were not overlooked. Warrants were promptly issued for the arrest of some five or six of these, one of them a minister whose offense was that he was engaged one Sunday in painting a meeting-house erected by his people.

The trial of these persons came off at Fayetteville, Ark., the first week in November, 1885. In making up the indictment, an observer of the seventh day was called in to testify against his brethren. The following examination substantially took place :—

"Do you know any one about here who is violating the Sunday law?—Yes. Who?—The Frisco railroad is running several trains each way on that day. Do you know of any others?—Yes. Who?—The hotels of this place are open and doing a full run of business on Sunday as on other days. Any others?—Yes; the drug stores and barbers. Any others?—

Yes; the livery-stable men do more business on that aay than on any other."

As these were not the parties the court was after, the question was finally asked directly, "Do you know of any Seventh-day Adventists who have worked on Sunday?" Ascertaining that some of this class had been guilty of labor on that day, indictments were issued for five persons accordingly.

At the trial, the defendants employed the best counsel obtainable—Judge Walker, ex-member of the United States Senate. The points he made before the court were that the law was unconstitutional,—

First, because it was an infringement of religious freedom, or the right of conscience, inasmuch as it compelled men to keep as the Sabbath a day which their conscience and the Bible taught them was not the Sabbath;

Secondly, because it was an infringement of the right of property, taking from seventh-day keepers one-sixth part of their time; and the time of a laboring man being his property, the law was in its nature a robber; and—

Thirdly, because it took away a right that God had given —the right to labor six days and to rest one.

All this was overruled by the judge, who charged that the law rested *equally* upon all, requiring that all men should rest *one* day, and that the first day of the week; which requirement rested alike on the Methodists, the Baptists, the Congregationalists, the Sabbatarians, the Jews, worldlings and infidels; and if our religion required us to keep another day, that was a price we paid to our religion, and with that the State had nothing to do. He ruled, moreover, that no one had a right to set up his conscience against the law of the land.

From these denials of the rights which the Author of their existence has given to all men—namely, their right to labor six days, and to rest on the seventh, and the right to obey God rather than man, when man's requirements conflict with his, tne counsel for the defendants of course took appeal; and the case went up to the supreme court of the State, to be tried in May, 1886.

After the argument of the counsel had been presented, the defendants were given opportunity to speak for themselves, whereupon the minister before referred to occupied about forty minutes in presenting to the court a clear and concise argument from the Scriptures, showing the duty of all men to keep the seventh day and that alone. By-standers remarked that the spectacle of a minister of the gospel pleading in court from an open Bible for God-given rights which the laws of men denied him, was one not often witnessed since long by-gone days of religious intolerance and persecution.

One other case besides those of the observers of the seventh day—that of a hotel runner, came up for trial; but he was cleared in about five minutes, while the seventh-day keepers were convicted. Many think this case was thrown in merely as an attempted cover of the true spirit of the prosecutions, which came from professors of religion.

During the same time a similar work has been going on in Tennessee, where seventh-day views have of late been more extensively agitated. Eld. S. Fulton, of Springville, Henry Co., Tenn., writes that eight in that State have been prosecuted for Sunday labor. Three of the number have been convicted on a charge of "flagrant violation of the Christian Sabbath." The charge was preferred by a professor of religion; but two of the men were quietly plowing in their fields a full half mile from the house of the one who lodged complaint against them. In these cases a fine of $20 and costs was imposed on each. Appeal has been taken to the supreme court of the State, which convenes in Jackson in May next (1886), the parties having meanwhile to give bail of $250 each for their appearance in court at that time.

In regard to the state of public sentiment in Tennessee on this question, Eld. F. writes:—

"Public sentiment is fast changing here in favor of Sunday legislation. Some seven years ago, a Mr. Thomason, a lawyer of Paris, Tennessee, in consulting with our brethren on the question of Sunday labor, advised them to pursue their work on Sunday, claiming that they could not be harmed for it, as the constitution granted them that right. Since then, he has professed religion and joined the Presbyterian church, and now says that we must quit work on the Christian Sabbath or suffer punishment by law; and there is no avoiding it."

Speaking of the trial, he says: "In the court room, the attorney for the defendant asked the question if Sunday was the Sabbath; and the judge ruled it out as not a proper question; neither would he permit a statement to be made why our brethren worked on Sunday. In his charge to the jury, it was easily seen that he was determined to have them punished. The jury had hardly left the room when they returned a verdict of 'Guilty,' and a fine of $20 and costs was imposed on each. Our brethren then appealed to the supreme court, in the hope that some justice may be shown them there."

It is the opinion of some that the decision will be reversed in the higher court. A prominent lawyer whom Eld. F. has consulted gives his views of the case in the following letter, which we are permitted to lay before the reader :—

"HUNTINGDON, TENNESSEE, Jan. 6, 1886.

"ELD. SAMUEL FULTON,

"*Springville, Tennessee.*

"*Dear Sir,*—

"Your letter of yesterday received and duly considered. In reply I have to inform you that I cannot furnish you with the opinion of the judges in Tennessee in relation to the statute under which members of your church are being prosecuted for working on Sunday, except in so far as the question has been before our supreme court. The constitutionality of our act of Assembly, making it an offense, punishable by a fine of $3, to work on Sunday, has never been passed upon by our supreme court. It has, however, been decided by our supreme court that it is not nuisance for a man to work on Sunday, and therefore not indictable. See 7th Baxter 95. In a later case the same court decided that 'hunting or fishing on Sunday may be done in such a manner as to subject the party guilty to indictment for a nuisance.' See 1 B. I. Law Reports, page 129.

"From what I have learned in relation to the prosecutions in Henry county, I would say that if our supreme court does not go back on the question decided in the case of the State *vs.* Lossy 7 Baxter page 95, before referred to, the case now pending on writ of error in said court will be reversed, remanded to the circuit court, and dismissed on the ground that to work on Sunday is not an indictable offense. But should the court overrule the case last mentioned, we may be able in that case to make the constitutional question; but inasmuch as I have not seen the record as made up, I cannot say positively. In the 7 Baxter case, the judge, delivering the opinion of the court, incidentally remarked that the defendant was guilty of violating the statute prohibiting work on Sunday, but that the offense was not indictable. The question of the constitutionality of the Sunday statute was not before the court in that case. It seems to me that if our Sunday laws, as against members of your church, can be sustained at all by the courts, it must be on the ground that the legislature possesses the power to require the citizen to rest on any one day in the week, Sunday, Monday, or any other one of the seven. I know our courts, both State and Federal, have gone a great way in upholding certain legislation on the ground of the police power of the States. However, I don't want to be understood as saying that the legislature possesses the power to pass the statute under consideration, as I have not had the time necessary to a proper investigation of the question. But I feel confident that if the question can have the consideration at the hands of courts that its importance demands, your people would be allowed to observe their Sabbath and to work the remaining six days of the week. I am, however, fearful that much prejudice, bigotry, and intolerance must be overcome before success can be predicted with confidence.

"Very respectfully, * * * *"

Still later reports from Eld. F. represent that the opposition there is growing still more active, and is becoming so persistent and bitter as to threaten serious injury to their work. Too many, under the most favorable circumstances, will quail before the opposition sure to be visited upon unpopular truth, in only a social point of view, from their friends and neighbors. But when, in addition to this, they are threatened with almost certain prosecution, fewer still will be found to yield to the voice of conscience, though they may be quite well convinced that the observance of the seventh day is in accordance with the Scriptures.

We do not apprehend that human nature in Arkansas, Tennessee, and Pennsylvania differs materially from human nature in any and all of the other States; and in every community there will be found plenty to oppress their neighbors in the matter of Sabbath-keeping, if once the law can be secured to give them that privilege.

The issue of these cases will be watched by many with great interest.

INDEX.

[282]

www.ingramcontent.com/pod-product-compliance
Lightning Source LLC
Chambersburg PA
CBHW021037030726
47496CB00006B/1584